Praise for Daniel Ingram-Br[...]
and *Rise of the Shadow Stea[...]*

'Daniel Ingram-Brown has an intriguing voice and [...]
matter and no little skill in the execution.'
Haydn Middleton, author

'Daniel Ingram-Brown is a creator of worlds a[...]
wonder...He entertains but is so much more than an e[...]
and theologian of the street, the home and the playgr[...]
Simon Hall, author and social commentator

'This is a very well written book. Quality. Grabs strai[...]
narrative, atmospheric, good dialogue, plenty of dr[...]
with a darkness. Can't fault it...'
Maria Moloney, author and editor

'Daniel Ingram-Brown has a deep appreciation and [...]
the importance of storytelling for the transmission an[...]
of eternal truths, for adults and children alike.'
Rev Canon Tony Bundock, Rector of Leeds

'Excellent writing...The descriptions, characters, dialo[...]
all first class.'
Krystina Kellingley, commissioning editor for Axis-[...]

'Daniel Ingram-Brown writes with conviction and br[...]
layers together...He brings his love of stories alive in h[...]
much to offer the reader.'
Beci Jamieson, Arts Development Manager, Doncaste[...]

'...Daniel Ingram-Brown...has the ability to weave pe[...]
worlds of myth, prophecy and archetypes.'
Mike Love, Chair of Leeds Christian Community [...]
Peace

The Firebird Chronicles:

Rise of the Shadow Stealers

The Firebird Chronicles:

Rise of the Shadow Stealers

Daniel Ingram-Brown

OUR STREET
BOOKS

Winchester, UK
Washington, USA

First published by Our Street Books, 2013

Our Street Books is an imprint of John Hunt Publishing Ltd., Laurel House, Station Approach, Alresford, Hants, SO24 9JH, UK
office1@jhpbooks.net
www.johnhuntpublishing.com
www.ourstreet-books.com

For distributor details and how to order please visit the 'Ordering' section on our website.

ISBN: 978 1 78099 694 3

A CIP catalogue record for this book is available from the British Library.

Design: Stuart Davies

Illustration: Shaeron Caton-Rose

Printed in the USA by Edwards Brothers Malloy

Contents

www.danielingrambrown.co.uk
Twitter: @daningrambrown
Facebook: www.facebook.com/danielingrambrown

For Kenneth, Sebastian and Alfie

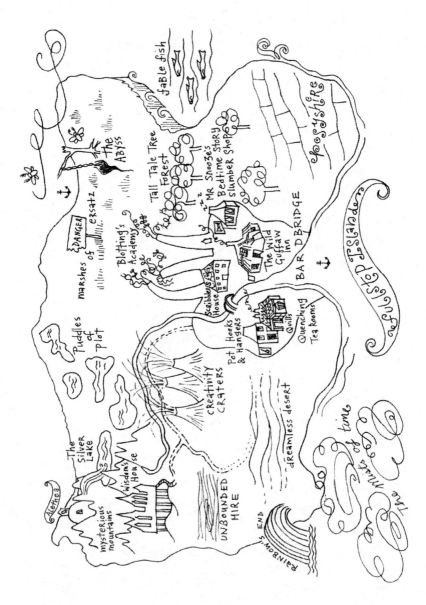

Chapter 1

The Ritual

'Curses,' the old woman spat, clutching a half-finished letter in her bony fingers.

She glared at Mr Bumbler. His dead body lay slumped across the grand writing desk in the drawing room of Chronicle Manor. Dusk light passed through the puzzle trees in the garden, casting eerie shadows on the portraits of his ancestors, shrouding their eyes from the foul scene.

Bumbler's pen was clasped in his podgy fingers. His head was twisted awkwardly, his jowly cheek pressing into the desk's burgundy leather. His startled eyes were fixed on a cut-glass tumbler. In it, the dregs of a dark-brown spirit slowly congealed. It had been laced with poison.

Outside on the window ledge, a flock of crows watched their mistress, Grizelda, with beady eyes. She pulled her cloak around her skinny body and re-read the letter for the third time:

Grammatax, old friend,
I have completed the report into the strange happenings that you asked me to make for Blotting's Academy; the report of disappearances and missing characters.

I have discovered that recently there has been an increase of activity along the fault line beneath the Central Chasm. I am afraid, dear friend, that our fears have been justified. Part of the fault line, the dark pit we call the Abyss, has been activated once more.

But I have also heard there is movement in Alethea. My sources tell me that the Storyteller is *preparing to set in motion the long awaited plan. They say, old friend, he believes that she will return — and when she does, the darkness of that pit will be closed forever.*

The old woman looked up, her eyes dark. It wasn't possible; Bumbler had to be wrong. Even the meddler, the Storyteller, wasn't able to make such a thing happen. She lowered her head and continued to read.

Keep your eyes peeled at the Academy, Gram, especially in the Department of Quests. My sources tell me that his plan depends on two children, Apprentice Adventurers...

There the letter stopped, punctuated by a scrawl where Bumbler had collapsed.

The old woman cursed again. If only she had waited a little longer before administering the poison. She knew enough, though. The Abyss was under threat and with it, her livelihood.

Grizelda was one of the few who dared to mine the Abyss for its great bounty. She served its lord in return for access to its treasures. she'd made sacrifices to keep herself alive and nobody was going to spoil her party.

It's time for a gathering, she thought to herself, crumpling the letter in her fragile fingers. *It's time for the ritual.*

Silently, the Abyss waited.

It was the next day and Grizelda moved slowly through the marshlands of Ersatz, her rough cloak dragging through the water, making it slurp. Her gnarled fingers and spindly body mimicked the wizened Barb Bushes that spotted the marsh. Above her head, her crows circled the empty sky.

Grizelda was tracing her way to a barren circle about a mile from the coast. This was the place, beneath a dead tree, that the Abyss plunged endlessly downwards.

She was not the only one heading towards the circle that evening. From a different direction, Knot lumbered through the marsh. He was a mountain of a man, with slabs for feet and a boulder head. He had known the old crone all his miserable life. She had nursed him from birth and in return he had served her, acting as her mule and muscle man.

He lurched from side to side, as if his weight might catch him off-guard at any moment and send him toppling into the muddy swamp.

Reaching the edge of the circle at opposite sides, the two figures stopped. Grizelda bowed her head, her eyes sly with mockery. Beside her, in the grass, there was a rustling. She looked down to see the long body of a snake slither towards her feet.

'There you are,' she cackled.

Knot, who was glaring from the other side of the circle, watched as another figure stood up from the tall grass. It was a slender lady, dressed entirely in green. He bared his yellow teeth.

'Melusine.' Grizelda nodded at the new arrival.

'Grizelda. Shall we?' Melusine hissed, stepping onto the dead circle.

'shoes!'

'Of courssse, *so* sorry,'

Melusine slipped off her green slippers and left them at the edge of the circle.

Grizelda and Knot followed suit, taking off their shoes and stepping onto the circle of death.

The three figures moved towards the centre. In front of them the Abyss opened, a jagged rupture in the ground, an unnatural well. By its side the dead tree pointed skywards. It had been stripped of all but one of its branches, the remaining one jutting

3

out over the hole. Tied around the branch was a thick rope, which dangled down, falling into the blackness and disappearing from sight.

Knot, Melusine and Grizelda reached the edge of the Abyss and stopped. There was a tiny sound.

Snicker, snick.

Something buzzed upwards from the dark. An insect. Recognising it, the three figures stepped backwards, fearful of the creature's deadly sting. It flew past them and disappeared into the grey sky. Grizelda looked up, her eyes dark.

'Well, we know what we're here for. Let's get on with it.'

'Firssst, let me see Bumbler's letter,' Melusine hissed.

Grizelda glared, but then reached into her cloak, pulled out the crumpled paper and handed it over.

Melusine scanned the words.

'He believes *she* will return? Imposssssible. She's gone. There is no way the princess can return.'

'I share your scepticism, but we cannot take any risks. And remember, even if that old fool is right and the princess does return, she belongs to the Abyss and we have the right to claim her. We must prepare for all eventualities.'

'And what is thisss about children?' Melusine scanned the letter again. 'Two children – Apprentice Adventurers?'

'How do I know? The old fool died before he finished it.'

Melusine shot Grizelda a daggered look. 'Such incompetence.'

'I remind you,' Grizelda replied, with an air of fake respectability, 'that I was the one who obtained the letter. If it had been up to you, we would have no idea of the situation at all. Because of me, we know we need to focus our attention on the Academy – on Apprentice Adventurers from the Department of Quests, to be precise. But we're wasting time,' she spat, dropping the act. 'Let's get on with it.'

Taking a deep breath the old woman let out a guttural, rasping word. It was the first word of a ritual that had been spoken many times around the Abyss. Melusine and Knot joined her, their voices lagging lazily behind. Together they sounded like a discordant choir, their dirge echoing across the Marsh of Ersatz.

'To the Abyss, I come.'

A low gust of wind rustled through the grass.

'With darkness, one.

I take from the thief what is rightfully mine.

I take as my master, unquenchable thirst.

I descend to the emptiness that consumes.

I return with the power to snare the prey.'

The ugly sound of the three rose, a savage hunger filling their voices.

'That I may feed.

That I may rise.

That I may rule from the heights and possess and consume.

To emptiness,' they cried, as if toasting victory.

'To darkness,

To absence,

To the Abyss.'

They stopped, the echo fading. Nothing in the marsh moved. Deep inside the pit, a mass of Shadow Grubs writhed and crawled across one another.

Eventually, there was a shudder, and slowly a whisper rose from the hole. The whisper spilled over the edge of the pit, blowing like death-sand across the surface of the circle. As it reached its edge, the grass withered and died and the circle grew a little bigger.

'Knot,' it whispered.

Knot knew exactly what to do. Greedily, he reached out and grabbed the rope. With a swing, he leapt into the centre of the hole, the tree creaking under his weight. Wrapping his legs around the rope, he slowly lowered himself down and disappeared.

Again, an insect buzzed upwards and escaped across the drab

marshland.

The women waited and watched.

After a while, Knot's white knuckles appeared again, clutching the rope. He strained, dragging his great weight upwards. His face was gaunt, sucked dry of its blood, his lips pale. The layer of Shadow Grubs that lined the walls of the Abyss had been fed. Knot stepped onto the ground and the rope swung back.

The whisper rose once more, calling Melusine next, and then Grizelda. One after the other, they descended into the blackness of the hole.

The sinking sun turned the marsh dirty orange.

When Grizelda finally re-emerged, like Melusine and Knot before, she looked sickly with pallor. Reaching into her cloak, she withdrew her hand and slowly opened her fingers. In her palm lay a number of small, shiny black pebbles.

Knot let out a low, half-witted grunt. He too reached into his pocket, but instead of pebbles, he produced some old frayed pieces of string. Smiling, Melusine held out her hand for the others to see. In it was a blood-red apple.

'Good;' Grizelda croaked, her voice weak, 'pebbles, string and an apple. The sacrifice has been made and we have what we need. Now we must stop the apprentices from playing their part – whatever it is – in the Storyteller's meddlesome plan. We must protect the Abyss at all costs.'

With that, the old woman turned and left the circle of death, the crows wheeling above her head as she moved back across the Marsh of Ersatz.

In the darkness of the Abyss the Shadow Grubs writhed, fat with new blood. With a snicker snick, another Shadow Beetle buzzed upwards and disappeared into the fading darkness.

#

On the other side of the island, the Storyteller watched as Grizelda, Knot and Melusine left the Abyss. He stared into the crystal pool at the centre of the banqueting hall of his castle, Alethea. In its waters he could watch any of the island's stories unfold; he could follow their twists and turns. He closed his eyes. In his hand was a silver cane, straight as a die and balanced perfectly. He held it out, its tip hovering just above the churning water.

'It's time,' he said.

There was nobody else in the castle, but the Storyteller knew he wasn't alone. Somewhere, beyond the Un-crossable Boundary, someone was with him.

He couldn't explain how, but he knew they were there.

Sensing energy pulsing through the silver cane, he opened his eyes. Shining in the crystal pool were two faces – a boy and a girl.

Surprised, he laughed. 'Of course – it's perfect.'

The girl's hair was a scribble of black, her features rounded like a question mark. The boy's eyes were sharp. He was thin and gangly.

An exclamation mark, the Storyteller thought.

In turn, he looked into their eyes. 'You are now members of Blotting's Academy, the place where all Story Characters make their first mark, where they undertake their training. You are Apprentice Adventurers from the Department of Quests.' He whispered into the pool. 'Your quest is to find me. Bring *her* back, and as you travel, you will come to know yourselves.'

Slowly, he lowered the silver cane and touched the surface of the crystal pool.

Chapter 2

The Spectre of Scribbler's House

The girl awoke with a start. Throwing off the bedcovers, she leapt to her feet and looked around. She felt as though she'd overslept. Had nobody called her?

I'm late, she thought, although she wasn't exactly sure what for. She peered around the room. For a moment it looked empty, hung with shadows.

What? Where's everything gone? She blinked, and the blurry outline of her furniture appeared.

I must be tired! Now, where are my glasses?

She looked down to see the fuzzy shape of some thick, black spectacles appear on the bedside table next to her. Reaching down, she picked them up.

These must be mine, but I can't remember... Putting them on, the room came into focus.

Ah yes, definitely mine.

Standing in the middle of the bedroom she looked around again. This was definitely her room; she knew that. It was part of a bigger house that had many rooms. Hanging on the wall was a picture of the house. It was a quaint, white building, lined with glowing windows. Below, "Scribbler's House" was written.

Ah yes, Scribbler's House, the girl repeated, with a smile that made her feel warm inside.

There was her bed hugging the corner of the room, and her chair. Beside it, flung into the corner, her bedclothes now lay in a heap. Opposite the picture of Scribbler's House, was a pinboard. From it, a poster read "MISSING" in stark red letters. A picture of a small tabby cat stared out with big, green eyes.

'You're a cutie, aren't you?' the girl said, going to examine the poster more closely.

"Have you seen Scribble, the house cat?" the poster read. "All sightings should be reported to Miss Dotty, the school secretary."

There was a tiny scraping sound behind and the girl turned round, half expecting to see Scribble the house cat scratching the skirting board. But there was nothing.

Suddenly, a loud knock made her jump. Quickly, she ran to open the door.

An older student with long, dark pigtails spoke shrilly as she poked her head around the frame:

'Come on, or we'll be late.'

'Late for...?'

'The First Word Welcome, dozy! It's your first day at the Academy! You haven't even done your hair yet. You look awful!'

'Oh, I've only just...Sorry, have we met?'

'What a silly question, I'm Head Girl, aren't I? Here, use this.' Her new friend thrust a hairbrush into the room. 'And don't forget your name badge.' She pointed at a bookmark-shaped label that was proudly pinned to her own tunic. It read, "Mythina, Head Girl."

The door banged closed, leaving the first girl alone again. Staring down at the brush, she suddenly felt sick with nerves.

My first day!

Outside in the corridor she could hear the sound of giggling, running and high-pitched conversation.

Quickly, or you'll miss out, she thought, anxiously.

Rushing to the mirror, she stopped. Something didn't feel right this morning. It felt like an itch that she wasn't able to scratch, or a slightly wonky picture. She tilted her head to one side, thinking that maybe that would straighten things out but then caught a glimpse of her reflection, gormless in the mirror. She shook herself and started to pull the brush through her unruly, thick, black hair.

Again, a scraping sound disrupted her thoughts. In the mirror, she caught sight of a movement in the corner behind.

Turning around, she peered at the place where the movement had been, but there was nothing there, just a dark patch of shadow. She stared into the gloom, but still there was no movement. Hesitating, she turned back to the mirror and continued to brush her hair.

Hanging on the wall next to her, she noticed a red tunic. She put it on. It had a gold emblem stitched into it – a book with a quill in the centre. Above it the words "Blotting's Academy" were stitched in fancy lettering. Looking at herself, she felt strangely proud. Her hair fell slightly out of place and she sighed, deflated. Carefully, she brushed it back into position.

What's going on? Normally all this beautifying would wind you up. You like your hair to be a mess! Oh, I feel all at sixes and sevens. She raised her hands to her head and ruffled her hair.

An image shot through her mind – a child caked in grime, hair matted and tangled, huddled in the dark corner of a cave.

The girl stumbled backwards, caught off-guard by the force of the impression.

She froze for a moment and tried to bring the image back to mind, but it was hazy and wouldn't form clearly.

What was that about?

The scraping sound disturbed her again.

Snicker, snick.

Jumping, the girl span round. The noise had been louder than before. But still the room appeared to be empty. She leaned forwards, peering into the corner again. She could have been mistaken, but the shadow seemed to have spread. She shivered.

Can't have.

Morning sunlight was streaming into the little bedroom. She looked at the shadow again. What was casting it? She glanced around but couldn't see what was.

There was running in the corridor outside.

What am I doing? she thought, irritated by her daydreaming. *Come on now, what was it Mythina said I needed?* She paused, thinking. *Of course, my name badge.* A sudden panic rose from the pit of her stomach.

'My name!' she said aloud, looking around helplessly. She'd forgotten. She'd forgotten her own name! How on earth could someone forget their own name? Her heart beating fast, she ran to the desk and scrabbled under a blank scroll of parchment. She lifted a notepad and there underneath, face down, was her own bookmark-shaped label. Picking it up, her hand trembling, she turned it over.

'Scoop,' she read aloud, exhaling a loud breath. 'Of course, what's wrong with you this morning, Scoop? It must be nerves. Now let's have no more of this silliness. Come on, or the others will have gone.'

She headed into the corridor to join her friends. As Scoop left, she glanced at the empty corner again. The shadow looked even bigger.

And weren't my bedclothes there earlier? she thought to herself. *I must have seen it wrong.*

Putting it out of mind, she dashed along the corridor to where she could hear her new friends talking and laughing.

'Watch out, or the spectre will get you,' Mythina was saying to a little girl with a round face. The young girl was looking nervous.

'There's no such thing!' one of the others butted in.

'So is,' Mythina replied. 'It's what's making everything go missing – haven't you seen all the posters?'

'Yeah, but...'

'But nothing, it's the Spectre of Scribbler's House. I know. I'm Head Girl, aren't I? Everyone knows it.'

Suddenly, a boy with a bedsheet over his head jumped out from a doorway and made a ghostly wailing noise. The round-faced girl screamed, her cheeks turning bright purple. Laughing, Mythina ran around the corner and thumped noisily down the stairs to the front door. Scoop followed with the others. Reaching the front door, they opened it and stepped out into the...

As the girls walked out of Scribbler's House they stopped. For the briefest of moments, almost too short to notice, it was as if they had run onto a blank piece of paper, upon which the world had not yet been drawn. Then, before they could blink, there it was – fluffy white clouds on a clear blue sky and in front of them, along a little track, the outskirts of the village.

'What was that?' Scoop asked, nervously.

'It was déjà vu,' Mythina replied, puffing herself up to sound clever. 'That's when you have an odd moment, like you've seen something or done something before, even though you haven't.'

It wasn't quite like that, Scoop thought, *although it definitely was an odd moment.*

Scoop wondered whether to challenge Mythina, but decided better of it.

Looking out of the window, just above where Scoop and her gaggle of friends had gathered outside Scribbler's House, was a boy. His name was Fletcher. He was wearing the same red tunic, which hung awkwardly from his skinny frame, but unlike Scoop, he was on his own. As those around him busily tried to make new friends, outdoing one another with practical jokes, loud stories and raucous laughter, he was in a thunderous mood and had let everybody know it.

Fletcher was a straight-to-the-point sort of person. He knew that he was the sort of boy who didn't mince words, and he didn't mind that it made him disagreeable to live with. The problem was, as he'd pointed out to the boy in the next room in an angry exchange, he didn't know exactly how he knew these things about himself in the first place. He had tried to explain what he meant, but the other boy had just muttered something about everyone feeling a bit weird on their first day.

'It's nothing to do with it being my first day,' Fletcher had said, angrily, 'the problem's not with me, it's with all this,' he had waved his hand around, irritably. 'Where's it come from? I can't remember! I can't remember anything before this morning. Can you?'

On waking up, it had felt to Fletcher as if the whole world had been created in that moment. It wasn't just that he had no memory; it was as though he had been picked up and dropped into completely alien surroundings. He had racked his brains, frantically trying to recall his past, but his mind was blank. All that he was aware of, somewhere deep below the surface of his heart, was a gnawing sense of anger; an anger he couldn't place. He ran his fingers across his scalp and looked at his pupils in the mirror. He looked fine and, considering his situation, felt well. And so he had concluded that the problem was not just with him; something else was going on, something bigger than just him. What irritated Fletcher was that nobody seemed to agree.

'There's nothing wrong with me,' he'd spat at his neighbour. 'I'm thinking perfectly clearly – it's all of you that are ignoring the facts.'

The boy had made an excuse and slipped away to join some lads who were planning to drop Gush Bombs on those in the lower rooms.

Fletcher sat on his bed and pondered the dilemma, finding himself looking at a poster that had been pinned to his notice-board. From it, the innocent eyes of a young lad with freckled cheeks looked out. Above the boy's head the word "MISSING" was printed in glaring red. Underneath, the poster read: "Have you seen Archie Squiggle? He was last seen at Mr Snooze's Bedtime Story Slumber Shop, in the village of Bardbridge. Archie's parents are offering a reward for his safe return. Any information of his whereabouts should be taken immediately to Miss Dotty, the school secretary."

Fletcher felt for Archie.

'It seems we're both lost,' he thought aloud.

Fletcher left his room and wandered around Scribbler's

House, his insides churning. The posters were everywhere: missing lunch boxes, missing furniture, even the house warden was missing. Fletcher peered nervously about the corridors. He would obviously have to be careful.

To his surprise, everybody else seemed to be treating the disappearances as a game. All around were whispers of a phantom – The Spectre of Scribbler's House – supposedly the explanation for the strange phenomenon. Fletcher overheard a group of students talking in hushed tones about how they'd seen it lurking in the basement. As he passed by, another student was talking excitedly about how he'd seen it appear in one of the upstairs windows. There were the cries of make-believe phantoms, followed by high-pitched squealing, around every corner. Fletcher was irritated. He didn't buy any of it and he wasn't going to fall foul of whatever was happening.

He stopped next to a window and looked out. It was a beautiful morning and as the sunlight warmed him, he felt the stillness of the day washing his irritation away.

In front of him, on the window sill, a pile of fliers and brochures had been left for the new students. Fletcher thumbed through them. There were tours of the local village, information about bands that were playing at the Wild Guffaw Inn, and a pamphlet written by Mademoiselle Belle about the local flora and fauna. At the back of the pile was a plain, hand-written notice that said "BEWARE" halfway down. It caught Fletcher's eye. He pulled it out to look more closely.

SENIOR LEVEL RESEARCH PAPER
The Shadow Beetle: Habits and Habitation.
Little is known about the reclusive Shadow Beetle. The population has recently seen a rapid growth and so the Department for Overcoming Monsters is undertaking specific research into these dark insects. Shadow

Beetles, as their name suggests, live in the shadows - or more accurately, they are shadows. They have no substance. Because of this they reflect no light. They are thieves, shadowy stealers that feed on words, which for an Island made of stories is a particularly dangerous habit! They erase meaning and turn all they consume into nothingness, leaving little piles of blankness in their wake. This means that they are very difficult to spot and even harder to catch. They do, however, become visible on contact with water.

BEWARE

The Shadow Beetle is extremely dangerous - its sting can be deadly. If you spot one, please do not attempt to catch it. Fill in the report form on the back and return it to the Department for Overcoming Monsters so that the insect can be caught and tested through dream analysis.

Form? Fletcher thought, derisively. *If they think I'm filling in a form they've got another thing coming. If I find one of these insects, I'm going to get it analysed myself. I can't trust anyone else.*

Fletcher folded the paper and put it in his pocket. He glanced at a "MISSING" poster above his head, his thoughts drawn to his missing memory. Frustrated, and more than a little nervous about the situation, he began to walk down the stairs towards the front door of Scribbler's House.

As Fletcher stepped into the air, something fell to the floor by his feet. It was a small, purple balloon, an unused Gush Bomb. He picked it up. Above his head, leaning from the window, was the boy from the next room. In his hands was a green balloon, which bulged with liquid. Behind him, another lad was pointing towards a group of girls who stood in a huddle in front of Fletcher. If there was one thing that irritated Fletcher more than not remembering where he'd come from, it was this sort of immature behaviour.

Scoop and her friends were still talking about the Spectre of Scribbler's House. Apparently, the Apprentice Fantasticals from the house next door, particularly those from the School of Horror, had said it could only be seen in mirrors, or in rooms where the temperature dropped below freezing. As they talked, Scoop became aware that she could hear a little scraping sound behind her ear.

Snicker snick. Snicker snick.

That's odd, she thought, feeling something tickling her back. She reached across her shoulder to scratch the itch.

Without warning, someone grabbed her arm and pulled her roughly across the path. Shocked, she turned. It was a boy with a thunderous look on his face.

'What you doing? Get off!' Scoop snapped, shaking herself free and rubbing her arm. As she did, there was a splosh behind her. She span round. On the floor where she had been standing was an exploded balloon and surrounding it, a pool of water. She looked up to see two faces duck behind a window frame, sniggering. She felt herself turn red with embarrassment.

'That's a Gush Bomb,' Mythina said, loudly. 'If it had hit you, it would have made you speak what's in your mind – you wouldn't have been able to stop yourself. You'd have been spilling a stream of consciousness for the next minute.'

Lucky that didn't happen, Scoop thought, aware of all the annoyances and insecurities that were flowing through her. Realising that the thunderous boy had just saved her from a drenching, she turned to thank him. As she did, he suddenly ran to where the Gush Bomb had landed and began to jump furiously up and down on the spot. His cheeks flushed and his hair flew about his face. It was quite a sight. The girls stared in amazement, smirking at each other and not hiding their giggles.

'What *are* you doing?' Mythina said with a sneer.

Fletcher didn't reply but continued to jump.

'Perhaps he's an Apprentice Clown!' Mythina pointed, laughing. 'Where are your big shoes, clown boy?'

Fletcher ignored Mythina completely. After a moment, he stopped jumping and stepped back. On the floor, in the pool of water under his feet, lay an insect – a big black beetle.

'I know what you are – visible on contact with water,' he muttered, under his breath.

Its skeleton was so well-armoured that Fletcher's jumping hadn't squashed it completely, but it was definitely dead. Smiling, Fletcher reached down and picked it up.

'Urgh!' A few of the girls stepped backwards in disgust.

Fletcher held the insect between his thumb and finger and stared at it for a moment. Then he raised his head, walked straight passed Mythina and strode off, without a word.

'Where are you going?' Scoop called after him, still shaken by her close encounter with the Gush Bomb and thankful for being saved from embarrassment.

'To the Academy,' Fletcher replied, turning but continuing to walk, backwards. He held up the dead insect, its broken wings dangling limply. 'I need to find somewhere to analyse this – with dream analysis. I think it's what's causing the disappearances.'

Mythina tutted.

'But what about the Spectre?' Scoop shouted.

'Oh, that – that's all rubbish.'

Mythina tutted again, loudly.

Turning, Fletcher strode away. Scoop's heart was beating fast. She wanted to follow him. She wanted to know more about the insect he'd caught. Was that what had been making the scraping noises? She looked at her friends and then back to the departing boy, but she knew that she was too embarrassed to leave them and run after him.

Maybe I'll see him at the Academy, she thought, frustrated with her lack of courage. Looking along the path, she watched as Fletcher walked through the gate at the end of the track and disappeared from sight.

In Alethea, high in the Mysterious Mountains, the Storyteller watched Fletcher and Scoop in the crystal pool.

Lowering the silver stick, he gently stirred the surface of the water, trying to gauge what he should do next. As the water bubbled and churned, his clarity grew.

He acknowledged his invisible ally beyond the Un-crossable Boundary.

Stilling the silver cane, he whispered, 'Ride, Auracle, to the village with speed. It is time to announce the good news.'

At once, wind whistled through the Alethean pass and something rode out from the tower. Below, the ground thundered and around, a gale blew. Looking down from above, it looked as if it was a storm beginning its journey across Fullstop Island – a white star spinning at great speed. Slowly, it moved towards the village of Bardbridge, home to Blotting's Academy. The people of the village had no idea what was going to hit them. Later, they would find out.

Chapter 3

An Old Island Rhyme

Scoop was still feeling embarrassed as she and the other girls headed away from Scribbler's House. At the end of the track from the house was the gate through which Fletcher had just vanished. Beyond it, a road crossed in two directions. In one direction, a number of thatched cottages lined the way to the village. As they neared the gate, Scoop peered along the road, hopeful to see Fletcher, but he was nowhere to be seen. Instead, she saw a stream of strangely assorted characters heading passed her, away from the village. Some were Academy students dressed in their red tunics, and others were obviously islanders or villagers. There were tradesmen and women: a baker, her apron and cloth-cap covered with flour; a cobbler, half-finished shoes hanging around his neck, and a man carrying an axe. *A woodcutter*, Scoop thought.

A group of students passed by: A boy with a hunched-back and thick tufted hair was watching a pale lad who seemed to be able to detach his hand from his arm and still make his finger wiggle. *They must be from the School of Horror*, Scoop smiled. A young lady rode passed, sitting side-saddle on a white horse, her golden slippers sparkling below her red tunic. As the horse trotted off by the hedge beyond its hooves, Scoop could swear there was a rabbit in a blue waistcoat. She thought she saw it bow courteously and then disappear into the bushes. Blinking, she looked back to Mythina.

'Where are they off to?' she asked, turning to the direction in which the crowd was heading; but before anyone had the chance to reply, she saw for herself. The road leading away from the village curved back, disappearing behind Scribbler's House. Rising up beyond the cosy student dwelling, towering over it, were three enormous rock-towers. From Scribbler's House, the towers hadn't been visible, but from here the quaint dormitories were dwarfed in their shadows. Scoop had never seen anything like them before. They weren't man-made but natural. The rock was dark and ridged, with tufts of grass and moss growing out of the cracks. The towers looked like someone had reached out of the sky and peeled back the ground like a banana skin.

'They look like frozen giants,' one of the girls said.

'Yeah, I can see that,' another agreed. 'It's like they're arching their backs, straining to look at the sky.'

'Oh yeah, with their hands on their hips!' the first girl added, excitedly.

'They are the Trichotomic Rock Cluster,' Mythina interrupted.

'The what?' The first girl looked bemused.

'The Trichotomic Rock Cluster – Trichotomic means three. They surround the opening to the Central Chasm. The Academy's built around them. The Hall of Heroes is in one of the towers – that's where the First Word Welcome is.'

'We'd better head in that direction then, hadn't we?' Scoop said, not wanting to hang around in case the boys with the Gush Bombs caught up with them, and secretly hoping she might catch up with Fletcher. She opened the gate.

Mythina shot her an angry look. 'Yes, I was about to say that.'

As Scoop stepped onto the track, a girl with fiery hair and emerald eyes smiled at her warmly. She was older than Scoop, having already finished her studies. As she sliced through the crowd, it parted for her. A swashbuckling sword hung from her side, and her armoured leather tunic was sharp-cut. Its back was decorated with studs, forming a picture of a golden feather. They sparkled in the morning sun. Scoop was intrigued.

'What's that?' she asked, pointing at the feather.

Mythina looked sulky. 'don't you know anything? It's the Golden Feather – one of the treasures kept in Alethea, although I don't hold to that. I think it's just a stupid myth.'

Scoop began to walk. Ahead of her, the golden feather flashed through the crowd. Increasing her pace, Scoop was able to follow in the girl's slip stream.

Just ahead, a frail old man, who walked with the aid of a long wooden staff, bobbed aimlessly along centre of the road. He was dressed in a bright golden-yellow kaftan, and on his head a purple and gold cloth-hat pointed cheerfully upwards, comical as a cockerel.

Unlike the rest of the crowd, he didn't move out of the way as the girl with the studded tunic approached him. She drew alongside the old man, who sped up to match her speed so that the two could walk together, his staff clacking jauntily.

He's very spritely for his age, Scoop thought, quickening her pace to keep up with them, her friends tagging along behind. The man glanced over his shoulder. For a moment Scoop thought he looked directly at her.

The red-haired girl greeted the old man.

'Ah, Rufina,' he replied. 'What a delight.' He spoke with a stutter, sending spit spraying into the air, but he emphasised his words with such relish that they seemed to Scoop to take on an almost magical quality. 'How are you, this fine morning?' he smiled.

'Worried,' Rufina replied. 'Have you heard about the disappearances?'

'One would have to be blind to have missed the posters – although sometimes I do fear that there is more blindness on the island than may be apparent from all the bright and eager eyes that surround us.'

'Precisely,' Rufina agreed, looking serious. 'The posters are everywhere. Has anything been said to the Academy staff?'

'I'm afraid not. Our old friend, Mr. Grammatax, has decided to treat the strange occurrences as nothing more than a few things being mislaid. But to his credit, he has agreed to look into the phenomenon further. He asked Mr. Bumbler to undertake a report, but I'm afraid he won't change the Academy's rather lax approach until he has received its findings.'

'It's so frustrating!' Rufina kicked a stone along the path. 'Everyone seems to be ignoring what's taking place right in front of them.'

'Distractions, distractions – the island is full of them. I'm afraid it is often easier to allow oneself to be distracted than to face up to a difficult reality, Rufina. Sometimes I wonder if the Academy itself isn't a distraction at times.'

Rufina looked at him, raising her eyebrows at what he had said.

'I know, I know, just ignore me – merely the ramblings of an old man.'

'It's not just the disappearances either, is it? There are other signs of instability. I've heard that the Fable Fish have tongue-tie.'

The old man gave a melancholy look. 'Yes, that's right. The fishermen tell me that the disease is spreading quickly, particularly in the shoals beyond the western cliffs.'

'And one of the Creativity Craters has burned out – I saw it myself.'

'Indeed, it is a sad sight,' the old man sighed. 'However, we must not let ourselves become discouraged. Fear is not our friend.'

There was a pause in the conversation. 'Is there any news from Alethea?' Rufina asked, turning directly to the old man and speaking quietly. 'What of the Storyteller?'

The old man grinned, almost mischievously. He leaned towards Rufina and whispered, 'I have heard rumours that he has sent out an Auracle, but as yet they are unconfirmed!'

'A wind messenger!' Rufina replied, loudly. A few people in the crowd turned to look.

'Shh!' the old man raised a finger to his lips. 'We don't want to spoil the surprise now, do we? I have put word out to my friends the talking animals to be on the lookout for the Auracle's cloud.'

Rufina smiled. 'I must tell Nib.'

Now it was the old man's turn to raise an eyebrow. 'Must you now?' he said with a playful air. Rufina blushed and looked away.

After a moment she looked back, her cheeks red. 'What's the message the Auracle will carry?'

'Haha! That I cannot say. I may be Ambassador of the Storyteller, but there are many things that even I do not know. We will have to wait to find out, along with everybody else.'

'Don't you have a sense, though – a Bard's guess?'

The old man paused. 'Well, there has been one thing going round and round in my head.'

'A loose cog?' Rufina grinned, cheekily.

The old man laughed. 'Many would say so, many would say so – but no – not as far as I'm aware, anyway.' He frowned, lifting his head and jiggling it around as if trying to listen for a rattle. 'No, all fine,' he said, falling still, but looking as if he had forgotten what they had been talking about.

'*So...*' Rufina said, impatiently, 'what *has* been going around in your head?'

'Ah, yes. Well, it's an old island rhyme, actually. You may have heard it. It goes something like this:

When Alethean bells chime,

And the Golden Feather shines,

All shadows will hide and flee,

And her face again we'll see.'

'Yes I know it,' Rufina replied, sadly. 'My mother used to sing it to me before...' she paused, looking down at the path, 'before...'

'Of course,' the old man interrupted, kindly. 'She was a great adventurer, your mother, and a wonderful singer as well, I'm sure. Well anyway, that is what has been flowing around my head.'

'And I know enough to take seriously what's flowing around in a Bard's head,' Rufina replied.

Whilst they were speaking, the crowd slowed down. They had reached the foot of one of the rock towers and people were slowly filtering through a pointed doorway at its base. Rufina and the old man disappeared behind a wall of heads, but just before they did, the old man looked over his shoulder and seemed to smile at Scoop.

What was that about? Was he smiling at me? Scoop wondered as she waited for her turn to enter the tower.

A child – an orphan dressed in rags – pushed past her feet and Scoop's heart leapt. Involuntarily, she reached out, the desire to protect the little orphan taking her by surprise. She stopped and quickly pulled back.

What am I doing?

She didn't know the orphan. Why had she reached out?

You could have scared the child, she chided herself. She glanced around, embarrassed by the force of her reaction.

The ragged child disappeared through the legs of the waiting crowd.

Disconcerted, Scoop looked up at the tower that loomed over her. Had the old man smiled at her? Why had she reacted to the orphan like that? She didn't feel in control. Looking back again into the black opening, she shivered. Scoop hated the dark. The feeling of unknowing, and the crowd closing in around her, was making her anxious. What was on the other side of that door?

She didn't know how, but she knew that she was supposed to be there. She knew that she was a part of something bigger than just herself. *But what exactly is it I'm part of?* She desperately tried to remember. *I hope, I really hope, that I'm about to find out.*

A few miles from the three towers of the Academy, at the Port of Beginnings and Endings, a ship swayed on the harbour waters. Along its gangplank shuffled travellers and seafaring folk arriving at Fullstop Island's main port, dragging their trunks behind them. Last in the line of passengers were a cloaked figure and a gigantic man. As they stepped ashore, a flock of crows, which had been perched on the bow of the ship, flew into the air and began to circle. Unseen, a snake slipped along the plank and disappeared into the shadows of a warehouse.

'Now, you know what to do?' Grizelda said quietly to Knot.

'Yeah. I'm to go to the Academy and...and...'

'And be on the lookout for Apprentice Adventurers,' the old woman yelled, causing the ship's boston, who was packing away the gang plank, to turn his head. 'How many times!' She swallowed her words and lowered her voice again. 'You're to look out for Apprentice Adventurers from the Department of Quests, remember?'

'Department of Quests,' Knot repeated, dully.

'Your job is to try and stop as many of them as you can from leaving the Academy grounds.'

'Yeah, that's right.'

'I know it's right! I'm the one who told you to do it, aren't I! The Storyteller's planning to use two of them in his plan to close the Abyss, remember? So if we stop the apprentices, we stop his plan, don't we? Get it? Dullard.'

'But which ones...'

'We don't know which ones, do we? So, just stop as many as you can from leaving the Academy grounds. It's not difficult. I can't be seen in the village, remember, and nor can that snake-in-the-grass, so *we'll* have to deal with the apprentices who manage to slip through your fat fingers. Get it? That will probably be all of them, won't it! But as soon as they leave the village gates, they're mine. And she,' Grizelda pointed to the warehouse, 'she is going to do what she does best – slither about and cause trouble. Now get going, yer lazy oaf!'

The old woman hobbled to a carriage and sped off. Alone, Knot began to lumber along the cobbled street – it wouldn't be long before he arrived at Blotting's Academy. He had his string and his instructions. All his life he'd been bossed about by the old woman. Grizelda's mocking voice screeched in his ears, calling him a dullard and a lazy oaf. Why couldn't she leave him alone? He felt hot with embarrassment. As he lumbered on, dull anger rose inside him. Silently, he vowed that he would prove himself. When he got to the Academy he would disable as many Apprentice Adventurers as he could and then, perhaps, the old crone would leave him alone.

Chapter 4

The First Word Welcome

When it was Scoop's turn to enter the rock tower, she took a deep breath and stepped through the dark opening. The sight that greeted her made her gasp. The atmosphere wasn't oppressive at all. It was amazing. Above her head, tall red banners hung, emblazoned with the Academy's golden crest. The rock walls were decorated with bright frescos of the great stories – whirl-winds, forest cottages, wardrobes and rabbit holes. The excited murmurs of students rose, making the hall hum and the banners swing gently. Scoop looked but could see neither Rufina nor the old man anywhere in the crowd. She peered around hopefully, scanning faces for Fletcher, but there were so many people it was no good.

At the end of the hall was a bizarre sight – a cloud of spray shone with little rainbows, as light poured through an enormous window.

'What's that?' she asked, as the girls caught up with her and sat down.

'Oh, that's the River Word,' Mythina replied, snootily. 'They engineered it to pass through here when the Hall of Heroes was carved out of the tower.'

'The river? But...'

'It's supposed to look like the Banquet Hall of Alethea.'

'What's Alethea?'

Mythina looked shocked. 'Don't you know anything? Alethea is the castle of the Storyteller, in the Mysterious Mountains. Legend says the river has its source in Alethea – apparently it flows from a pool with water as clear as crystal. From there it passes underneath its east window and sweeps down through the valley to the village, and then onto the Oceans of Rhyme – so they say. This hall is supposed to look like that one.'

Along the walls, stone seats were carved into the rock. On them sat a number of quirky-looking characters, who seemed almost to blend into the stone. There was a tall stony-faced man wearing a black cloak; two ladies wearing identical lace aprons – one tall and thin, the other short and round; a woman with flowing sapphire hair, and next to her an old man with twinkling eyes. He appeared to be dressed for bed, wearing a white nightgown and a pointed cap. As Scoop looked at their faces she had the strange sense that she could see beyond them, or through them, to something else; something with which each of them shone.

'Who are they?' she asked Mythina, pointing.

'Oh, they're the Bards, Teachers, Dwellers and Keepers.'

'Shopkeepers?'

'Well yes, but they're more than just shopkeepers – they're the keepers of the keys to the island.'

Just as Mythina was finishing her sentence, a man at the front of the hall, by the cloud of rainbows, rose to his feet. He stood behind a lectern, on a raised platform.

'Shh! Mr Grammatax is getting up – he's the Headmaster,' Mythina hissed, as if Scoop were the one who had been speaking.

Mr. Grammatax stood solid as a blackboard, his frame stocky and square and his fingers as stubby as chalk. On his head perched a meticulously level mortar board. He tapped the lectern firmly with his stick and a wave of hush rolled across the hall.

'Settle down now, settle down,' he boomed, his voice echoing around the chamber. 'Welcome to this remarkable...'

'Exciting,' interrupted Miss Merrilore, in a high voice. The Deputy-Headmistress sat behind Mr Grammatax, slightly to one side. She couldn't have looked more different. She was maypole-thin, her colourful robes swirling to strawberry hair where, entangled, a garland of leaves and bright berries rustled. She craned her neck around Mr. Grammatax, causing a titter of laughter to spill around the hall.

Mr. Grammatax continued, ignoring the interruption, '...this remarkable and *prestigious* centre of learning, to which people travel from across the four corners to hear stories passed down through the generations – the ancient establishment of Blotting's Academy!'

At this, a group of fairytale trumpeters (who sat on a balcony just to the right of the lectern) rose to their feet and blasted out a bright and breezy fanfare, to which many students broke out in a joyful splattering of applause.

'Many stories are to be found here at the Academy. Some are from the Hills of History...'

'Things that have actually happened!' interrupted Miss Merrilore, again.

'Yes, thank you, Miss Merrilore.'

'Quite alright, quite alright.'

'And some are from the Creativity Craters.'

'Stories of the mind!'

'Yes, indeed, stories of the mind! There are stories of mystery and romance,'

'Giants and Dwarfs,'

'Courage and suspense,'

'Puppy dogs and pigs!' At this interruption, Miss Merrilore leapt to her feet, possessed with such an excitement that she snorted like a pig and then proceeded to bark as if the snort had been a deliberate part of the speech. The hall erupted with a great burst of laughter.

Mr. Grammatax's face swelled up like a big red balloon.

'Miss Merrilore, please!' he exploded. 'We must have some order here. Imagination is all very well, but it must be kept in check by the logical rigour of language.'

'Sorry, Mr. Grammatax,' Miss Merrilore mumbled, retreating to her seat.

'Thank you. As I was saying, you are now students of this

historic Academy. Whilst you are here you will study many narrative disciplines. You will tell, be told, and even become part of, many varied stories. Your tutors will share their knowledge with you, and you will learn from the masters. The great Cadmus Reed, wordsmith and Head of the Department for Overcoming Monsters, will teach the arts of tyrant toppling and monster slaying.' He signalled to a broad-shouldered man, wearing a leather apron, who sat on one of the stone seats. By his side rested the most enormous broadsword Scoop had ever seen. Cadmus grinned at his wide-eyed audience, and for a moment Scoop thought she could see a resemblance to Rufina in his face.

Mr Grammatax continued, 'Mr Snooze is Head of the Department of Dreams. He will take you on adventures to the Land of Nod, where you will learn the art of dream analysis and explore the stories of Voyage and Return.'

I bet I can guess who Mr Snooze is, Scoop thought, turning towards the man in the white nightgown, whose little eyes twinkled at the watching faces.

There was a disturbance towards the front of the hall as a boy suddenly lifted what looked like a mirror into the air. The mirror seemed to be shouting at him. There was a bustle and then the mirror disappeared again into the crowd.

'Shut up, I'm trying to listen about dream analysis,' Scoop heard the boy's muffled shout. His voice was familiar. She stared at the back of his head. Was it Fletcher? It could have been, but everyone looked so similar in their robes.

'Settle down now, settle down,' Mr Grammatax boomed. The ruckus died down and the Headmaster continued. 'The Head of the Department of Quests is the Yarnbard, Ambassador of the Storyteller, Guardian of the River Word...' the Headmaster's voice trailed off as he turned towards a stone seat which stood empty. 'Yes, well,' he blustered, turning red. 'Well, you will no doubt run into the Yarnbard in good time – he is never one to remain in the same place for too long. The point is that all twelve of the

Academy's departments are overseen by experts in their various fields. Whether you are part of the Department of Everyman, Underdogs, Heavenlies, Royal Rehabilitation, Lovers and Comics, Detection, Tragic Turnaround, or even the Department of Oddities, there are many resources at Blotting's Academy to draw upon, so use your time well. But as Mortales – as Story Characters who dwell this side of the Un-crossable Boundary – you will...'

Story Characters, Scoop repeated to herself, no longer listening. *I wonder what it really means to be a Story Character. I suppose that's what I'm here to learn. I wonder what exactly I'm an apprentice of – and what department I'm in? Surely I should know already.*

She wracked her brains but couldn't remember having been told.

Let's be honest, it's not the only thing you can't remember, is it? Scoop thought, sharply. *This morning you couldn't even remember your own name, could you?*

She chided herself. All morning she had been trying to ignore the black hole inside. There had been so much going on to distract her that for a while she had succeeded in putting it totally out of mind.

Come on, Scoop, stop trying to kid yourself. Admit it. You can't remember anything before this morning, can you?

She cast back, desperately groping the darkness, searching for something, anything, a little shard of light to chase, but there was nothing.

Her shoulders dropped and she shrank down, fear pressing in on her.

Surely, every character has a beginning? Why can't I remember mine? She fought back a tear. Looking around, she felt suddenly out of place.

Fletcher was also feeling that he was in the wrong place. He was in the Hall of Heroes as well, and had found himself sitting beside a girl with a magic mirror. The mirror wouldn't shut up. It kept looking at him and spouting nonsense about him being bound for glory, having been chosen for something or other, destined to meet...blah, blah. Fletcher had threatened to smash the shiny piece of glass if the girl didn't make it shut up. She looked hurt and the mirror had huffed and looked away, saying that it hoped it had been mistaken.

Fletcher was annoyed, he hadn't intended to come to the First Word Welcome at all; he had more important things to do – to find out about the disappearances and to analyse the Shadow Beetle – but he'd been swept along by the crowd, and although he had tried to push in the other direction, he had found himself in the hall with everyone else. The one useful thing that *had* been said – the fact that Mr Snooze carried out dream analysis – he'd almost missed because of the blasted mirror's incessant monologue. As soon as the First Word Welcome finished, Fletcher had decided he would find Mr Snooze and ask him to analyse the beetle. He would have left there and then, but the little man in the nightgown was in the hall, so there was really no point.

He zoned back in to the Headmaster's voice.

'...your tutors will not just tell you what you need to know; that is not their job, but they will guide you. Ultimately, you must make your own discoveries, for you must learn to live your own stories. Now, I will hand over to Miss Merrilore to explain the structure of this ancient establishment of Blotting's Academy.'

Mr. Grammatax waved impatiently towards the lectern and Miss Merrilore stood up.

Scoop tried to concentrate on the First Word Welcome again. Surely something would be said that would shed some light on her situation. She watched, numbly, as Miss Merrilore made her way to the lectern.

'Err, thank you, Mr. Grammatax. Well now, my dears, in order to release our students to explore this magical island in full, every student is assigned a mentor, an ancient guide with whom you will explore and train. Depending on your department, you will either work alone with your guide or be partnered with another student. Apprentice Heroes, for instance, work solo, without friends and against all the odds. Apprentice Adventurers, however, must work in pairs – for a Quest will never succeed without the strength of companionship and camaraderie. And, of course, we mustn't forget your other invaluable guide to this mysterious island – tutors, if you would.'

She waved her hands and a great number of robed, bespectacled figures rose from their chairs to hand out battered copies of a small, old brown book. On receiving her copy, Scoop blew the dust away from the cover to reveal the title, "Bumbler's Guide to Bardbridge."

She leaned across to Mythina. 'Who's Bumbler?'

'He's the Academy's historian. I heard he's gone missing though – hasn't been seen for days. Hopefully that'll save us from some very boring lessons!'

The spectre of Scribbler's House has been busy! Scoop almost replied, but she decided that she'd probably annoyed Mythina enough for one day.

The pages inside her copy of the guide were well-thumbed, a list of names written in the front, crossed off as each year passed and each student moved on. Scoop squinted at the list. At the bottom in small, neat letters, her own name had already been written. She looked up, surprised. It seemed that the guides were being given out randomly. How had she got the book with her own name in it? She looked back at the list. Seeing her name made her feel a little better. At least someone knew she existed. Mr. Grammatax moved to the lectern for the final time that morning and Scoop closed the book.

'Thank you, Miss Merrilore. Well, I think that's enough explanation, now for some exPLORation. Let the adventure begin!'

The hall broke out in a sudden rush of noise and movement as students began to rise and scurry around, leaving through different doorways and gathering together in tight groups.

'Is that it?' Scoop leaned across to Mythina, still feeling shaken.

'Yes, it's amazing, isn't it? I've sat through five First Word Welcomes now – but they're still so exciting.'

'Yes, but...'

'But what?'

'Well, I was hoping for some answers, you know, about the missing things, that déjà vu moment and...stuff,' Scoop said, not wanting to admit to anybody else that she had no recollection of life before that morning.

'Oh that, I'd forgotten all about having déjà vu.'

Before Scoop could ask how she could have forgotten something so odd, a flustered-looking lady approached the group. Her grey hair was tied up in a dishevelled bun, and she wore a black dress covered with large, white polka dots. She gave a little cough.

'That's my job done,' Mythina whispered, standing up.

'What?' Scoop looked confused.

'Well, you don't think I'd sit with new apprentices out of choice, do you? I'm Head Girl, I had to look after you – show you to the Hall of Heroes. Now I'm done and I'm going back to my friends. I'm from the Department of Tragic Turnarounds. I'm a Snob – didn't you know?'

Although Scoop had found Mythina annoying, she had still thought of her as a friend. Now she felt even more alone and miserable. She found herself hoping that she was in one of the departments where apprentices worked together in pairs.

The flustered lady gave a little cough again and glared at Mythina. The Head Girl smiled sweetly before running off to join a group of meticulously groomed students who were looking down their noses at a gang of orphans carrying bowls of gruel.

'Hello. I'm Miss Dotty, the Academy secretary,' the flustered lady said in a small voice to the group of apprentices that Scoop was with. 'When I call your name you must go through the door to our left and wait on the benches in the corridor, ready to be introduced to your pair and then collected by your mentor.'

Scoop's heart leapt. She *was* in a department where she would get to work with a partner. She looked around nervously, wondering who it might be, really hoping that whoever it was they'd get on.

Miss Dotty began to read names from a clipboard she was holding. When Scoop's name was called, she walked nervously to the corridor and sat on a bench. The lady with the sapphire hair, whom Scoop had seen sitting on one of the stone seats in the hall, rushed past, accompanied by two excited students.

'You must be careful,' the blue-haired lady was saying. 'If you see any dark patches of shadow in the Botanical Gardens, come and tell me immediately...' Her voice faded away as she disappeared along the corridor.

Other students and their mentors came and went. Scoop watched the man with the nightgown introduce himself as Mr Snooze and lead two apprentices off to experience their 'first adventure in the land of dreams'. But Scoop's mentor was nowhere to be seen and neither was her pair. She felt tearful again. She'd been abandoned. Anxiousness rose from deep inside her. Nobody seemed to be paying her any attention. Was everyone else in their lessons? She wasn't even sure exactly what she was supposed to be studying. Her friends had all left and, worse than that, none of her questions had been answered. She wondered if anyone even cared about them. Looking down, she opened the battered brown book that was in her hand.

Perhaps this will have some answers, she thought, although she didn't feel hopeful. She flicked to the first page and began to read.

The ancient establishment of Blotting's Academy is a place as thin as paper, if indeed it can be described as a place at all. It is a light place, often disappearing in a puff of air and reappearing in some forgotten corner or unnoticed crack...

'Have you been left behind?' a boy asked, abruptly.

Scoop looked up to see Fletcher staring at her.

'Oh, it's you,' she replied, taken aback. 'Thanks for earlier. I'm sorry I...'

'It's alright,' Fletcher interrupted. 'You look like you've been abandoned.'

'Abandoned? Oh, I don't think...' Scoop trailed off, looking around. The corridor was empty apart from the two of them.

'Well, there's no one else here, is there?' he said flatly. 'I'm Fletcher, by the way.' He held his hand out. 'What's your name?'

'Scoop,' she said, shaking it gingerly.

'I don't suppose you've seen Mr Snooze have you? I'm trying to find him. Did he come this way?'

'Yes, he did, actually.' Scoop pointed. 'He went in that direction.'

'Thanks. Catch you later,' Fletcher said, starting to leave.

Before he could, Miss Dotty appeared. 'Ah good, you've found each other,' she said, scuttling over to them.

Scoop looked confused. 'What?'

Fletcher furrowed his brow. 'Well, she seems to have been abandoned and I'm going that way, so I'm not sure that "found each other" is how I would describe it.'

'Yes...well...all the same. At least you're together.'

'Why's that good, then?'

Scoop raised her eyebrow and Miss Dotty gave her a weak smile.

'Well...you are one another's pair. Scoop and Fletcher, that's what it says – Apprentice Adventurers in the Department of Quests.'

As Miss Dotty read their names together, the two apprentices glanced at one another, an unexpected flicker of familiarity sparking for an instant.

Scoop's heartbeat quickened. 'My pair?' she asked, awkwardly.

'That's what it says.'

'I see,' Fletcher replied.

'What about our mentor then?'

Miss Dotty threw her hands into the air. 'Goodness only knows where your mentor is. They were supposed to be here ages ago. All the others have come and gone.'

'Well, who is it? What's their name?'

Miss Dotty consulted her clipboard. A knowing frown spread across her face. 'Ah, I see – your mentor is the Yarnbard. Wait here, I'll go and find him.'

Turning, she walked away, shaking her head.

When she was out of earshot, Fletcher turned to Scoop. 'Well, I'm afraid I'm not waiting around here for anybody – mentor or not. I've got something important to do.'

'Analyse that insect,' Scoop said, sounding interested.

'Yes, that's right.'

'Well, perhaps I could come too. We could find the Yarnbard together. I'm not sure Miss Dotty is going to find him here – he obviously wasn't at the First Word Welcome.'

'Oh, I don't think...' Fletcher looked uncomfortable. 'I'd prefer to work on my own and, besides, I'm not bothered with the Yarnbard – I just need to get this insect analysed.'

'But we're partners,' Scoop said, disappointed, 'and Miss Merrilore said...'

'I'm not really bothered with Miss Merrilore, the Yarnbard or the Academy to be honest. I don't even really know how I ended up here.'

Scoop paused. What did that mean? Was it possible that like her, Fletcher couldn't remember anything before that morning?

She froze, unsure whether she could trust him. What would he think if she told him that she couldn't remember either?

'Well anyway, I'd better be going,' Fletcher said, turning to leave.

'It feels like you've forgotten something,' Scoop blurted out.

Fletcher stopped in his tracks.

'What?' he said, turning back.

'It's like you've forgotten something. All morning I've had this strange feeling like something's wrong. I can't remember the most basic of things. Why I'm at the Academy, for instance, or what the village is called – or even my own name, for that matter!'

'I knew it!' Fletcher hissed. 'Something's going on. I'm not the only one.' He looked Scoop in the eye. 'That's why I have to analyse this insect – I think it will tell me something about what's going on – why we can't remember – and why everything's going missing. But look, I have to do this alone. You understand?'

'But...'

'I'm sorry,' Fletcher said. Then he turned and began to walk away.

Scoop stood up. 'But I've heard some things that might help,' she called after him. 'Something about a rhyme – when Alethean bells chime and the Golden Feather shines...' But Fletcher didn't turn around. He opened a door and vanished. 'And we're partners,' Scoop's voice echoed along the empty corridor – 'Apprentice Adventurers.'

She collapsed back onto the bench, crestfallen. What was she supposed to do now? She was alone – no mentor, no pair, no idea what to do. With a sigh she slumped forwards, her head in her hands. As she did, out of the corner of her eye she noticed something hidden on the floor just underneath the bench – a small piece of knotted string. It was odd. It wasn't anything special – rubbish really – just a frayed piece of brown twine, but for some reason Scoop felt drawn to it. Perhaps it was just a distraction from her disappointment or from the questions swimming around in her head, but as she sat on the bench feeling angry and tearful, she really wanted to pick it up. She moved a little closer. The string was twisted into an odd shape, and as Scoop peered at it, she thought it looked almost like a person.

It's a doll – a string doll, she thought.

She looked around furtively, wanting to pick the doll up and have a proper look without anybody seeing. Slowly, Scoop shuffled along the bench to where the string was hiding. With another quick look, she bent down and picked it up.

At the other end of the corridor, unnoticed by Scoop, someone was watching. A gigantic man sat in the shadows against the opposite wall. He stared at Scoop as she picked up the string, and almost toppled from the bench. He could have been mistaken...but no, his eyes weren't deceiving him. He recognised the girl with the scruffy black hair.

*It's...*He was too excited to even think it.

Was he seeing things? He rubbed his bleary eyes and opened them wide. No. It was definitely her. He couldn't believe his luck. He clapped his hands and lurched to his feet with uncharacteristic coordination. This was definitely something Grizelda would want to hear about. He had to find her. Where was she? The old crone hadn't let him know where she was going.

But she told me to stay here, he thought, confusing himself. *She definitely said I was to stay at the Academy. 'On no account leave, dullard,' she said. I remember that.*

He scratched his head and thumped back onto the bench. The girl was more important, surely. What to do? He wasn't used to making his own decisions.

As soon as I'm sure the girl's captive, his ponderous inner monologue creaked, *I'll find the old woman. Yeah, that's what I'll do.*

Finally, he'd done something right. He bared his yellow teeth and pulled his mouth into a tombstone smile. He hadn't been this clever for years.

Actually, he thought, slowly, *I don't think I've been this clever at all.*

On the other side of the island, many miles from where Scoop sat holding the brown twine, a hedgehog scurried across a dust track. It was on its way home from a meeting. The meeting had been with the ducks of the River Word and now the hedgehog was feeling intensely anxious. The chatter in the undergrowth was that the shadow was spreading fast. Already, many animals had gone missing. The hedgehog's own cousin had unexpectedly disappeared while crossing the Dreamless Desert – this is what had alerted the little creature to the gravity of the situation.

At the meeting, a message from the Guardian of the River Word, the Yarnbard, had been delivered. He was asking that if any animal saw anything out of the ordinary, they report it to him, via the ducks, who were expert in blabbing stories along the entire course of the river. The hedgehog had agreed.

The little creature was now replaying the meeting in its head as it scurried home. Suddenly it stopped, its senses on edge. There was a tremor. The ground under its feet was rumbling. Something was wrong. It looked along the road nervously, its nose snuffling, fearful, its eyes wide. In the distance, it could see what looked like a cloud. Around it, the trees leaned away, as if raising their hands to shield their faces. The sky above the cloud was dark, every so often broken by a silent flash of lightning. It was a storm, and it was getting closer.

Quickly, the hedgehog scurried towards the safety of the long grass by the side of the path, but again it stopped. There was more danger, *in* the grass this time – something black and slithering – a snake.

Just my luck, the little creature thought. *A snake to eat me or a storm to sweep me away!*

The snake raised its head towards the cloud, its whole body

alert. It, too, was distracted by the approaching storm and so the hedgehog decided to continue towards the grass as quickly as its little legs could take it. The cloud was drawing closer – it seemed to be travelling at great speed.

As the hedgehog reached the grass, the wind blew, whipping up fallen leaves, sending them swirling into the air. The snake slithered backwards, deeper into the foliage. The earth pounded. Whatever was at the centre of the cloud was powerful.

The air became thick and the storm hit. Trees leaned back and the grass whirled around the hedgehog's little face. Just before curling into a ball, it caught sight of what was at the centre of the storm: bearing down was a fearsome sight – a stallion, its nose flared as if it were charging onto the battlefield. It strained on its reins, thrusting forwards, its muscles rippling. Snorts mixed with the sound of hooves as they struck the ground, causing sparks to fly from the earth.

On the horse, leaning forwards, eyes focused ahead, was a rider. He wore a thunder-cloak and tricorn hat. A silver bugle was in his hand, and slung over his shoulder was a cylindrical case, decorated with gold. Horse and rider were low to the ground, both charging forwards, their eyes unflinching.

Then, in a second, the storm passed. The wind circled and the dust cloud slowly settled again, leaving the path quiet. The first danger had passed.

Unrolling, the hedgehog turned to face the second, but the snake had disappeared. Instead, standing in its place was a tall, slender woman. Her face was dark as she watched the horse and its rider disappear along the track in the direction of the village.

Taking his chance, the hedgehog ran passed her feet and scurried into the undergrowth.

'The Yarnbard will want to hear about this and no mistake,' it said under its breath. 'I must get a message to the ducks as quickly as possible. An Auracle is definitely on the move.'

Chapter 5

Dreams

Scoop held the string in her hand. Again, her mind cast back, searching, trying to remember life before that morning. What was her beginning? Frustrated and sad, she ran her fingers along the string, feeling the rough prickles of the twine. Her hands reached a place where the twine had been knotted and she stopped, running her thumb back and forwards across the bump. It was a pleasing sensation.

An image flashed into her mind.

She was a baby in her mother's arms. Her mother was singing to her.

Yes that's right, my mother was a wonderful singer, Scoop thought to herself, *and a great adventurer too. She used to sing island rhymes to me. Yes, island rhymes.*

She smiled.

Taking the string in both hands, she began to tie another knot, pulling it tight and feeling the tension of the twine between her fingers, taut and strong.

Another image flashed through her mind.

She was a young child, outdoors in a garden. Birds chirped and her mother's voice could be heard singing sweetly through an open window. The house was a quaint, white building with glowing windows. The sight of it made her feel warm inside.

Across a vivid green lawn, her brother...

– Yes, that's right, my brother –

...came running towards her, a sheet over his head.

Scoop laughed.

Her brother always played tricks on her, dressing up as a ghost and jumping out from behind corners. Scoop loved it.

Quickly, she tied another knot.

And, she thought to herself, *we used to have a rabbit.*

She saw the rabbit snuffling across the lawn, nibbling the grass. *I used to dress him in blue waistcoat. Yes, a blue waistcoat, that's right.*

Scoop was grinning, a wide, blank grin. Her eyes glazed as she stared at the string, its knotted story consuming her. She felt hungry to know more, the images causing a fire inside her – a fire she didn't want to put out.

I had a white pony too, she thought, seeing herself aged seven, sat primly on a horse, her golden slippers sparkling. She sat up straight and pushed her shoulders back, regally.

Suddenly, she noticed a little old man with a long wooden staff smiling kindly at her across the little picket fence that surrounded the garden.

Who's that? she thought, angrily. *I wish he'd go away.*

He looked directly at her, his eyes deep, as if he was trying to tell her something.

She looked away and tied another knot.

A tabby cat with big, green eyes ran across the lawn to greet her. The young Scoop knelt down to pick him up. Sitting in the sun with the cat on her knee, she stroked his soft fur and the cat purred.

'Hello, Scribble,' she heard herself say. 'You're a cutie, aren't you? But you are naughty – you know that scratching the skirting board makes Mother mad.'

Scoop's fingers were working quickly now, tying knot after knot in the rough brown twine.

She saw her father – a woodcutter – come striding towards the house. He was carrying his axe and his leather apron was bloody.

Must have killed another wolf, Scoop thought with pride. *My dad can overcome any monster he likes.* Hanging from the woodcutter – her father's – belt, Scoop noticed the most enormous broadsword.

There was the old man again. She could see him out of the corner of her eye. He was interrupting her; closer now – his stupid pointy hat making him look ridiculous. He smiled again.

I wish he'd stop doing that! What is it he wants? She tried to ignore him.

Her fingers were now becoming red from playing with the twine. Still she twirled and manipulated it, pulling and knotting it again and again, completely transfixed.

The gigantic man on the bench against the opposite wall watched. Scoop's head was bowed low and her shoulders hunched. She was well and truly captive, playing incessantly with the string, twisting it into different patterns, matting it into a web. He knew that she wouldn't want to let it go now. He smiled and rose from the bench, his work done. Lumbering off, he headed towards the Academy's western entrance as quickly as he could. From there he would leave Bardbridge and find Grizelda. She would be pleased with his news, he was sure. As he disappeared, Scoop was left alone, her hands still knotting the string and her mind lost in its own tangled fantasies.

Meanwhile, Fletcher had discovered where he could find Mr Snooze. He was planning to persuade the Head of the Department of Dreams to analyse the Shadow Beetle. Driven by his instinct that the missing posters, his missing memory, and the little black creature he'd caught were all connected, he marched on, his brow furrowed.

He had received directions from an older student. Following them, he made his way to a little shop just beyond the boundary of the Academy grounds.

Ducking under the low beam of the door, he found himself in a room filled with bunk beds and couches. A warm fire blazed in the hearth and the air was filled with the smell of incense. The bare walls and wooden floorboards reverberated with the soft humming, the almost melodic rising and falling, of the many snorers. The atmosphere was hypnotic. Little candles burned by each of the beds. Above them, small crystal dishes hung, their contents gloopy and brown. Wisps of smoke floated from the dishes, rising from the bubbling brown liquid that each of the candles heated, and passing by the noses of the dreamers.

Fletcher could see Mr Snooze tiptoeing expertly around the shop, adding little drops of Munchkin Seed here, or Faraway Juice there, guiding his sleepers on their forays into the land of dreams.

Noticing Fletcher, Mr Snooze held a finger to his lips and signalled for him not to make a sound. Silver hair framed his impish face, which reminded Fletcher of the crescent moon.

After a moment, Mr Snooze beckoned him, before disappearing through a doorway in the side of the room. As quietly as he could, Fletcher followed. He stepped through the doorway into a tiny store room, covered with shelves and racks. On them, hundreds of glass bottles and tubes stood, filled with colourful potions and powders, crystals and liquids.

'Welcome,' Mr Snooze whispered. 'This is my Bedtime Story Slumber Shop. How may I be of service?'

'I want to get something analysed – through dream analysis,' Fletcher whispered.

'Of course,' Mr Snooze beamed. 'Do you have a specimen you wish to analyse? I can analyse any living, or once living, Mortale, as long as I am able to extract its essence.' He opened a drawer and pulled out an empty glass tube.

'Yes, I have a specimen,' Fletcher answered. 'So, how does it work then, this dream analysis?'

Mr Snooze grinned at the invitation to talk about his favourite subject. He lowered his voice to an excited whisper.

'Well you see, in the land of dreams, the barriers between one thing and another dissolve – one is able become a different person, or an animal, or even an object – and yet still be uniquely oneself. Last night, for instance, I dreamed I was Dorothy – from the Wizard of Oz – you know?'

A faraway look entered his twinkling eyes and he tilted his head, as if being carried away.

'Oh, how I love those ruby slippers,' he said, whimsically.

There was a long pause and for a moment it appeared that Mr Snooze had fallen asleep. Just as Fletcher was about to step forwards and tap the moon-faced man's arm, the proprietor of the Bedtime Story Slumber Shop awoke with a splutter, shook himself and turned back to Fletcher.

'Yes well, anyway,' he muttered, 'in dreams we are uniquely able to step across the threshold of another's life and experience reality through their eyes. All we need is to be able to extract the essence of the creature, using its blood or spit for instance, and we can step into its world through a dream, and analyse its story.'

He opened another drawer and took out a pestle and mortar, which he placed on the shelf by his side.

'So, where is your specimen?'

Fletcher pulled the Shadow Beetle from his pocket and held it up for Mr Snooze to see.

Mr Snooze blinked quickly and then, looking a little flustered, began to clear the pestle and mortar away again.

'Yes, well, I'm sorry...I'm not really...'

He opened the drawer again and placed the glass tube back inside.

'What are you doing?' Fletcher hissed. 'I need to get this analysed. can't you do it?'

'Yes, yes, I can do it – of course I can, but...'

'But what?'

'Where did you get...where did you get *that* from?' Mr Snooze pointed nervously at the Shadow Beetle, keeping his finger well back from the insect.

'I caught it – outside Scribbler's House.'

'Scribbler's House?' The silver-haired man blinked again, his twinkling eyes in obvious distress. 'Oh dear.' He dropped his head and muttered, 'That's bad. Scribbler's House. It's worse than they're saying, then.'

'What is? What's worse?'

'They said it was just a few things being mislaid. But Shadow Beetles – around Scribbler's House. Oh dear.'

'Can you analyse it or not?' Fletcher said, firmly. 'I think it's going to tell me something about the disappearances that are happening on the island.'

Mr Snooze looked at Fletcher. 'You know what it is, don't you, boy?'

'It's a Shadow Beetle.'

'Quite. One of the darkest creatures on the island – I'm afraid it won't take you to a pleasant place. This won't be a Dorothy dream with rainbows and comical creatures – *this* will be a nightmare.' A dark cloud passed across Mr Snooze's face. 'And once you willingly enter a nightmare, you make yourself suscep-tible to the influence of dark dreams in the future. I cannot guarantee your safety.'

Fletcher looked directly at Mr Snooze. 'I don't care,' he spoke quietly. 'It can't be any worse than the nightmare I'm in right now – what with the disappearances and...' Fletcher's mind turned to his missing memory, a great emptiness stretching backwards. 'And...well, I have my own reasons.'

Mr Snooze examined the face of the young apprentice standing in front of him and then slowly opened the drawer again, taking out the pestle and mortar.

'I'm not at all sure about this you know,' he muttered, shaking his head. 'But if you insist. Pop it in there,' he signalled to the mortar.

Fletcher dropped the insect over the ceramic bowl. It fell into it with a clink.

Mr Snooze picked up the pestle and began to grind the beetle with vigour, black bile oozing from its body. After a moment, its wings and legs, horns and abdomen were so thoroughly crushed that everything had dissolved into sticky black goo.

'I'll tell you what,' Mr Snooze said, stopping abruptly and looking up. 'I'll add some Alethean Crystal to offset the effect of the Shadow Beetle. Yes, that's what I'll do, Alethean Crystal.' He reached to the top shelf and picked up a glass jar full of tiny white crystals. 'The purest you will find,' he said with a nervous smile.

Taking a pinch, he sprinkled them into the black goo and stirred the potion with the pestle. Taking out the glass tube again, he raised the mortar and poured in the contents.

'You're sure?' he asked, looking serious.

Fletcher nodded.

'Well then, follow me.'

Mr Snooze led Fletcher out of the store room and back into the shop. He signalled to an empty couch and motioned for Fletcher to sit and put his feet up. Doing as he was instructed, Fletcher reclined and closed his eyes.

As he lay on the couch, he could feel his breathing slowly adjust to the rhythmic pattern of the other sleepers in the shop.

With a nervous look at Fletcher, Mr Snooze held the tube over the crystal dish that hung next to Fletcher's couch. A candle flickered below it, ready to heat the mixture. He paused, the tube hovering for a moment, and then decisively poured the black contents into the shallow vessel. Some of the liquid ran down the outside of the dish, dripping onto the candle, which hissed angrily. Sitting down gently beside Fletcher, Mr Snooze watched the dark liquid and waited, twiddling his fingers nervously. Slowly, the Shadow Beetle potion began to churn, moving with the heat. A thick bubble split the top of the viscous mixture. Then, almost unnoticeably, a wisp of black smoke rose from the dish and began to twist through the air towards Fletcher's face.

As Fletcher took a deep breath, he tasted the bitter smell of the smoke on the back of his tongue. A feeling as cold as poison slid down his throat and into his chest. The room around him disappeared and he was alone.

Chapter 6

Secrets from the Shadows

As the Shadow Beetle potion dissolved into his lungs, Fletcher was enveloped by darkness. For a moment nothing happened. He waited, not breathing; listening.

There was movement around him, he was sure of it – slow, imperceptible movement.

What had he done?

His heart quickened.

Something was in the darkness with him. He could sense it watching – its eyes silently on him – penetrating, unflinching. Its gaze surrounded him. He tried to stare back, to catch a glimpse of whatever was hiding in the shadows, but it was no use, the darkness was all consuming.

Fletcher's muscles tensed. He hated not being in control. Fighting the panic that was rising from the pit of his stomach, he attempted to silence the fears that sprang unbidden into his mind, assassins from the depths of his subconscious. Perhaps he was trapped, unable to escape. What was this darkness anyway, so deep and thick? It surrounded him totally, pressing in on him. Where on earth was he?

Under the earth, one of the assassin voices whispered.

As a single crack can break a whole dam, Fletcher's defences fractured and panic rushed over him, a smothering torrent of fear.

He struggled to move but his body wouldn't respond. He had been buried; buried alive, encased in the earth, surrounded by a great weight of soil, crushed like a pip between layers of history. What tiny life he had was being snuffed out, suffocated. He was nothing, his life as insignificant as his memory was short. He tried to call out, every fibre of his being suddenly wanting to run, to claw its way out and find light again. He strained, his mind now racing, unnaturally alert, and yet his body pinned to the spot, every sinew rigid, his skin prickling and his flesh hot. Blood thumped through his head as the darkness crept closer, closing inwards, covering him, its weight crushing.

Fletcher's breathing was loud and rapid. But above the sound of his own respiration, he became aware of another noise. It was making the ground around him buzz with tiny vibrations. Paralysed, he listened.

What was it?

Through the earth, low ticks and taps were being sent. It was the sound of clicking. With a shudder, Fletcher recognised the noise and began to struggle. The knowledge of what was approaching assailed him: a swarm – an army of a million tiny creatures surging through the earth. The clicking was unmistakable. It was the snicker and slither of insects, and they were getting closer.

Suddenly, Fletcher felt movement on his skin. Something crawled across his hand, and then a moment later an insect scuttled over his face, touching his eyelids. Antennae tickled his mouth and spindly legs tried to push themselves between his lips, hoping to gain access to the warm, moist cavity. He blew, half spitting, and dribbled down his chin.

Out of the earth they emerged: cockroaches, Dull Worms, lice and mites, grubs, termites, maggots and Shadow Grub – larvae of the Shadow Beetle – creeping and crawling through the darkness.

He was in its nest, the nest of the Shadow Beetle. The smell was disgusting. A nauseous feeling rose from the pit of his stomach and he made an effort not to breathe too hard, for fear that one of the insects would get sucked into his mouth or pulled up his nose.

He could hear the creatures rustling and writhing over one another.

Then, with a sickening lurch, he realised that the sound was more than just random insects – the scratching and scraping formed a pattern. This wasn't just an unthinking swarm; the insects were working together, moving as one. The swarm was a single organism in the darkness – a many-bodied creature – and it was whispering.

Fletcher gagged.

'She,' the whisper rustled. 'She is mine.'

There was a pain in Fletcher's head as the many-bodied creature invaded his thoughts. As insects surrounded him, digging their claws into his flesh and stinging his skin, he could feel the creature taking control. He fought, but it was no use; he was being pulled into the blackness of its mind.

What sort of creature was this? As it took control, Fletcher knew without doubt that the swarm of insects was just one of its disguises. He could feel its power; the power to transform at will, to change its form, to become smoke, putrid air – even darkness itself. He could feel the weight of the creature's own history crushing it, making it writhe with pain – a history that stretched back before Fullstop Island had existed, to another time and place. He felt the gravity of that history, and realised he was being pulled back – back through time, back through the memory of the creature's many forms, back to the beginning of its life.

He opened his eyes and found himself looking out from what appeared to be the body of a large beast with black fur. It was prowling, cat-like, close to the ground. It was in the shadows of a forest of gracefully arced trees. Through the branches the cooing of wood pigeons echoed and grouse rustled in the undergrowth. In the distance, the low, coarse call of a stag could be heard.

This place felt different to any Fletcher had experienced. The light was somehow richer and more vivid than the light of Fullstop Island. Looking up, Fletcher realised why: two suns hung in the amber sky – two bright orange orbs of equal size, one directly above and the other lower, near to the horizon. It was as if he'd stumbled onto the pages of an ancient decorated book – all the colours were emerald and deep red, golden and earthen brown. High silver trunks reached towards the sky, their delicately shaped leaves framing the image before him. The beast, through whose eyes Fletcher was seeing, clawed at the earth, scraping against the dry ground and ripping the soil. It was in pain.

The beast was looking onto a bright clearing in the forest. Fletcher could see the sun's rays slicing through the trees, pouring dappled light onto the ground. The brightness hurt his eyes.

In the centre of the clearing, resting against the trunk of a tree was the most beautiful woman. An unexpected surge of emotion flooded through Fletcher as the beast's eyes fixed on her. Fletcher felt strangely drawn to her, sadness and joy assailing him all in the same instant. He wanted, from somewhere deep inside, to reach out to her. His feelings shocked him. Who was she?

The woman was young, her skin soft and her body full of life. She wore a long dress, which flowed onto the bright, cushioned grass. The dress was white and intricately embroidered with images of golden feathers. A rich trim lined the edges of the dress, drawing out the woman's elegant figure. Fletcher felt the beast's insides wrench, its whole being pulled towards her with compulsive and irresistible desire. Everything in Fletcher wanted to restrain the creature, to drag it away from that place, but he was powerless.

At the woman's side lay a man, his back towards Fletcher. He was dressed in a fine, thigh-length tunic. It was also white and gilded with golden trim. His long auburn hair fell over his shoulders and heavy leather boots rose to his knees.

The two were laughing and talking together. From the way they looked at one another, Fletcher could see that they were lovers. They reminded him of a prince and princess of old.

A scream exploded through Fletcher's head. The creature was

enraged by the sight of the lovers. Fletcher tried to cover his ears but it was no use, the scream pulsed through his body, tearing at his flesh, shooting painfully through his veins.

In agony, the beast circled the clearing, watching, waiting for an opportunity to act on its desire, to strike.

Suddenly, the man sprang to his feet, his voice full of excitement. It resonated through the boughs of the trees.

'I cannot wait any longer.'

'For what?'

'To tell you.' The man smiled broadly. 'My father has a gift for us – a wedding gift.'

The woman sat up straight, her eyes bright.

Fletcher felt the beast's fur bristle with fury.

'What gift?'

'A tree,' the man replied with delight, 'planted for us with his own hands.'

The young woman slouched back against the trunk. 'A tree?' she asked, a trace of disappointment in her voice.

'Yes,' the man said, stepping towards her. 'But this is no ordinary tree. This tree is filled with life – with the power to create. From its silver branches I intend to fashion a cane. With it we will summon whole worlds – together create universes. And its fruit...well, you shall see!'

'Can I see now?' the woman replied, greedily.

'Now?'

'Yes.'

'Of course, if you wish.'

She smiled, her eyes wide, filled with hunger.

The man nodded and then turning, left the circle of trees. The woman held him in her sight until he faded into the distance and disappeared. Left alone, she sighed and stretched backwards against the trunk.

Taking its opportunity, the beast leapt into the centre of the clearing. Fletcher could feel it change; somehow transform. It stood upright now, strong and proud, energy surging through it. Fletcher could see its body below him and it appeared to be human.

The woman was in front of Fletcher. She was young, barely more than a girl. Shocked by his sudden appearance, she rose to her feet and, looking around, checked to see that they were alone. Once satisfied that nobody was watching, she looked directly at him. In her eyes, Fletcher could see inquisitiveness; longing even. Blushing, she turned away, her dress fluttering in the wind. For a moment she stood with her back to the creature. It waited, aware of its own power. After a moment, the girl looked over her shoulder and smiled, biting her lip. Her look was one of challenge, of invitation, and it was directed straight at the beast.

'What have *you* brought me?' she asked, playfully.

Fletcher felt the hand of the beast reach out. In it lay a fruit, red and shining in the sun.

'My gift is knowledge. Eat this. Once you do, your eyes will be open and you shall see what I see. You will see what life truly is.'

No, Fletcher silently urged, *don't do it*. He tried to fight the beast, but felt as if its words were pouring from his own mouth. He felt sick.

The girl paused for a moment and then lifted her head slightly, beckoning. The creature stepped forwards. Reaching out slowly, the girl took the fruit. She held it up, studying its blood red skin. Drawing it closer, she breathed deeply, savouring the smell. Fletcher felt the creature grow taller. This was unbearable. He didn't know why, but he felt connected to the girl in the white dress. The desire to protect her was overwhelming. But he could do nothing.

'Eat,' the beast commanded.

Moving the fruit to her lips, the girl took a bite.

Fletcher shuddered.

Instantly, the creature exploded with desire. She had chosen it, accepted its gift above the other. Transforming again, it collapsed into a million tiny creatures and swarmed over her.

Crying out in surprise, she stepped backwards; but it was too late, the creature was fast and powerful. It flowed over her, consuming her life, feeding on her beauty.

'Now you see,' Fletcher heard it whisper. 'Life is no more than decay. The end of the story is darkness and death. That is the truth.'

The girl lay limply on the ground.

For a long while the creature stayed in the clearing, basking in the sun, gorging itself and satisfying its appetite.

Fletcher was bereft.

After what seemed like an age, the void was broken by the man's return. His auburn hair shone in the sunlight. Fletcher could sense the beast smiling, glutted and victorious, surrounding its prize.

The man let out a cry, overwhelmed by the horrific scene before him. It was a cry of anguish and pain. The cry grew louder and, as if in response, the earth began to rumble. The trees shook, branches falling, the forest collapsing about them. The land itself began to move below Fletcher's feet, great waves of motion rolling across the earth as if it was merely a sheet being shaken.

The beast transformed again. It leapt from the ground and flew high into the air, screeching, gripping the girl in its sharp talons. Below, the land was rupturing, the whole world breaking apart.

Fletcher felt as if his brain was being shaken from him. The pain was excruciating.

The beast pushed onwards, driven by a desire to hide, to protect its prey. A crack in the sky had opened and the great wings of the creature beat towards it. Surging forwards, furious energy forced the creature through the rupture. The clouds surrounded it, consuming it – and then everything changed.

The light dimmed. One of the suns had been extinguished from the sky. The rich forest below disappeared. The ruptured land split, dispersing across an ocean, forming a scattering of islands. One island, barren and sandy, lay below, a deep gash to its north-east. Seeing the gash, the beast swooped towards it. It plunged downwards, the girl still gripped in its talons. It passed the surface of the land and disappeared, vanishing into the darkness of a deep chasm. As it did, shadows began to spread across the island in dark clusters emanating from the Abyss, into which the beast had vanished.

Mr Snooze watched as Fletcher's body shook and twisted in agony, the nightmare gripping him.

The silver-haired man's impish face was pale. He shook his head intermittently, muttering under his breath. Not able to bear the sight any longer, he rose and scurried to the store room, returning with the jar of Alethean Crystal.

'Not enough,' he muttered, 'not enough.'

He pulled the lid and it came off with a pop. Taking a big pinch of the crystals he sprinkled them into the mixture that bubbled next to Fletcher's couch. The liquid's colour lightened and Mr Snooze watched, holding his breath. After a moment, Fletcher's body calmed and his face softened.

Slowly, the pain subsided. Fletcher was shaking. In his sleep, he could hear the sound of bubbling water, and then intense peace swept through his bones. All around him, bells began to ring – the pealing of bells, joyful and bright. Before him, Fletcher could see a light, a fire burning brightly, a numinous glow emanating from its flames. In the centre of the fire was a feather. It was the most beautiful thing Fletcher had ever seen – long and slender, shimmering with a thousand shades of glistening gold. Jewel-like swirls decorated its spine. The fire seemed to be flowing from the feather, and yet it wasn't being burned up in its heat.

'I have hung a bell from the top of the Alethean tower,' a voice said. 'On the day I see her again, it will ring – it will ring a splendid song – and we *will* be together. When it finally does sound, the whole island will be filled with joy, for on that day all that is broken will be fixed, all that is missing restored, and all that has been forgotten will be remembered.'

Fletcher awoke.

He felt drowsy and tried to stand up, but a hand reached out and touched his shoulder. Mr Snooze was sitting on a chair beside his couch.

'Pause for a moment,' the silver-haired man whispered. 'You are not fully awake. Wait and let the effect of the dream wear off.'

Fletcher sat for a moment in silence, his head beginning to clear but his thoughts hazy, the dream only partly remembered.

So the Shadow Beetle he'd caught had been part of a bigger creature – a creature that had travelled to the island through a crack; a rupture in the sky. And the rupture had been caused by the separation of the woman and man he'd seen in the clearing. Who were they? Who was so powerful that even the land reacted to his cry?

And what were the bells he'd heard afterwards, and the golden feather?

Hadn't Scoop shouted something about a golden feather as he'd left the Academy?

He turned to Mr Snooze. 'Do you know anything about a golden feather?' he asked, bluntly. 'I saw one in the dream.'

'Ah, that will be the Alethean crystal.' Mr Snooze smiled. 'The feather is one of the Alethean treasures – the greatest of its treasures, some people say. It is said that whoever possesses the feather can look into their own heart – they can understand all that has past and know themselves fully. Because of this, the feather holds great power. But I don't think the treasure is a physical...'

Fletcher stood up.

'I have to go,' he said to Mr Snooze.

The silver-haired man looked at him, his eyes twinkling. 'But you should rest.'

Ignoring Mr Snooze, Fletcher stepped away from the couch.

'Be careful,' Mr Snooze whispered. 'Whatever the Storyteller has in store for you, it's important.'

Without replying, Fletcher walked across the wooden floor, past the beds of the dreamers, and ducked under the low doorway, leaving Mr Snooze's Bedtime Story Slumber Shop. He had to get back to Scoop – to find out what she knew about the feather. Her memory was missing too. Perhaps they should work together, after all. He needed to know about the man and woman he'd seen in the forest clearing – the girl who'd had such an effect on him and the man whose cry could shake worlds. But above all, he needed to find the Golden Feather. Wherever this treasure was, it would help him remember – remember who he was and how he'd ended up here. Perhaps Scoop knew something that would help him find it – he had to get back to her.

In the banquet hall of Alethea the Storyteller smiled, his auburn hair shining in the sunlight. The first part of his story had been uncovered. The plan he had set in motion was moving forward. Soon all the threads of his story, a story that had been buried beneath the island long ago, would be unearthed. And then the great reversal would begin.

Chapter 7

Plot Knotters

While Fletcher had been at Mr Snooze's Bedtime Story Slumber Shop, the sky had grown darker. Retracing his steps to the Academy, Fletcher decided to head back to the place where he'd left Scoop and begin his search for her from there.

She can't have gone too far, he reasoned.

When he returned to the corridor, he was surprised to see Scoop still in exactly the same place. She was surrounded by a crowd of young apprentices all peering at her and whispering behind their hands. Some of the smaller ones craned their necks from the back of the crowd, trying to get a good look at whatever was going on. But Scoop stared downwards, as though she didn't even know the crowd was there.

'Get going, there's nothing to see here,' an older boy suddenly called, standing up from where he'd been kneeling in front of Scoop and causing the crowd of apprentices to jump backwards.

The instruction had come from Nib, the stable boy at the wordsmith's yard.

'I'll call the Headmaster if you don't scarper,' he called out with feigned threat.

The crowd of bystanders yelped and dashed away noisily, leaving Scoop and Nib alone. Nib knelt back down, but Scoop didn't acknowledge him.

As Fletcher drew closer, he could see that she was staring at something clutched in her hands. It was a mess of knotted string. Scoop was frantically tying it into a tangled web.

'Hello, Scoop,' Fletcher said as he reached them. 'So I came back – I think we should work together, after all. What's going on?'

Scoop didn't respond.

'Oh, not another one,' Nib sighed, looking up. 'I thought I told you to scarper. There's nothing to see here. Get back to your mentor – and your pair if you have one.'

'Good advice,' Fletcher replied, sarcastically. 'I'll do just that.' He stepped closer to Scoop. 'Well here I am! Tada!'

'What?'

'This happens to be my pair. So it seems that I was following your advice even before you gave it, doesn't it?'

'Oh, I see. Well, where have you been?'

'Never mind – it's a long story. Who are you, anyway? And what's up with Scoop – what's that in her hand?'

'It's a Plot Knotter. Haven't you heard? They're all over the Academy.' Nib tapped a loose fabric bag that was tied to his belt. It was filled with old brown pieces of twine just like the one Scoop was playing with. 'I've been sent to clear them up. I'm Nib, by the way.'

He held out a grimy hand for Fletcher to shake and gave a friendly grin, his teeth white against his blackened skin.

Fletcher grudgingly shook Nib's hand.

'So what's a Plot Knotter then?' Fletcher asked, reaching out to the string. Like a shot, Nib grabbed him.

'What...?'

'Don't touch it.'

'What..? Why?' Fletcher shook himself free.

'It's dangerous.'

'Dangerous?'

'It's covered in Talejacker Spiders, microscopic insects that jump off the thread when it's disturbed in some way – by tying a knot for instance. They climb into your ears and from there take over your story – adding their own embellishments. Clever little things really – take your own memories and weave them into new ones. It's like an enchantment – have you going round in circles.'

Nib knelt down and took Scoop by the elbow. 'Come on now,'

he said gently. 'Let's get you up – we need to find someone who can help you.' He lifted his hand and Scoop rose without resistance. But still she stared at the brown string, looking blank, her hands moving quickly, adding yet more knots.

'She's going to be alright though?' Fletcher asked, looking at Scoop and feeling worried.

'Yeah, right as rain I shouldn't wonder. She just needs a Sight Draught. Who's your mentor?'

'The Yarnbard.'

'Brilliant.'

'Really? We haven't even met him yet. He wasn't at the First Word Welcome and he hasn't come to meet us.'

'Yeah well, I've heard he's waiting on some important news.' Nib quietened his voice to a whisper and leaned forwards. 'Apparently, the Storyteller is sending an Auracle!'

'A what?'

'A wind messenger – a message from the Storyteller is about as big as it gets. That'll be why the Yarnbard wasn't at the First Word Welcome and why he hasn't met you. He won't have forgotten you though.'

'Yeah, whatever.'

In the distance there was a low rumble of thunder.

'He'll have been keeping an eye on you, somehow.'

Fletcher raised his eyebrows. 'So what do you suggest we do with Scoop?'

'Well, if the Yarnbard's your mentor, best thing to do will be to find him. He'll have a Sight Draught, I'm sure, and she'll be back to her usual self in no time.'

'But we don't know where he is.'

'Well, I suggest we take her to the Wild Guffaw Inn then. If there's one person in Bardbridge who knows more about folks' comings and goings than anyone else, it's the barman. I'll bet a tankard of Noveltwist he'll know exactly where the Yarnbard is.' Nib paused, looking torn. 'Only thing is, there might be more of these lying around,' he patted the bag of Plot Knotters, 'and I should really be clearing them up – we don't want anyone else picking one up, do we?'

'I can take her.'

'Really? On your own – you sure?'

'Of course – I'm not stupid! I assume the inn's easy enough to find?'

'Yeah, it's by the river – you can't miss it. It's a crooked house with criss-crossed black beams, overhanging windows and a precariously leaning doorway.'

'Ok,' Fletcher replied, bluntly.

Without saying goodbye, he began to lead Scoop along the corridor. She continued to knot the string and put up no sign of resistance.

A thought occurred to Fletcher and he turned back.

'But how will we recognise the Yarnbard?'

'Oh, you'll recognise him alright. He's a little old man with a thin beard, a golden kaftan, and pointed shoes. The rumour in the village is that he's as old as the hills – he certainly looks it.'

Fletcher turned back to Scoop. 'Come on then, partner, let's try and sort this mess out. Then you can tell me what you know about the Golden Feather.' He took her by the arm again. Stepping slowly, so as not to trip Scoop up, he led her along the corridor and out into the heavy air.

After following the course of the river into Bardbridge, Fletcher and Scoop reached the Wild Guffaw Inn. It stood alone on the bank, just as Nib had described. As Fletcher approached the ramshackle edifice, he thought he could see its walls wobbling, as if the house of hospitality was quietly chuckling to itself. It looked as though it might suddenly collapse into a forward roll, stand up and shake itself down, before freezing again.

Leading Scoop to a crooked, open window in the side of the inn, Fletcher peeked through. Instantly he was hit by noise: a gigantic roar of laughter, the clattering of plates and tankards, loud conversations, and shouts from the bar, all competed with one another. Revellers sat on barrels and leaned on one another's shoulders. They were a ragged but jolly bunch, many sporting peg-legs or eye-patches. Fletcher had the impression that everybody at the inn knew each other. A sign above the bar read:

"Whether you're missing a leg or an eye, your teeth or your hair, or you're just a few cards short of the pack, welcome friend!"

Fletcher walked Scoop to the front of the inn. It looked as if the door was grinning at him. Quickly, he ducked through it.

At once the raucousness stopped and every eye turned towards the two apprentices, curious to find out who the new visitors were. Chairs scraped as the patrons twisted their heads to look at the pair in the doorway. Fletcher wondered if this was how the patrons of the Wild Guffaw always greeted new visitors. Behind the bar, a man with a shaved head, tattooed arms, and a blue and white striped apron leaned forward and growled, 'Can I help?'

Taking a deep breath, Fletcher walked to the bar, Scoop by his side. Everything was quiet, apart from a loud snoring that emanated from one of the alcoves. The sound of Fletcher's steps crunched on the bulrush covered floor.

'Yes,' Fletcher said, confidently, his voice loud in the watching quiet. 'I've been told that you are the person to speak to about trying to find somebody.'

'I might be.'

'Well, I'm looking for the Yarnbard. Do you know where he is?'

A few of the inn's patrons chuckled. The sound of snoring from the alcove grew louder.

'Do I know where the *Yarnbard* is?' the barman repeated. 'Well – let – me – think.' He scratched his bald head, over-exaggerating the movement. The chuckling increased and whoever was snoring snorted loudly. 'Well I might do,' the barman grinned, drawing his face close so that Fletcher could smell his pie-soaked breath. 'He's a long way from here,' he whispered. The inn's patrons giggled. 'A long, long way from here – in a whole other world, actually. And yet,' he paused and held up a finger, 'and yet, he's so close. In fact, if you listen hard you can hear him exploring that other world right now.'

The inn hushed. In the background the snoring rose loudly again and people began to point and gesticulate towards the alcove. Fletcher looked. Poking out was a pointed, golden hat.

'He's here?' Fletcher spluttered.

The Wild Guffaw exploded with laughter.

'Yeah,' the barman beamed, wiping a tear from his eye. 'The old buzzard only come in a few moments ago. He sat down and went straight to sleep. He's been snoring so loudly that I'm worried he's gonna drive away me trade.'

The inn's patrons guffawed joyously.

'Right – thanks,' Fletcher replied.

Ignoring the hilarity, he turned to the alcove.

'Wake him gently now,' the barman intoned, 'wake him gently. And watch out when he speaks. Words aren't the only things to come out of the Yarnbard's mouth when he gets going. Veeery good.'

Knowing giggles tittered around the room. Fletcher shrugged and led Scoop to the alcove, ignoring the barman's cryptic warning. The patrons of the inn returned to their various pursuits and the rumble of conversation grew again.

Fletcher peered around the corner. Leaning against the wall, his purple and gold cloth-hat draped over his face – its point just poking out from the alcove – was a little old man wearing a golden kaftan, his pointy grey beard rising and falling in time with the sound of his snoring.

This is our mentor? Fletcher thought, disapprovingly. *Well, I don't hold out much hope of getting answers from him!*

Walking straight to the sleeping Yarnbard, Fletcher lifted the hat from his face.

The old man sputtered and his eyes sprang open.

'Ah, there you are!' he cried, jumping to his feet and grabbing a staff that rested in the corner.

'There *we* are?' Fletcher replied. He wiped spit from his face, quickly understanding what the barman had been trying to warn him about.

'Yes, that's what I said,' the Yarnbard continued, 'there you are. I've been waiting for you.'

'Waiting for *us*?!' Fletcher turned red.

'Yes, exactly.'

'But we're the ones who've been waiting for you! You should have been at the Hall of Heroes to collect us. We've been all over the Academy looking for you.'

'That sounds like fun! I was going to take you on a tour myself, but it sounds as if you're one step ahead of me already.'

Fletcher paused, thrown off-guard by the apparent compliment. He wiped spit from his face again. 'Well...I suppose...'

The Yarnbard grabbed his hat from Fletcher and placed it on his head.

'So, are you ready?'

'Ready..? What?'

'I said are you ready? Sit Scoop down here, there's work to be done. We need to administer the Sight Draught as quickly as we can.'

Fletcher was taken aback. 'The Sight Draught – but how do you...'

'I've been keeping my eye on you both. I'm afraid I wasn't able to meet you at the Hall of Heroes – well you know that – my apologies for being remiss, but the ducks were insistent.'

'The ducks?'

'Yes, exactly, the ducks – they had a message for me, from a talking hedgehog who lives in the north. Anyway, that's why I was asleep. As I couldn't meet you, I've been keeping an eye on you both from a distance. It's very tiring having to sleep all the time, but I've been preparing Scoop to take the Sight Draught.'

'Preparing...But how?'

'Mr Snooze told you, didn't he? Keep up, keep up! In dreams we are able to step across the threshold into another person's story. I've been keeping watch on you both from the Land of Nod. Scoop's just getting used to having me with her – she should be willing to take the Sight Draught from me without us having to force it on her.'

'But how did you know that I'd been to see Mr Snooze?'

'He told me. We meet regularly in the land of dreams. We're old friends, you know,' the Yarnbard smiled, fondly. 'Although I do wish he'd stop dressing as Dorothy – it's very off-putting. Now sit her down. I'll find her again in Nod and you administer the draught.'

'But don't you need essence – the crystal dish and stuff,' Fletcher asked, absently obeying the instruction. He sat Scoop down at the table, his mind racing to catch up with events.

'No, no, no, they are only needed when one first begins their explorations. But I am a master of the art of dreaming.'

Without a moment's pause, the old man slipped a small silver bottle and tumbler from his pocket and set them on the table. He pulled the cork out of the bottle and poured a shining silver liquid into the tumbler. Then he picked up the glass and handed it to Fletcher.

Fletcher took it, looking bemused. 'But how will I know when to...'

'She will reach out for it,' the Yarnbard interrupted. 'When she does, give her the draught. It's as simple as that. Now, I'd better get back to her. There's no time to lose. I am expecting the arrival of a very special visitor any minute. I've been told that this is where he intends to make his announcement and I don't want Scoop to miss out on what he has to say.'

With that, the Yarnbard sat down, lay back against the alcove wall and closed his eyes. Within seconds he was snoring loudly again.

Scoop was sitting on the green grass of her family's front lawn with her best friend (a girl with long, dark pigtails) and her brother. They were being entertained by a passing clown.

'Dance for us, clown boy,' her best friend called out, shrilly.

The clown began to jump and twist awkwardly in front of them, tripping over its large, red clown shoes.

Scoop clapped. She loved these sunny days when she could sit at home in the garden and relax with her friends.

When the clown finished his act, he bowed dramatically.

'Who's next?' Scoop called out, eagerly.

An old man hobbled towards them. He was bent over double and walked with the aid of a long wooden staff. It looked as if a puff of air might blow him over at any moment.

'Who are you?' Scoop asked, frowning. She felt as if she'd seen the old man before.

'You might say I am a conjurer,' he replied.

The sun slid behind a cloud and the bright colours of the garden darkened.

The conjurer reached into his pocket and slipped out a silver tumbler. He held it out towards Scoop.

'Drink,' he whispered.

Scoop looked into the old man's eyes. Something strange was happening. She couldn't put her finger on exactly what. She glanced at her best friend and her brother. They were both glaring at him.

'Drink, Scoop,' he whispered again, reaching his arm out further.

Scoop looked into the old man's eyes. They were kind. She stared at his long yellow kaftan. The cloth was so delicate and rich that she had to blink. As she did, she thought she saw the threads of the kaftan move, as though they were alive. Then there was a flash of silver, followed by a golden flare of light, but with a swish the kaftan rustled and fell silent again.

Scoop reached out and took the tumbler.

Fletcher watched as the Yarnbard slept. Outside the inn, the wind had whipped up and the shutters were beginning to rattle in their fixings. Fletcher was nervous. Both his mentor and Scoop were oblivious, but there was tension in the air. The inn's atmosphere was charged, as if a storm was about to break.

His eyes moved from the Yarnbard to Scoop and back again. Perhaps he'd been wrong about the old man after all, but the Yarnbard looked so comical in his kaftan and cloth-hat that it was hard to take him seriously.

Scoop's head was still hung low, her whole focus on the Plot Knotter, her eyes darting frantically as she twisted the string. As Fletcher watched her, however, he noticed a change pass across her face. Her hands slowed a little and her eyes settled for a moment, becoming still.

She blinked.

Then, hesitantly, one of her hands left the Plot Knotter and began to reach upwards.

This is it, Fletcher thought. Reaching out towards her, he placed the tumbler carefully into her hand. Her finger's closed around it.

'Drink,' the conjurer said again.

Slowly, Scoop lifted the silver glass to her lips and took a sip. She licked her lips. The taste of the conjurer's drink was very odd. She felt the liquid slide down her throat and began to feel nauseous. Lowering her hand, she rubbed her stomach, feeling hollow. She'd felt like this before, hadn't she?

An image of a long, wide corridor flashed into her mind – a piece of string and an empty bench.

Scoop's head was fuzzy. Dizziness hit and the garden began to spin. She tried to stand up.

'I'm just...' she slurred, reaching out for her brother's hand. She looked to her side but there was nobody there.

The garden was dark now. Beyond the fence, heavy rain had started to fall, the drops drumming, an oncoming army to cleanse and to wash.

Fletcher watched Scoop's face. Almost as soon as the silver liquid had passed her lips, her skin turned pale.

Suddenly, her fingers became limp and the Plot Knotter fell to the floor. The tumbler looked as if it was going to slip from her grasp and so Fletcher reached out to support her hand, closing his fingers around hers.

Scoop tried to stand up.

'Scoop,' he whispered, concerned.

Her mouth moved but no sound emerged.

The garden span in Scoop's head: her mother's house, the glowing windows and the picket fence, all spinning in the dizziness, losing their substance. Gradually they were disappearing. Her world was collapsing upon itself. In its place a whirlpool circled her. Scoop felt as if she was swimming, trying to pull herself up through water, trying to find air. Her body strained, paddling upwards. Then, through the whirling motion, something caught her eye.

In the throne room of Alethea, the Storyteller looked into the crystal pool. It was swirling. In its centre an apprentice was swimming, fighting for her life. The Storyteller knelt over the water, his eyes wide. He hated to see such struggle and wanted nothing more than to reach into the pool and pull the apprentice to safety. But he knew that he had to wait, for now was not the time for them to meet.

But perhaps, he thought, *this is a time for me to reach out. There's something I can do; something that will be of help in time.*

Picking up the silver cane, he held it out. It hovered just above the surface of the pool.

'To unlock what you see, Isaiah is the key,' he whispered.

From the end of the cane something emerged. It fluttered down into the swirling current. It was a scrap of paper. It drifted into the pool and was consumed by the water.

As Scoop swam upwards, she noticed something coming towards her. It was being swept by the current. She watched until it was close enough for her to see. It was a scrap of paper. For a moment it looked as if it was going to slip passed her, but quickly she reached out, stretching her arm as far as she could, and grabbed. As Scoop closed her fist, something crumpled in her hand. She drew her hand back, and sure enough, caught between her fingers, was the scrap of paper.

Bit by bit shapes began to form in the pool, as if they were on the other side of the water. They were just outlines at first, but gradually they were gaining substance. There were tables and barrels, a room filled with people, tankards and a bar.

Scoop was still holding the silver tumbler, but around her fingers another hand was wrapped. It was steadying her. As she focused, she could see the hand clearly and feel the heat radiate through her skin.

She followed the arm, and there in front of her was Fletcher's face, his expression concerned.

'Are you ok?' he was saying. 'Wake up. Scoop, wake up.'

'Fletcher...?' Scoop asked, dazed. 'What's happening? Where am I?

'We're at the Wild Guffaw.'

Fletcher became aware that he was gripping Scoop's hand tightly. Embarrassed, he loosened his grip and she slumped backwards against the wall.

Scoop's other hand was clenched. As she relaxed it, something fell to the floor. It was a scrap of paper. She picked it up and glanced at it.

Something was written on the paper in neat handwriting:

"To unlock what you see, Isaiah is the key."

Shaking her head with puzzlement, she stuffed it into her pocket and looked round.

The whirling pool had completely vanished now. She was at an inn. It was full of people drinking and talking loudly. 'But how...' she stammered.

The Yarnbard had woken up and was getting to his feet.

'This is to blame,' he said, his voice croaky.

Pulling a pair of tweezers from his pocket, he bent down and picked up the Plot Knotter in its tongs. He held it up. It dangled in front of Scoop's face.

'The string...Oh yes...I remember, but...'

'It's a Plot Knotter,' Fletcher interrupted. 'It's covered in Talejacker Spiders. They climb into your ears and create false memories.'

Scoop paused. 'False memories? But my mother, the house...' she looked at the Yarnbard.

The old man shook his head, kindly.

Scoop's heart dropped and she stared at the floor. Her head was still spinning, trying to take in all the information. 'Spiders?' she muttered, lifting a hand to brush at her ear, distractedly.

'The spiders have gone now,' the Yarnbard assured her.

'You're the Yarnbard,' Scoop said, looking up, her thoughts fragmented and her eyes furrowed. 'Our mentor?'

'Indeed I am.'

'You weren't at the Hall of Heroes to meet us.'

'No, I'm sorry, Scoop. The ducks...'

'But you were in the garden...'

'Yes, I was in your dream.'

Scoop paused again. 'But, how did I get *here*?'

'I brought you,' Fletcher smiled. 'We are partners, after all. We needed to find the Yarnbard so that he could give you a Sight Draught.'

'Partners, yes...' A faint smile flicked across Scoop's face and then her head dropped again. 'But you left me.'

'I came back – and I've discovered some things that are going to help us – things about the disappearances.'

Scoop looked from Fletcher to the Yarnbard. 'So it was all a dream then – the garden, my brother, my mother singing?'

The Yarnbard looked serious. 'I'm afraid so, Scoop. An illusion created by the Talejackers. But you're back now. It will take a little time for your head to clear, but soon you will see the illusion for what it was.'

Scoop could see it already. The illusion seemed garish to her now – shallow. She couldn't understand how she'd ever been fooled by the dream. Although a sense of emptiness filled her again, she knew it was better to see things as they actually were than to live in a dream, even if her reality was full of uncertainty.

A strong gust of wind blew the inn's door open and a large man with an eye-patch peered out before pulling it closed again.

'There's a squall brewing out there,' he said, in his thick island accent. 'It's gonna be a whopper, mark my words.'

'I think perhaps we should have a tankard of Noveltwist Cordial to raise our spirits,' the Yarnbard smiled, rising from his seat.

'But this is an inn,' Scoop said, looking around nervously. 'Should we really be here at all?'

'Of course. Academy students are welcome at the Wild Guffaw. Only juices and cordials served here. The only intoxicating substances you will find in the Wild Guffaw are its stories – the barman sees to that.'

Scoop looked around with disbelief at the buxom women and

tattooed men.

Picking up his staff, the Yarnbard clacked across to the bar. Fletcher and Scoop followed. The smell of sweat and stale heat hung in the air.

'Three tankards of Noveltwist Cordial, barman,' the Yarnbard squawked.

'Veeery good,' the barman replied.

Pouring the jugs of syrupy-looking liquid, the barman passed one to Scoop.

As she took a sip, Fletcher turned to her. 'So I was wondering, now that you're ok...You said something earlier about a golden feather – what do you know about it?'

Scoop was only half listening. Through a steamed-up window, she was watching the dark sky flicker with sheets of lightning.

'About the Golden Feather, I mean,' Fletcher repeated.

'Hmm? Oh...err...Mythina said something about it – that it's a treasure – and that it's kept at Alethea.'

'You know where it's kept?' Fletcher said, eagerly.

Scoop ignored him. Outside, she could see a bartender being buffeted by the wind. He pulled one of the shutters closed and disappeared from sight.

'Scoop, are you still feeling ill? Maybe we should sit down again?'

'Sorry, Fletcher, what's that...? Oh, no it's alright, I'm feeling fine now.'

'Well, I said...'

'Listen, can you hear something?'

Distractedly, Fletcher tilted his head. He wanted to steer the conversation back to the Golden Feather and to Alethea – if that's where the treasure was to be found, what was to stop them heading there right now? He hated wasting time. It seemed to him that the feather was their best opportunity to recover their missing memory and Fletcher, for one, intended to find it. But as he listened, in the distance, getting louder by the second, he *could* hear something – it was the sound of horse hooves.

A clap of thunder broke directly overhead.

Scoop was right. Something was approaching the inn.

Chapter 8

The Auracle

The sound was growing nearer. Every so often it was accompanied by the impatient cry of a bugle. It grew louder, closer, until, with the powerful neigh of a steed brought to halt, the hooves stopped outside. Instantly, heavy rain started to hammer the little inn. The closed shutters rattled violently. Fletcher watched with surprise as Nib slipped in through the door. It slammed behind him.

He gets around.

Shaking water from his clothes, Nib rushed over to the bar and leant across it to speak.

'What's going on out there?' the barman hissed, obviously concerned that whatever the commotion, it might hamper his flourishing trade.

The inn's patrons continued to talk loudly, laughing, oblivious to the noise outside.

'It's an Auracle, sir.'

'An Auracle?'

'Yeah...A wind messenger – from the Storyteller.'

'The Storyteller, blimey! What's a messenger of the Storyteller doing here?'

'He's just tying up his horse. He's carrying a scroll.'

'Flippin' heck! Okay, better go and make sure he's properly looked after. Thanks for letting me know.'

Nib nodded and disappeared back through the door.

Scoop turned to the Yarnbard.

'Yarnbard, I overheard you talking to that girl called Rufina about the Storyteller earlier. Who exactly is he?'

'He's obviously important,' Fletcher interrupted, watching the barman frantically tidy and wipe down the bar.

'Important? Yes, that would be somewhat of an under-statement,' the Yarnbard replied. 'Without him none of us would be here, but *exactly* who he is I cannot say. The Storyteller is a mysterious being and goes by many names.'

'I thought you were his Ambassador,' Fletcher said, a sardonic tone to his voice.

'That's right, Fletcher, I am.'

'But you've never met him?'

'Nobody has ever met the Storyteller, other than in one of the disguises he is said to wear, least not me.'

'How is it you're his Ambassador then?'

'A good question, Fletcher, a very good question – I must admit to asking the same thing myself, daily.'

Suddenly, the door of the inn banged open. Wind whistled through it, sending hats and napkins flying into the air. A couple of the tankards nearest the door fell over, their contents spilling across the floor. Immediately, the Wild Guffaw fell still – only the sound of the wind and rain, and the rattling of the shutters remained.

Outside, Scoop could see a grey cloak billowing in the squall. Whoever was wearing it must have been very tall, for she could only see as far as his chest. Through the rain, she watched him raise his hand; in it a silver bugle. All at once, a sonorous blast split the air. It was deafening. Scoop almost jumped out of her skin and, along with everyone else, raised her hands to cover her ears. The inn shook with the sound.

The Auracle stepped through the door, his head low. As he rose, he towered above all others, having to stoop so as not to hit his head on the low beams. He slid a golden cylinder from his shoulder. Opening it, he pulled out a scroll. There was a crash of thunder and a violent gust of wind – those who still had hats, held on to them tightly.

'Dwellers, Keepers, Bards and Teachers, students and inhabi-tants alike,' the Auracle bellowed, his voice blowing through the

Wild Guffaw like a hurricane. 'I am a servant of the Storyteller.'

Nervous glances darted around the room.

'I have been sent to Bardbridge-By-The-Word with a Royal Proclamation. So hear ye, hear ye, young and old, rich and poor, hear ye the Royal Proclamation of the Storyteller!'

A bolt of lightning split the air, followed by a ground-shaking thundercrack. Tables shook and the inn's patrons ducked, grabbing hold of whatever supports were in reach.

Without flinching, the Auracle continued: 'The Storyteller requests that all islanders attend his forthcoming wedding banquet.'

As the Auracle spoke these words, the wind fell still, the shutters stopped banging and the inn's patrons froze. Only the sound of the rain beating the thatched roof remained.

Scoop was spooked by the sudden stillness. The storm seemed to be responding to the messenger's announcement, providing a red carpet of silence for his words. The patrons of the inn stared open-mouthed at the Auracle, as if he'd just announced the presence of a ghost in the room, rather than news of a wedding.

'What's going on?' she whispered,

'Shh.' Fletcher raised his finger to his lips.

Slowly, the Auracle spoke into the quietness, his words hanging motionless around the low beams, hovering on the stillness of the air.

'The Storyteller welcomes all – the lame, the blind, all who have lost, who are poor or without. This banquet will be for the restoration of things that are missing. Nothing is required of those who make the journey to Alethea.' The Auracle paused, as if to underline his words, 'nothing except that they wear robes woven with the silver thread of the Storyteller – a silver thread made gold.'

Fletcher looked down at his Academy robes.

I wonder what that means.

'The feast will commence in three nights' time. It will be held in the throne room of Alethea, atop the Mysterious Mountains. Three midnights from hence the great Alethean bells will chime and the Storyteller *will* be wed. The banquet is prepared and the Storyteller commands your immediate attendance. And now, I must away!'

Turning, the Auracle nailed the proclamation to a wooden wall panel with precise blows, silver sparks flying as the hammer struck the nails. The wind whistled through the door once again, causing it to bang open. The Auracle stepped through it, and was gone.

There was a moment's silence and then the inn exploded; a cacophony of shouts and slamming tankards filled the air. There were loud conversations about the proclamation, the banquet, and if this was some sort of practical joke. Arguments broke out about whether the Storyteller could really expect everyone to make the journey, and people shouted loudly from one side of the inn to the other about the credentials of the Auracle himself – was he really one of the Storyteller's messengers, or was he a charlatan in fancy dress, as some of the islanders seemed to fear?

Fletcher's eyes were wide. 'We have to go,' he shouted over the noise, pointing at the proclamation. 'Alethea – that's where the Golden Feather is – that's what you said, wasn't it! We've *got* to get there.'

'What are you talking about?' Scoop shouted back.

'I saw it in my dream – the feather. It will help us remember. "Those that possess it can look into their own heart" – that's what Mr Snooze said. We need to get going. In three nights' time the banquet starts. That's not long, and Alethea must be miles away.'

Scoop looked flustered. 'But it's late – and what about the Academy? We're supposed to be studying, aren't we? Shouldn't we be having lessons or something?'

'Scoop – you are an Apprentice Adventurer,' the Yarnbard squawked, puffing his chest out like a peacock. 'Stories aren't confined to the classroom! It is your job to hunt the Academy out

79

– to follow its trail of clues wherever they lead. Its lessons may be given at any time and in any place. The Academy is carried on the air, disappearing and reappearing in the most unlikely places. It cannot be confined to bricks and mortar. You must trust it to lead you. Follow your heart, for that is where real learning is to be had. That *is* your training!' The old man thrust his chin high into the air, as if he were a king delivering a battle speech.

Scoop stared at the Yarnbard, bewildered.

'So we can go to the banquet?' Fletcher asked, suspiciously.

'Of course, we couldn't ignore a royal proclamation, could we?'

The old man lowered his head again and looked at his apprentices.

'But now is not the time. We must be practical. It's late and it has been a long day. We will need all our energy to begin the journey to Alethea. There are guest rooms here at the inn reserved for pilgrims and wayfarers, and although we are at the very start of our journey, we are now, none-the-less, travellers.'

The hubbub of the inn had died down, villagers disappearing in different directions to gossip and spread the surprising news of the Storyteller's wedding banquet. In the dimming light, the barman lit candles in lamps that hung from the beams.

The Yarnbard pointed. 'Candlelight is the ideal accompaniment for a good story, don't you think? And there's a story that you must share with us, Fletcher. We need to hear all you have discovered about the Shadow Beetle. I suggest we retire. Tonight, you will tell us your story – tomorrow we will set our sights on the banquet and on Alethea.'

Adrenalin pumped through Fletcher's veins. The banquet was an opportunity he couldn't miss. He would get to Alethea and find the Golden Feather. In three nights' time he would discover who he really was and why he couldn't remember.

Beyond the gates of Bardbridge, Knot lurched, silhouetted by the moonlight. He had finally tracked down Grizelda.

Why didn't she tell me where she'd be? he grumbled to himself.

It had taken him all day to find her, but rumour had finally led him to the place where she had laid her trap for unsuspecting apprentices. It was by a fork in the path, just before the foothills of the mountains. As he neared the fork, he slowed down, quietly repeating the news he carried under his breath.

He could see the old woman's dark outline ahead. She was sitting on a little stool, her cloak wrapped around her skinny body to protect her from the chill of the night, her murder of crows perched on a nearby tree.

Around Grizelda, a number of squat, black rocks jutted up from the path, making it uneven. Among them, a lone apprentice stood – she was stock still, her features grey. Knot could see Grizelda watching the young apprentice with satisfaction. Slowly, the girl's face was darkening.

As Knot approached, the moon slid behind a cloud.

A twig cracked and the old crone span around.

'Who is it?'

'It's me...' Knot panted.

Grizelda flew into a rage. 'What are you doing here, you moron! I told you to stay at the Academy. What is it you want?'

Knot was out of breath.

'Speak up!'

Grizelda waved her hand at the black rocks, which looked like heaps of melted wax. 'Look!' she yelled. 'These are all apprentices you've *failed* to stop. What have you been doing, dullard?'

Knot looked. The lone apprentice, who had been standing by Grizelda, was blending into the stones that surrounded her – becoming one of them.

Grizelda cackled.

'Have you never seen a child being petrified before?'

Her thin lips turned upwards into an ugly grin. The sound of cold cracking rose from what had once been the girl's toes, through her legs, and across her whole body.

'Anyway, I take it you're not here for a pleasant conversation! What is it you want – out with it, you great oaf!'

'I've got some news.'

'Well it had better be good. You shouldn't have left the Academy! And if I find out...'

'I've seen one of them,' Knot blurted, interrupting Grizelda's tirade. It was dangerous to interrupt the old woman, but if he didn't speak, he was going to burst.

Grizelda narrowed her eyes, menacingly. 'What are you talking about? Who have you seen?'

'The chattels. The ones we...' Knot's voice faltered as he saw the old woman's face contort with fury at his words. Fearfully, he waited for a response.

Grizelda's rasping breaths echoed in the cold night.

I was right to come. I was right to tell her. I know I was. Knot repeated over and over in the silence.

'The chattels?' the old woman said, finally.

'Yeah,' Knot replied, tentatively. 'It was the girl what I saw.'

'Where?'

'At the Academy. I got her with a Plot Knotter.'

Grizelda fixed Knot with her beady eyes. 'Was the boy there too?'

'I didn't see. I come straight here.'

The old woman spat on the ground with contempt. 'Well, well, well. So that meddler thinks he's found a use for those two, does he – after all these years? I thought they were dormant, that their stories had been de-activated.'

Knot didn't reply.

Grizelda glared. 'Well it looks as if I've stopped all these apprentices for nothing, doesn't it! Sorry, my dears,' she called over her shoulder.

Behind her, the lone apprentice had disappeared, merged into the black rock.

'If those filthy chattels are involved,' Grizelda crowed, pointing her bony finger at Knot, 'they're the ones we have to watch for – mark my words. They're the ones we have to watch.'

In the Mysterious Mountains, the Storyteller focused his attention on the three travellers at the Wild Guffaw. He smiled, his heart warmed. He had always felt misunderstood – unknown, perhaps even unknowable. But as Fletcher told Scoop and the Yarnbard all he had discovered that day, the Storyteller knew that finally a connection had been made.

A connection to you too. He directed his thoughts to the invisible presence he felt flowing from beyond the Un-crossable boundary.

In Scoop's pocket a note nestled, crumpled and unseen. The Storyteller recalled its words and whispered them into the crystal pool.

'To unlock what you see, Isaiah is the key. Follow the thread, Scoop. Follow it, Fletcher. Trust your hearts and I *will* be waiting.'

Chapter 9

Pot Hooks and Hangers

Fletcher opened his eyes. Sunlight was streaming through the leaded panes of the window of the Wayfarers guest room at the Wild Guffaw. Outside, the trees were filled with song birds. It was morning. There was no trace now of the storm that had accompanied the Auracle; it was as if the wind messenger had never even visited the inn. Everything was so peaceful. Shadow Beetles, proclamations, and the dark feeling of unknowing he'd felt yesterday, all seemed far away.

Suddenly, the door flew open and Scoop rushed in.

'He's gone,' she yelped.

'Shh!' Fletcher replied, bleary eyed, raising his hand.

'But he's gone!' she repeated, loudly.

'Who? Who's gone?'

'Who do you think? The Yarnbard! His bed was made this morning and there's no sign of him anywhere.'

Fletcher sat up.

'Look, he's left this.' Scoop held up a yellowed envelope. Fletcher reached out and she passed it to him. In curly lettering, the apprentices' names were written.

'Should we open it?' Scoop asked.

'What else would you suggest?' Fletcher ripped the fragile paper and pulled out the letter. He was about to read it when Scoop snatched it from him.

'What does it say?'

'I don't know – you didn't give me a chance to—'

'Dear Scoop and Fletcher,' Scoop interrupted, perching on the edge of the bed and starting to read. 'My apologies, but I have had to leave early in order to pay an urgent visit to an old friend of mine.' She looked up. 'You see, I told you he'd gone!'

'I didn't say he hadn't, did I? What else does it say?'

Looking back, Scoop continued to read. 'You made such a splendid start to your adventure yesterday that I have no doubt you will make an equally good start to your Alethean quest.' She looked up again. 'He's left us!' she squealed, agitated.

Fletcher grabbed the letter. 'While eating breakfast, which I have arranged for you at the inn, I suggest you take a look at the last stop in Bumbler's tour of Bardbridge, which is to be found in his guide. I think you will find it of interest. It is a place where I believe you might discover more about the silver thread of the Storyteller – the thread of which the Auracle spoke.'

'Oh yeah – what was it he said again?'

'That to get the banquet, we needed it sewn into our robes. A silver thread made gold.'

'What does that mean?'

'No idea.'

'Has the Yarnbard written anything else?'

'No, nothing. He's just signed it.'

Scoop snatched the letter back and scanned it to check there was nothing else.

'Breakfast?' Fletcher repeated, feeling suddenly hungry.

Scoop sprang up. 'Have you got your copy of Bumbler then?'

'Hold your horses! You heard what he said – *over breakfast.*' Fletcher's belly rumbled. 'Anyway, I was in such a rush yesterday, I left my book in the Hall of Heroes.'

Scoop tutted. 'I'll just have to get mine then. Come on, quickly – I've been up for ages.' She picked up Fletcher's tunic and flung it at him. Leaving it dangling from his head, she left the room, the door banging loudly behind her.

As soon as the barman had brought their breakfast to them, Scoop laid Bumbler's Guide on the table and the two apprentices leaned over to read. Fletcher had to be careful not to drip egg yolk on the book as he munched his "What Came First?"

Sandwich. Scoop pushed her plate to one side, mouthing the words as she read.

POT HOOKS AND HANGERS. CIPHER'S DEPOSITORY.
Keeper: Mr. Isaiah Scriven

The last stop of note on this rudimentary tour of the village is the Cipher's Depository, called Pot Hooks and Hangers, which stands next to Quills' Quenching Tea Rooms. This is the place to discover stories that are not yet understood.

Built to house the records of dreams, as yet un-deciphered codes and partially blotted or obscured letters, diaries or ancient texts, Pot Hooks and Hangers is filled with mysteries that the island's inhabitants have chosen to keep locked away. Its blacked-out windows and pulled-down shutters hide a myriad of secrets. Behind the long, black marble counter that one is confronted with when entering the shop, a dark doorway leads to the vaults. These are filled with locked containers and caskets, each veiling one of the hidden secrets of the village. The front of the Depository is stark and bare, decorated floor to ceiling with polished marble.

Mr. Isaiah Scriven, the Depository's Keeper, is stony-faced, but delve below the surface and you will find...

Scoop turned the page.

...often protected by an alpha-numeric code in which the letters of the alphabet are substituted for...

'Hang on,' she looked up, 'that doesn't make sense.'

Peering closely at the book, she noticed that a page had been ripped out. She showed it to Fletcher.

'You'll have to tell the Yarnbard about that – get a new one.'

'Yeah.' Scoop looked distracted. 'So do you think he means for us to go there – to this Pot Hooks and Hangers, I mean? Sounds scary to me.'

'Why else would he mention it?'

'I don't know.'

'Is there a map in there?' Fletcher pointed to the book.

'Think so.' Scoop flicked through the pages. 'Yes, here it is.'

Fletcher squinted at the book and pointed, mumbling, his mouth still full of toast.

'Careful,' Scoop said, brushing his hand away. 'You'll get the pages dirty.' She looked at where he'd been pointing. 'Yes look, I've found it. Pot Hooks and Hangers. It's the other side of the river. Come on,' she said standing up and grabbing her breakfast sandwich, 'there's no time to lose.'

In the mid-morning haze, Fletcher and Scoop ducked in and out of the shade, navigating the cobbled streets of Bardbridge as they headed towards Pot Hooks and Hangers. In the brightness, it was hard to believe the island was under threat at all. But every so often, Fletcher caught sight of a sign of danger: a boarded-up shop covered with missing posters; a cordoned-off alleyway with yellow hazard signs depicting Shadow Beetles; a wiry gentleman on a soapbox shouting at the islanders to open their eyes and heed the coming apocalypse.

Every few minutes, Scoop stopped to turn the map upside down and then back again, trying to work out the directions. Fletcher was preoccupied with the events of the previous day. He brought the image of the Golden Feather back to mind and it renewed his energy. He *had* to find the treasure. The first night had passed, which meant they only had tonight and then the banquet would start the following evening – that didn't leave long.

I hope this silver thread isn't a distraction, he thought, swerving to avoid a throng of people who scuttled out of a shop. Everyone seemed to be going in the opposite direction. Horses, carriages and bicycles zoomed past, throwing him off balance.

No, he reassured himself, *we need to get there and that's what the Auracle said was needed. I just hope it doesn't take all day!*

Scoop stopped suddenly. Fletcher almost bumped into her. Looking up, he found himself outside two shops. To the right was Quills' Quenching Tea Rooms. A large pink cupcake decorated its bay window, and outside little round tables were busy with villagers eating breakfast. Next to it, cold and lonely, was an austere building. Its shop front was obscured by long black blinds. Gold writing on the door read, "Pot Hooks and Hangers. Proprietor: Isaiah Scriven."

Taking a deep breath, Scoop entered through the ebony door. The bell rang. Fletcher took a wistful look at the tea rooms and followed. As the door shut, the sound of the birds and the people at the tea rooms disappeared. Warm sun was replaced by cold, black marble. Everything was silent.

In a doorway behind the counter, there was movement. Slowly, a tall dark figure in a cloak and top hat emerged from the shadows. Scoop recognised him from the First Word Welcome; he'd been sitting on one of the stone seats. He looked straight forwards, his eyes not meeting Fletcher or Scoop's.

'May I help?' he asked, his low voice echoing from the marble walls.

Scoop wriggled behind Fletcher and pushed him forwards. Fletcher shot her a look but then turned to speak.

'Yes, err, hello...'

The cloaked figure of Mr. Scriven didn't turn to him. Motionless, fixed straight ahead, he appeared to be listening intently.

'Err, well, yes. We were told to come here...by our mentor from the Academy.'

'Apprentices, I see.'

Reaching out a hand, Isaiah placed it on the counter and turned towards Fletcher and Scoop. But still he looked past them, his gaze above their heads.

He's blind, Scoop realised.

As if reading her thoughts, the Keeper of Pot Hooks and Hangers spoke:

'I am Isaiah Scriven. As you will realise, I am blind. It is perhaps because of this that I am trusted with the island's secrets. Many mysteries wait in the vaults to be uncovered. What is the mystery for which you seek revelation?'

'We're trying to find out about the silver thread of the Storyteller,' Scoop said nervously, before Fletcher could speak. 'We need to have it woven into our robes so that we can go to the wedding banquet...It says so on the proclamation.'

'The silver thread?' Isaiah's voice rose, almost imperceptibly. He paused, silence falling around him. Fletcher and Scoop held their breath. 'Not many apprentices make such a request.'

Although Mr Scriven was blind, Scoop had the unsettling feeling that he was able to see right through her.

'I may not have sight, but I hear many things. The shadow is encroaching. The villagers are disconcerted. They fear the disruption it is causing across our quiet island. Many would prefer to pretend the shadow does not exist at all. But for one who lives in the constant darkness of blindness, perhaps even shadows lose their torment.' Mr Scriven took a long, deep breath. 'The banquet is a sign that the Storyteller intends to confront our fears, for the wedding will transform the shadows. But only those carrying the silver thread of the Storyteller can fully appreciate the power that moment will bring. The ancient rhyme speaks of its importance: "When Alethean bells chime and the Golden Feather shines..."'

'All shadows will hide and flee,' Scoop interrupted, 'and her face again we'll see.'

'Yes,' Isaiah said, gravely.

Fletcher looked at Scoop curiously; she hadn't mentioned the rhyme since he had left her alone at the Academy.

Isaiah Scriven continued. 'The islanders do not understand

the tales of old. They believe the silver thread to be nothing more than a story. They trust only their eyes.' He paused again. 'But I believe there is one artefact in the vaults that will help you discover the truth about the Storyteller's thread. Wait here.'

Turning, he disappeared through the doorway. Footsteps echoed and then faded as Mr. Scriven made his way down a steep, stone staircase into the vaults.

Fletcher and Scoop waited, not daring to speak.

After what seemed like an age, they heard the sound of footsteps emerge again and Mr. Scriven appeared in the doorway, carrying a small wooden casket. He placed it on the counter.

'Many of the secrets left here are hidden in some way. They are coded or un-deciphered, abandoned or forgotten – relics, which remain in my care until the time comes for their mysteries to be unlocked.'

Suddenly the casket jumped, rattling, as if something alive was locked inside. Scoop leapt as the clatter resounded from the marble walls. Mr Scriven placed his hand on the small wooden box and it fell still.

'What's in there?' Fletcher asked, suspiciously.

'This casket contains a distillation – an early attempt by the Hermits of Hush to brew Noveltwist cordial – an attempt that did not succeed.' The casket shuddered under his hand, and Scoop felt her skin prickle with nerves. 'Noveltwist must be brewed with great precision. It is made from the waters of the River Word and the river is laced with the silver thread of the Storyteller.'

'The silver thread is found in the river?' Scoop asked.

'Yes, but its extraction is a dangerous business, which is why the brewing of Noveltwist is such a risky undertaking. When performed wrongly it can have a deadly effect – which brings me to the casket.' The wooden box rattled again. 'In here is the result of that early, failed attempt of the Hermits of Hush to distil the cordial. Instead of Noveltwist, the experiment created...' Mr Scriven stopped. 'Well, I shall leave you to find out for yourselves,' he said, his voice barely above a whisper. Scoop thought she noticed a smile flick across his face.

'But be careful,' Isaiah continued, 'the thread of the Storyteller is incredibly powerful – perhaps the most powerful force on the island. It should be handled with care.' Isaiah pushed the casket towards the apprentices. As it slid across the counter it shook, urgently.

'You're giving it to us?' Scoop asked, scared.

'Yes. You may take the casket – it is my choice to give or to withhold the artefacts left in my care, and on this occasion I choose to give.'

Scoop was unsure. She couldn't fathom the Keeper of Pot Hooks and Hangers. Was this a gift of generosity or malice? Fletcher hesitated and then picked up the casket, tucking it under his arm. He held it tightly to stop it from shaking.

'There is one more thing you need to know,' Isaiah growled. 'This secret will only reveal itself to the ones for whom it was intended. As you will see, the casket is protected with a lock.'

Looking at the box, Fletcher noticed that it was held shut with a rusted padlock. On the front of the padlock were six small wheels, each circled with numbers. Above each of the wheels was an arrow.

'Only those possessing the key will be able to open the lock. If you cannot open the casket within the next hour, it will explode into flames and the secret will be lost. If you try to tamper with the lock, or force it open, it will ignite in your hands and be destroyed.'

'What's the key?' Fletcher asked.

'That I cannot tell you, but if you are the intended recipients, you will already have it.'

With that, Isaiah Scriven turned and disappeared through the doorway, leaving Fletcher and Scoop alone. They looked at one another, bemused.

'What now?' Scoop whispered. 'Are we free to go?'

Fletcher shrugged. They waited a moment longer, but no movement or sound came from the dark doorway.

'Come on,' Fletcher said. 'You heard what he said, we only have an hour.' Turning, he opened the door, and with a last look over his shoulder, stepped back into the sun, the casket still gripped under his arm. Scoop followed. Unseen, behind the dark opening to the vaults of Pot Hooks and Hangers, wrapped in shadows, Isaiah Scriven listened as the door closed and the apprentices disappeared.

Chapter 10

Opening the Casket

'What are we going to do now?' Scoop asked, as she stepped into the light. 'I don't know what I think about that casket,' she pointed at the wooden box, which wriggled under Fletcher's arm. 'Or him,' she signalled back to Pot Hooks and Hangers. 'He's scary. How do we know we can trust him?'

'We don't,' Fletcher replied, simply.

'So what are we going to do?'

'We need somewhere to sit and think,' Fletcher said, turning to the tea rooms next to Pot Hooks and Hangers. 'Let's go in there.' He headed off in the direction of the bay window decorated with the pink cupcake.

'What did he mean, we already have the key?' Scoop asked, following Fletcher through the maze of little tables to the entrance. 'What key? I don't have a key, do you?'

'No,' Fletcher answered as he stepped into the shop.

Quills' Quenching Tea Rooms was a quaint little establishment full of doilies, floral designs and frills of every kind. It had a homely ambience, with the gentle sound of clinking teacups and the hush of polite conversation.

'Welcome!' said a tall lady, who was standing by the door. She was wearing a frilly apron, which was pulled tightly across a bright red dress. Her white hair swirled upwards and was held together with a cherry-coloured clip. She reminded Scoop a little of a Knickerbocker Glory, a tall ice cream with lots of fruit and lashings of strawberry sauce.

'And twice welcome, duckies,' said a round lady, who waddled towards them from the other side of the room. *Chocolate cake!* thought Scoop, with a smile, looking at the woman's rich brown dress and dark, bobbed hair.

'We are Molly and Mabel Quill,' the ladies spoke together. 'Keepers of Quills' Quenching Tea Rooms.'

'Take a seat,' the Knickerbocker Glory lady said as she pulled out a chair, ushering them to sit down. Before they had a chance to say anything, Fletcher and Scoop found themselves sitting at a table in the bay window, in front of the large pink cupcake. Molly and Mable stood before them, each holding a waitress's pad, their heads cocked to opposite sides, ready to take the order.

'What can we get for you?' the round lady beamed.

'Epiphany tea...?'

'Blank-verse Buns...?'

'Hum Jam...?'

'Jotted Cream...?'

'Sonnet Scones...?'

'Or Rhyming Couplet Cake?' they ended together like a little theatrical troupe. Scoop wanted to applaud.

'Well actually, we just popped in for somewhere to sit and talk,' Fletcher replied, suddenly aware that they had no means of paying.

Quickly, the sisters put their pads away. The tall lady smiled. 'I see. Well, your wish...'

'...is our command,' the round lady finished.

Fletcher felt awkward. 'It's just that...well, we don't have any way to pay. I'm not even sure how one does pay on this island.'

'Ah, I see,' the tall lady beamed. 'Of course, you are new apprentices. Well, it may surprise you to know that my sister and I are actually...'

'...rich' the round lady whispered, leaning forwards. 'Princesses, actually.'

Fletcher shot Scoop a smirk.

The tall lady continued, 'And so we have a policy of not charging new apprentices.'

'Everything is free.'

'Our gift.'

'On the house.'

'Oh,' Scoop said, surprised.

'We will bring you our lunchtime tea selection. Sister...' The Knickerbocker Glory lady held out her hand and the chocolate-cake lady waddled off towards the kitchen.

'Do you think they're really princesses?' Scoop whispered when they were both out of earshot.

'I very much doubt it,' Fletcher replied. 'I think they're off their trolleys – but whatever – we have more important things to think about.' Lifting the casket, he set it on the table. It wriggled and he held it down firmly.

'What do you think we should do with it?' Scoop asked.

'Well, I don't think we have many options,' Fletcher replied. 'We have to try and open it. What else can we do?'

'I don't know. I don't really trust Mr Scriven, but the Yarnbard seemed to want us to go there, so I suppose we should try to open the casket – if we can.'

'What's the time?' Fletcher looked at a clock, which read five past twelve. 'He said we had an hour. It's been at least five minutes since we left Pot Hooks and Hangers, which means we have to open the casket by one o'clock, otherwise it will burst into flames.' Fletcher paused; he hadn't noticed it before, but the casket was getting warmer. He could see the nerves on Scoop's face and decided not to mention it.

'So what's the key? That's the question,' Scoop asked, intensely.

'Well, there's no hole in the padlock, so I don't think it's physical,' Fletcher reasoned. 'I think the key must be to do with these wheels.' He pointed at the little circles on the front of the lock. 'There are six of them. It looks as if we need to turn them, so that the each arrow points to one of the numbers. Each wheel has the numbers one to twenty-six on it.'

'Why twenty-six?'

'I'm not sure.'

'Do you think when all six are lined up correctly, it will open?'

'That would be my guess.'

'So the key is a series of six numbers.'

'Yes, I think so.'

'Here we are,' the round lady said, appearing by the side of the table with a trolley of cakes and delicious treats. The tall lady popped up on the other side of them and began to lay out plates, knives, forks and napkins.

'Could we move this out of the way?' she said, motioning to the casket.

'No,' Fletcher and Scoop said loudly, both at the same time.

The sisters paused, and villagers sitting at some of the other tables turned their heads to look.

Scoop lowered her voice. 'We need to look at it, sorry.'

The sisters smiled. 'Your wish...'

'...is our command.'

Busily, they began to fill the plates with buns and cakes.

Time was passing. Scoop looked up at the clock and noticed it was now a quarter past twelve.

'Here we are, duckies,' the round lady said, placing a little pot of cream in the centre of the table. 'A traditional Fullstop Island lunchtime tea – Hum Jam, Jotted Cream, Sonnet Scones...'

'...and, of course, our famous Rhyming Couplet Cake,' her sister finished with a flourish.

'Thanks,' Fletcher said, hoping they would go away.

'Is there anything else we can get you, duckies?'

'No, that's everything, thank you,' Scoop replied.

'We just need some space to talk,' Fletcher added, pointedly.

'You're wish...'

'... is our command.' The sisters wheeled the trolley away.

Fletcher glanced at the clock. It had taken them a whole five minutes to set the table and lay out the food – how could they have been so slow? He brought his mind back to the task in hand. 'If we're the right people to have the casket – and Mr Scriven must think we are – then somehow we already have the key with us. Has anyone mentioned numbers?'

Scoop racked her brains. She couldn't think of anyone who'd said anything about numbers. What on earth could this key be? In silence, the apprentices ran over the past day's events in their minds, searching for any clue that could lead them to the number they needed. Fletcher picked at the food, distractedly.

After a moment, Scoop looked up. 'There was one thing about keys yesterday. When we were in the Great Hall, Mythina said that Keepers hold the keys to the island.' She paused. 'But we've only met one Keeper and that's Isaiah Scriven. He didn't say anything about numbers. And he was the one who said that *we* had the key! This is so confusing.' She looked down at the casket again.

The hands of the clock ticked steadily onwards... twenty-five past twelve... half past twelve. Fletcher noticed that the casket was getting much hotter now. It was making his hand uncomfortable. He lifted off the pressure and the casket rattled, angrily.

'This is ridiculous,' Scoop said, suddenly. She had been replaying the same events in her mind, over and over again. 'We must be getting something wrong. I can't think of anything we've done that could help us guess this number. There must be something else – something written on the casket perhaps – some other clue. Here give it to me.'

Reaching out, she grabbed the casket, but as she did, she was taken by surprise. The casket was blazing hot. She dropped it, and it clattered to the floor, where it began to shake furiously. The customers in the tea rooms glanced at the commotion, edging away.

'It's hot,' Scoop exclaimed.

'Yes, I didn't say because I didn't want to worry you.'

'Worry me? What about? That we're fifteen minutes away from failing our second task. Fifteen minutes from this stupid casket going up in flames? Fifteen minutes from failing to get to

the banquet? Why on earth did you think that would worry me?'
She sat down and folded her arms, agitated. Fletcher picked up
the casket and put it back on the table.

'I'm sorry – I forgot,' a sugary voice said from behind Scoop.
She looked around to see the tall lady standing behind her with a
big pot of tea. 'Your Epiphany Tea – you can't have a traditional
Fullstop Island afternoon tea without the tea, now can you?'

'Here we are, duckies.' The round lady appeared again and
began to lay out cups and saucers.

'We don't want it,' Scoop said, irritably.

'Just put it there,' Fletcher said, looking at the sisters'
wounded expressions.

'I'll pour you a cup, duckie. It won't take a moment. Your
wish...'

'...is our command.'

The round lady poured the tea and the sisters disappeared
again. Fletcher looked at the clock. It was now ten to one. His
head was aching and he was starting to lose hope. Picking up the
cup, he took a sip.

'Hang on,' he said, suddenly. 'I've thought of something.'

'What?' Scoop looked up.

'This morning, when you were reading about Pot Hooks and
Hangers, there was that missing page. didn't the bit after that say
something about an alpha-numeric code?'

Scoop grabbed the book from her bag and rifled through it to
where the page had been torn out. 'Yes,' she said, excitedly:

...often protected by an alpha-numeric code in which the letters
of the alphabet are substituted for numbers.

'Does it say how the code works?'

'Yes. It looks pretty simple actually – when you know about it.
Basically you substitute the first letter of the alphabet for one, the
second for two and so on. So A is one, B is two, C is three...'

'Of course, that's why the wheels have the numbers one to twenty-six on them – that's the number of letters in the alphabet.'

'So each number stands for a letter.'

'Exactly. So, perhaps it's not a number that we're looking for – perhaps it's a word.'

At the same time, Fletcher and Scoop looked at the clock. It was five to one.

'Quickly,' Scoop said. 'We only have five minutes. What words have been significant to us? Scribbler? Storyteller?'

'It needs to be six letters,' Fletcher interjected.

'Surely if we had been given a key we would have noticed it? We could be here all day trying to think of six-letter words, and we don't have all day. We can't just pull a key out of thin air!'

As the words left her mouth, it hit Scoop. She had been so stupid! A six-letter word pulled out of thin air. She plunged her hand into her pocket and pulled out the scrap of paper that had been hidden there. She'd forgotten all about it. She stared at it:

"To unlock what you see, Isaiah is the key."

Isaiah had six letters.

'It's Isaiah!' she shouted, urgently.

'How do you know?'

'I'll explain later. We only have a minute left. I'll work out the numbers and you turn the wheels.'

Fletcher was struggling to hold the casket in place now. It had started to shake more violently and was so hot that he had to keep swapping hands to prevent his skin from burning. Scoop pulled a pen out of her bag and began to scribble furiously in the margin of Bumbler's Guide.

'Ok, the first and fourth wheels need to point to number nine,' she instructed.

'Ouch,' Fletcher yelled as he turned the first wheel. The metal was scorching.

'The second wheel needs to point to nineteen, and the third and fifth wheels need to point to number one.'

In turn, Fletcher adjusted the wheels so that the arrows were pointing to the right numbers. 'Last one,' he said, looking up. He and Scoop stared at each other nervously. The minute hand of the clock was about to hit the hour.

'The last wheel needs to point to the number eight,' Scoop whispered.

Fletcher turned the wheel to the right place, and as he did the lock clicked. The padlock fell to the floor with a crack.

Without warning, the lid of the casket flew open, and upwards leapt a great stream of silver threads. They poured towards Fletcher and Scoop's faces like a million silver tentacles. The two apprentices jumped up from their chairs, knocking them over, but the threads were too quick. Before Fletcher or Scoop could do anything about it, the threads had wrapped themselves around their bodies, crawling over them, binding them as bandages bind a mummy. Scoop could feel the threads weaving into her tunic, connecting with her clothes. She could feel them on her face. The image of Isaiah Scriven filled her mind, his blind eyes, white and motionless. Then suddenly, the threads reached *her* eyes, and everything around began to spin, whirling into a tunnel of silver. She felt herself being pulled into the twisting mass. The power of the threads was impossible to resist. Before she knew it, Scoop's feet had left the floor and she was flying; flying along the tunnel of silver; flying towards a time and a destination unknown.

Chapter 11

The Silver Tunnel

The tunnel felt unstable. On its walls, images flickered into view and then vanished almost immediately. The effect made Scoop feel nauseous and she closed her eyes. Like the whirlpool caused by the Sight Draught, the tunnel span about her – but its force was unpredictable, more volatile. Suddenly Scoop shuddered to a stop, her stomach lurching.

When she opened her eyes, the image of a desert at twilight filled the tunnel walls. Scoop felt as if she was actually standing in the wilderness. To one side of her, endless dunes stretched away and to the other side, a high cliff loomed. Scoop heard the wind whisper and a ghostly finger of sand blew past her feet.

All of a sudden, the image flickered. The ground jolted and Scoop stumbled. The tunnel was obviously still unstable. She stood up again, her heart beating fast.

The flickering stopped.

On the desert's horizon, a figure had appeared. It was a man, a Stranger, and he was coming towards her.

Scoop tried to move away, but as she did the image adjusted around her and she found herself standing in exactly the same place.

The Stranger was still approaching.

I can't get away, Scoop thought, looking for an escape. It was no good; she was trapped in the tunnel.

She turned back to the Stranger. He appeared to be dragging something behind him. Although the figure was distant, Scoop could hear what was being pulled as it scraped across the sand. But the sound was loud, as if it was right next to her. The noise set her teeth on edge.

Again, the desert jolted and the Stranger flickered out of view.

He reappeared again, closer than before.

He was leaning forwards, clutching a rope that passed over his shoulder to the object he was pulling. Scoop could see what it was now. It was a boat – a long, wooden rowing boat.

In the desert?

Unbeknown to her, Fletcher was experiencing the same thing – but, unlike Scoop, Fletcher recognised the Stranger. There was no mistaking it – it was the man he'd seen in the forest clearing.

What's he doing here?

Unlike in the forest, he could see the Stranger clearly. He was a young man, lean, perhaps even thin, but time had taken its toll. His clothes were ragged and dirty and his long auburn hair, dank and unwashed. He looked weathered, his skin leathery and his hands rough. His shoulder was bleeding from where the rope cut into him. He looked as if he'd been travelling for miles.

The Stranger drew near and stopped.

This is the place, he thought, bending down to catch his breath. Scoop jumped. She could hear his thoughts in her head.

The boat tipped to one side as the rope slackened.

Scoop watched as the Stranger scanned the contours of the jagged cliff.

There it is, she heard him think.

The place where his eyes settled was jet black; there was no rock there. Instead, the foot of the cliff gave way and plunged into darkness, revealing the mouth of an oily black cave. In front of the cave the land dipped down, creating a large bowl in the earth.

Again, the tunnel jolted.

Fletcher's body jerked, Isaiah Scriven's words resounding in his head:

"The river is laced with the silver thread of the Storyteller. But its extraction is a dangerous business...When performed wrongly it can have a deadly effect."

Well, let's hope we get out of this alive, Fletcher thought to himself, dryly.

As the tunnel stabilised, it became clear that the scene had jumped forwards. The Stranger was now sitting *in* the boat, which he had dragged to the centre of the bowl in the earth.

What's he doing? Fletcher frowned, staring at the surreal scene. *Why's he got a boat in the desert? And why's he sitting in it?*

The Stranger reached down, pulling out an object from beneath the boat's bench. It was wrapped in an old oil cloth. Carefully, he removed the covering. Inside was a small book – a journal. It had a thick red binding, which had been decorated with a crest. When Fletcher saw it, his heart leapt.

It can't be!

He stared at the journal. There was no mistaking it – the crest was of a golden feather, surrounded by fiery flames.

Adrenalin pumped through Fletcher's veins.

Open it, he urged the Stranger silently, hungry to see what its covers concealed.

The Stranger ran his fingers lightly over the crest, his eyes shining with sadness. As if yielding to Fletcher's urge, he tenderly opened the journal.

Inside, the book was filled with close handwriting, the words flowing into each other like a long string of ink. The scarlet pages were spotted with small watermarks, tears having fallen upon the page. In the desert light, the words sparkled – for they had been written with silver ink.

Fletcher wanted with all his heart to read what was in the journal. He tried to move forwards, but the scene adjusted around him. Frustrated, he clenched his fists.

The desert flickered again but quickly stabilised.

The Stranger was now holding the journal against the side of the boat. Moving his eyes closer, he made a delicate sewing motion, as if pushing a needle through the corner of the page. As he did, he nipped the edge of the very first letter of the very first word that was written in the journal. Fletcher watched in disbelief as the letter slowly peeled away from the surface of the paper, becoming a fine silver thread, held between the Stranger's thumb and finger.

The silver thread! This must be it. It's made from whatever's written in that journal! Somehow it's connected to the Golden Feather.

Fletcher's mind buzzed as he tried to work out how.

Mesmerised, he watched the Stranger draw his hand back a little further. A second letter peeled away, making the thread longer. A third letter, then a fourth joined the thread, until the Stranger held a whole word in his hand, pinched between his thumb and finger, the other end still delicately connected to the page of the journal. The Stranger lifted his hand. A string of words disappeared from the page – a sentence, and then a paragraph. As he drew the string of ink away from the book, the place where it had once formed words was left blank.

The thread of our story, the Stranger marvelled. *I am pulling the ink right from the page.*

Our story, Fletcher pondered. *Exactly whose?*

He thought back to the forest clearing, suddenly remembering something from the dream. The young woman he'd felt such a strong bond with – she'd been wearing a dress decorated with golden feathers. Perhaps the book was hers. It made sense. Perhaps the silver thread was their story.

The Stranger let go of the end of the thread, hanging it over the side of the boat. He moved his hand back to the journal and, taking the middle of the thread, gave it another tug. More sentences unwound and disappeared. They slid down the side of the boat, making the thread's own weight enough to pull the words and letters from the journal by itself.

Slowly at first, but trickling faster, the words began to flow by themselves from the page. The unwinding thread of ink gathered speed, words disappearing from the journal, its pages turning of their own accord. It was as if a vein in the book had been opened and it was bleeding, its silvery story trickling freely from the page and splashing to the ground. But the pool that was forming as it fell to the floor was not a pool of blood, nor was it a pool of ink: it was a pool of silver threads; threads containing the story of the Stranger and the young woman. As the threads gathered around the bottom of the boat, they looked like silver water, sparkling and shimmering in the desert.

The Stranger held on to the journal with both hands as the thread turned into a trickle and then to a stream. It splashed into the silver pond that was forming. With every drop the book shed, the stranger grew weaker, weariness overtaking him. As the words flowed, the pond grew. Then with a rock, the little boat freed itself from the land and began to float on the silvery water.

All of a sudden, the whole desert shook violently. Fletcher fell over, scraping his knee.

'Ouch!'

As the tunnel shook, the image of the Stranger and the boat flared and then disappeared completely.

Fletcher felt as if the tremor was trying to shake him from where he was standing. The ground was disappearing and he feared he was being pulled back into the silver tunnel. He didn't want to go yet; there was more to see, he was sure. He held on to the image of the desert, resisting the force of the tunnel. A sharp pain flowed through his temples. Then all at once, solid ground returned beneath his feet.

There had been another glitch in the story and time had moved on. It was night now, just before morning. The spreading dawn was visible just beyond the cliff.

The lake had grown; it lapped at the mouth of the cave. But the boat still floated on the water. The Stranger had obviously held the journal throughout the night as it poured out its story. He looked exhausted.

Another flick of silver light flashed across the desert.

Above the cliff, the horizon started to transform, turning from silver to deep blue to purple, before a band of golden yellow light spread along the cliff-top. In the centre, bright rays of sunlight emanated from a dazzling point and hit the water. As they did, the silver threads began to glow and the whole lake exploded with dancing golden light.

When the Stranger saw the lake glowing, he stood up, balancing himself as the boat rocked. Still holding the book in one hand, he lifted his other. In it was gripped a cane made of silver wood.

Fletcher recalled his dream again, remembering the Stranger's words:

"This is no ordinary tree. This tree is filled with life – with the power to create. From its silver branches I intend to fashion a cane. With it we will summon whole worlds – together create universes."

The Stranger held the cane high and, in a voice that bounced from the cliff, called out:

'Flow river. Carry our thread throughout this island. Water the land with our story. Bring life, and one day return to me.'

The Stranger fell silent, the echo fading. For a moment the land was still. Then above the cliff, directly over the mouth of the cave, a drop of water fell. Like a tear it plunged downwards and splashed into the silvery lake. An instant later, a whole sheet of water tumbled over the cliff-top. The lake churned as the waterfall mingled with the silver thread.

Opposite the cave, where the rim of the earth was lowest, the lake burst over the side of the bank. It flowed across the dunes, creating a brand new stream. As the waterfall fell from the cliff, the stream flowed away from the lake, carrying the silver thread of the Stranger in its sparkling waters.

Seeing the new stream, the Stranger opened his mouth in an ecstatic moment of joy. With a deep cry he threw the journal into the depths of the water.

No, Fletcher reacted, his body straining to reach out and grab the book. But it was no good. It hit the surface of the water, floated for a moment, and then sank, its heavy cover weighing it down. The image of the golden feather faded into the depths.

Fletcher slumped back.

A river of words, the Stranger thought, looking to where the new channel of water inched forwards, baptising the earth on its maiden voyage.

'The River Word,' he spoke aloud.

The desert began to shake again, this time jolting with bone-breaking force.

The image of the golden feather disappearing below the surface of the water impressed on Fletcher's mind and he allowed his body to be pulled away, back into the tunnel.

Fletcher and Scoop flew back along the whirling silver. Again, images flickered on its wall. The Stranger's face was there, large and vivid, his eyes piercing, his hair like fire. In the confusion, Scoop thought she saw his features merge and blend with another face, as if someone was behind him, or through him – or somehow in him. The figure inside the Stranger was different, though – small and slight. Scoop tried to focus and just for a moment she saw her.

Her? she thought, surprised.

In Alethea, the Stranger fell to his knees, sweat pouring from his forehead. What had just happened? It was as if Scoop had been able to see through him, beyond his flesh – to the other side of the Un-crossable boundary.

'Impossible,' he said, looking up, his eyes darting. 'The boundary's impenetrable.'

But was it? Part of him had long suspected that it wasn't as solid as everyone believed. After all, he sensed so clearly the presence that flowed through him from beyond its limitation. But what *exactly* was out there – that was a mystery.

His heart beat fast.

'Who are you?' he murmured. 'I know you're with me – that

somehow I speak the words you give me. But I want to see you. I want to see your face.'

Instinctively, he looked into the crystal pool. From its waters a visage reflected. The Storyteller gazed into its eyes and deep peace filled him.

From the crystal liquid, a whisper rose, 'It is good. The second part of our story is uncovered. Only a day remains until the appointment we've longed for arrives. Keep them safe. It is crucial the apprentices make it to the banquet alive.'

The Storyteller didn't speak. He didn't need to, for he knew that the face in the pool already knew exactly what he would say.

Chapter 12

Pigtail Tips

Through the swirling silver, familiar shapes began to form. After a moment, Fletcher and Scoop found themselves standing once again in Quills' Quenching Tea Rooms. The casket was on the floor in front of them, broken into splinters, and behind them, their upturned chairs lay. The silver threads were unravelling from their clothes and being sucked back into the broken box. With a slurp, the last of the threads retreated under a splinter of wood and disappeared from sight.

'Are you alright, duckies?' a kindly voice called from across the room.

The apprentices turned to see the lady with the chocolate-coloured dress waddling towards them.

'What happened? Was the tea too hot? Have you spilled something? Not to worry, it happens all the time.'

'No...' Fletcher began, 'it was the casket.'

'Oh dear, you've broken it,' she said, arriving at the table and crouching down to pick up the splinters of wood. 'I hope it was nothing precious.'

'Sit down, sit down,' her sister appeared, picking up Scoop's chair and ushering her to it. 'we'll have it cleared up in no time. Your wish...'

'...is our command.'

'But, how long were we away?' Scoop stuttered.

'Away? Whatever do you mean, duckie? I just popped into the kitchen for a moment and next thing I heard the crash and came straight over.' She smiled, reassuringly. 'No damage done – other than the casket of course. What a shame. Never mind, everything will be right as rain in no time.'

Scoop looked at the casket. Under the shards of wood, she

could see something glistening. Fletcher had spotted it too.

'We'll bring you a new pot of tea – a nice calming blend of Posyshire Rose...'

'Ouch,' the round lady suddenly exclaimed, quickly withdrawing her finger from the shattered casket and putting it in her mouth.

'Sister, what's wrong?'

'It's nothing.' She looked at her finger, 'Just something sharp in the box.'

Her sister bent over the fragments of wood and gently moved some of the splinters away. 'Yes, look, it's a mirror.'

Fletcher and Scoop glanced at one another.

Carefully, the tall lady reached down and picked up the glass. It was a small, round mirror. It had been fractured along the centre and was now in two sharp pieces. She laid the broken glass on the table.

'Let's get the rest of the box cleared up and then I'll dispose of these.'

'No,' Fletcher and Scoop replied together, stepping forward and both picking up a piece of the fractured mirror.

'Oh...well it is your mirror, I suppose. But you must be careful – it's sharp.'

The Quill sisters headed back to the kitchen, taking the splinters of the casket with them.

The apprentices looked into the glass.

'What..?' Scoop whispered, surprised.

The reflection in the mirror bore no resemblance to the little tea shop, and their faces were nowhere to be seen. Instead, the mirror cast an image of another place, as if it were a window. From the snatches they caught, the place on the other side of the glass had a tall stone ceiling. It appeared to be reflecting the inside of a large circular hall. All of a sudden, a face appeared. Fletcher and Scoop sprang back. From the other side, the face squinted into the mirror. It was the Stranger. He blinked, and then his lips began to move.

'He's talking,' Fletcher whispered.

Scoop leaned in. Sure enough, through the glass, muffled but still intelligible, she could hear the Stranger speaking.

'I don't know if you can hear me...if you're there,' he said, his eyes darting, as if trying to see through the glass. 'The threads still have a little energy, so it is possible. If you *can* hear me, there's something I want you to do. You've seen what the silver thread is – my story – my love's story. The river has carried it throughout the island. It has brought life to what was once a barren land. Now, I want you to bring it back to me. Bring it back bright and alive, for now it is pale, just the moonlight of our love. Make it glow once again and bring it to me. Take this mirror with you. In the darkest place it will reflect the truth. Seek Wisdom. She will help you. I will be waiting – waiting for you both. Seek Wisdom.'

As the Stranger finished speaking, the mirror clouded over and the apprentices' faces appeared in the glass, wide eyed. They stood fixed for a moment, staring at themselves. Then Scoop turned her piece of mirror over to check the back. It appeared to be completely ordinary.

The tea-room door opened, disturbing her thoughts. An Academy student walked in. Scoop recognised the pigtails instantly; it was Mythina. Walking to the counter, Mythina picked up a little bell and rang it loudly. The tall lady rushed across to her.

'Welcome!' she said, beaming, 'How can I...'

'I hear that you're doing free food,' Mythina interrupted.

'Yes, for Academy...'

'Good. Well I want two Blank-Verse Buns and a packet of Rhyming Couplet Cakes.'

The round lady joined her sister. 'You're wish...'

'Is our...'

'And be quick – I'm late.'

The Quill sisters disappeared into the kitchen. Noticing Scoop, Mythina strode over to her, a fake grin on her face.

'Scoop!' she said in a high voice. 'How *are* you? How have you been?' She held Scoop by the shoulders and looked her up and down as if she were her mother. 'You *must* tell me. What's your partner like?'

Scoop stepped back. 'This is Fletcher.'

Mythina glanced at him dismissively. 'So, what *have* you been up to? I'm on my way to the wedding banquet. My new mentor – that foreign idiot, Thumbandingo – has been going on and on. He's created...' she laughed, annoyingly, '...he's created this new packet of sweets for his Tall Tale Tuck Shop, especially for the royal wedding – what an idiot. He's spent all this time distilling the Story Threads from different tales relating to the Storyteller – tours of Alethea, that sort of thing – and putting them in his sweets.'

Fletcher's ears pricked up. 'What do you mean he's been distilling Story Threads?'

'He's calling them "Auburns",' Mythina continued, ignoring Fletcher, 'after the Storyteller's auburn hair. How ridiculous is that?'

Fletcher stepped aggressively forwards. 'What do you mean – distilling Story Threads?'

Had Scoop just heard Mythina correctly – the Storyteller had auburn hair?

Mythina glanced at Fletcher and then looked straight back at Scoop. 'You know what distilling is, don't you Scoop, dear? Everyone knows what distilling is.'

Scoop looked distracted.

'It's when you boil something down to its essence, silly. Stories can become unstable when you distil them – downright dangerous sometimes – but if you're careful you can boil them right down to the threads from which they're made – their core. Anyway, that's what he's been doing – distilling some of the tales of the Storyteller and putting them in sweets. When you eat one, you get pulled into the thread and it feels like you're seeing the story as it unfolds. What a waste of time.'

'Could you put a story thread in anything?' Fletcher interrupted, again. 'Something like a mirror, say?'

'I suppose so – although, who would want to do that?'

At that moment the tall lady emerged, holding a bag of cakes. Walking to her, Mythina grabbed them.

'Anyway, I've managed to get rid of Thumbandingo. As if I need him to get to the wedding. I mean, you just have to follow the river to get to Alethea, don't you?'

'Well not exactly, dear,' the tall lady interrupted. 'There's a fork in the path just before Wisdom's house and...'

Mythina cut her off. 'I don't remember ordering advice. I thought I'd just ordered cakes.' She smiled, sweetly.

'Oh well... yes,' the tall lady's voice wavered. 'Of course, your wish is...'

'Anyway, I'd better be going.' Mythina waved at Scoop. 'See ya.'

She stepped through the door of the tea rooms and headed off alone towards the Mysterious Mountains.

As the latch clicked shut, Fletcher and Scoop were left staring awkwardly at the empty doorway.

Still a little distracted, Scoop turned to the tall lady. 'If you don't mind me asking, what was that you just said about Wisdom?'

'Hmm? Oh, just that the path to the Mysterious Mountains goes past her house – Lady Wisdom's, I mean.'

'You mean Wisdom's a person?'

'Of course she is, dear. She's one of the oldest inhabitants of the island – like all the Guardians, she possesses youth and age in equal measure. Here have a look at this.' She pointed at a framed map of the island that hung on the wall. 'You see, that's her house there. To get to it, you follow the path from the northwest gate of the village.'

The round lady appeared with a cloth and began to wipe a table. 'That path leads between the Creativity Craters and the Puddles of Plot, duckies. But be careful – part way along, it splits in two.'

'That's what I was trying to say a moment ago. Oh, I do hope that girl will be alright.' The tall lady glanced nervously at the door.

'You see, duckies, the left-hand fork looks wide and easy on the feet, but although it *seems* to head towards the mountains, it doubles back on itself.'

'That's right, sister. Travellers who take that path soon find themselves lost in the Unbounded Mire, from which very few ever emerge.' She peered at Scoop, a ghostly look in her eye. 'If you go that way, you must take the right-hand fork. Promise me you will.'

'That's very important, duckie. The right hand fork. Do you understand?'

'Yes,' Scoop replied.

'*If* we go that way,' Fletcher added, pointedly. He looked irritated.

'I think you'll find there's a map in Bumbler's guide. It would be best to have a map with you for the journey, don't you think? Do you have a copy with you?'

'We're not going that way,' Fletcher objected, but the others weren't listening. Scoop had already pulled the book out and handed it over. The tall lady flicked through it. 'Ah yes, here we are.'

Scoop leaned over to have a look.

Fletcher was angry now. 'Ok well, we'd better be going.'

'But...'

Before Scoop had time to finish her sentence, Fletcher turned and stormed out of the tea rooms. Flustered, she took her book back, made excuses and followed Fletcher into the street.

Outside, the sun had begun its afternoon descent across the sky.

Fletcher was marching down the road, already a little way off.

'Where are you going?' Scoop shouted after him, annoyed at his rudeness.

Stopping, Fletcher glared at her. 'I suppose you want to go look for this Wisdom woman, do you?'

'I don't know, I suppose...'

'Because I don't.'

'What *do* you want to do, then?' Scoop marched over to him.

'I want to find the Golden Feather. I want to know why I *still* can't remember anything. It feels like we keep getting distracted.'

'But to find the feather, we have to get to Alethea, right?'

'Yeah, so what's that got to do with running some errand for a Stranger we've seen in a mirror?'

Scoop was cross. 'Not just any Stranger.'

'What?'

'didn't you hear what Mythina said?'

Fletcher looked blank.

'The Storyteller – he has auburn hair! And you know what that means, don't you?'

Fletcher didn't answer.

'It's obvious, isn't it? It's him we've been seeing. It's was him we saw in the desert. Him you saw in the forest clearing. It's his story in the journal.'

Fletcher's mouth opened but no sound emerged.

Scoop continued. 'To get to the banquet we have to have robes woven with the silver thread of the Storyteller – a silver thread made gold. That seems to me to be exactly what *the Storyteller himself* has just asked us to do – to bring his story back to him bright and alive.' The enormity of what she was saying impressed on her – the Storyteller had spoken to *them*.

Fletcher looked overwhelmed. 'But how? Who are we? We

can't even remember our own past, can we? Why on earth would the Storyteller be asking us to do anything?'

'I don't know.'

Scoop stared at the ground. Perhaps she was wrong.

'That's why we need help, isn't it?' she mumbled.

Fletcher's expression changed.

'You're right. I'm sorry. I didn't hear...I didn't...'

'It's ok.'

He straightened up, his face grave and determined.

'There's no time to lose then, is there, partner? I don't know why the Storyteller's asking us for help, or how we can – but whatever the reason, this is too big for us to do alone – we're going to need all the help we can get.'

He looked up at the waning sun.

'Come on, it's getting late – let's just hope we can make it to the house of Wisdom before nightfall.'

Chapter 13

Trinkets

As Molly and Mabel Quill had suggested, Fletcher and Scoop left Bardbridge through the northwest gate. Once beyond the village, the path was quiet, only lone travellers passing from time to time. The sound of the river bubbling beside them was peaceful. It sparkled in the late afternoon sun.

The apprentices walked in tired silence. Just as the Quill sisters had described, they passed between the Creativity Craters (a range of volcanic cones that jut from the land, every so often emitting a belch of colourful smoke) and the Puddles of Plot (a series of enormous clear blue puddles, shaped like letters that meander across some vast green fields).

One of the Creativity Craters was blackened; no smoke puffed from it. The scorched earth looked out of place on the gentle landscape. Scoop remembered what she'd overheard Rufina saying to the Yarnbard only yesterday:

"There are other signs of instability...one of the Creativity Craters has burned out – I saw it myself."

"Indeed, it is a sad sight." Scoop recalled the Yarnbard's downcast expression.

Where was the old man? They could do with his help right now. She looked at the crater. He was right. It was a sad sight.

Shivering, she turned away from the charred rock. Her shoulders were tense. This wasn't a game. For some unfathomable reason, the Storyteller was putting his trust in her and Fletcher. This was so much bigger than she could cope with. She felt so small and inadequate in the vast landscape.

As they reached the western edge of the Puddles of Plot, the fields began to rise and fall, turning into the foothills of the mountains. The sun was falling behind the peaks, casting long shadows onto the track. Around them, birds sang their evening songs, bobbing from tree to tree. Above, wild geese flew in tight arrow formations. And in the heights far away, the eagles soared.

Farther along, where the foothills began to grow steeper, Scoop could see what looked like a fork in the path.

That must be the place Molly and Mable warned of.

As the apprentices neared it, they could see what looked like a squat, black stone, surrounded by a sparkling pool of water. The stone stood out from its surroundings, darker than the other rocks. But as they got closer, Scoop realised it wasn't a stone at all, but an old woman hunched over, huddled in a black cloak. The cloak was pulled so far over her head that only the whites of her eyes showed. She was perched on a small wooden stall and around her feet was not a sparkling pool, but an array of ornaments and trinkets. They shone in the light of the low evening sun.

Grizelda watched as the two apprentices drew closer.

Is it? she wondered, her beady eyes like razors.

She couldn't be sure. She didn't trust Knot as far as she could throw him and she'd only half believed his news. But as the apprentices came farther down the path, it was unmistakable – it was definitely them – both of them. She'd recognise them anywhere. After all, they'd been in her care for all those arduous years.

Her mind now alert, she peered at the sky. *Well, well, well – perhaps I can do some meddling of my own, eh? Better be careful they don't recognise me, though.*

She pulled her cloak closer.

As Fletcher and Scoop drew within earshot, Grizelda began to cry out, her voice rasping.

'Come 'n' get ya souvenirs, silver-plated crowns, miniature scrolls, replica regal regalia – two for the price of one!'

The old woman's croaking made Scoop recoil. An image hit her from nowhere – it was the same one she'd seen at Scribbler's

House while brushing her hair. This time it hit with greater force. The impression was clear. A cave – it looked like a dungeon, a thick door guarding its entrance. Huddled in the corner, alone and afraid, a girl with matted, dirty hair. Who was she?

Scoop stumbled.

'Hello, my dears,' Grizelda said, catching Scoop by the elbow and gripping her tightly.

For some reason, Scoop wanted to run away.

Come on, she chided herself, *she's just an old lady.*

'Hello,' she replied, forcing herself to be polite.

'Take a look at my souvenirs – two for the price of one for you.'

Scoop really wanted to move on, but she made herself bend down to look at the peddler's jewellery.

It was laid out prettily by the old woman's feet. Among the ornaments and trinkets, Scoop found a replica silver tiara. It was inlayed with shiny black pebbles. She ran her fingers across them. Ordinarily, the tiara wouldn't have been her sort of thing, but she found herself drawn to it. She imagined herself wearing the silver crown and was suddenly overwhelmed by a strong desire to put it on.

'Go ahead – try it, my dear,' Grizelda croaked softly. 'Tell me, what brings you here this evening?'

'We're going to Alethea, for the wedding banquet of the Storyteller.'

Grizelda cackled and her crows took to the sky with much flapping and cawing.

'Are you, now? Well, each to his own, each to his own. I myself am as happy as a bard just sittin' here in the sun. It's a beautiful evening.'

It was indeed a beautiful evening; the rich yellow sun was fading to orange. It shot intense beams between the mountain peaks. Scoop put the tiara on and stared at herself in a tray the old woman had balanced against a rock to act as a mirror.

I would look beautiful wearing this at the banquet, she thought, suddenly tired.

She could feel her legs aching. It was as if her feet were sticking to the floor. She sighed, melancholy seeping through her body.

Who does the Storyteller think he is, making us walk all this way?

Glancing to one side, she noticed a rock that reminded her of something.

It looks as if it's got pigtails. I wonder if Mythina and all the others are being made to work so hard. What's all the rush, anyway?

Scoop felt heavy. She tried to yawn but even that was too much trouble.

In the background Fletcher was talking. In his hand, a silvery pendant swung. Holding it up, his eyes followed the black amulet stone. Beyond it he could see Scoop starting to dose.

Good idea. We've walked an awfully long way. Where were we going, anyway?

He sat down, yawning.

As the apprentices fell still, a dark cloud rolled over the mountains, blocking out the sun. A cold evening wind whipped up. A moment later, a splattering of big, heavy raindrops started to fall on Fletcher and Scoop's darkened frames. Grizelda looked up; how quickly the weather could change in these parts. She glanced at her victims.

Halfway to stone already, she smiled to herself. *Soon be done. No point in hanging around longer than I need.* She began to pack away her trinkets.

A snake slithered through the scrub to the fork in the path. It slid across the black rocks and over Fletcher's rigid feet. A moment later Melusine joined Grizelda. Resting a hand on Scoop's frozen head, the two women glared at each other.

'So thessse are the children?'

'Yeah, this is 'em. Looks like it's all over, thanks to me. You and that oaf have been as helpful as a sieve in a fire – can't trust anyone but myself, can I!'

Melusine hissed angrily.

'I sent that lumbering fool to get food ages ago, but there's no sign of him anywhere. I'll be blowed if I'm waiting around 'til he gets back now these two have been dealt with.'

'You've silenced them for good?'

'Course I have. They're Deathstones they are,' Grizelda signalled to the black pebbles. 'Full of fossilised Dull Worms. Once they've had their effect, there's no coming back. Just wish this had happened first time round – then perhaps we wouldn't have had all this bother. Now get going you snake-in-the-grass, up to them hills where you can slither about to yer heart's content. Gimme some peace, won't yer – it's been a long day.'

With a flick of her forked tongue, Melusine disappeared, her snake body slipping over the black rocks onto the path to the Mysterious Mountains.

Fletcher and Scoop were unable to hear the conversation between the two women, for slowly they were being transformed into cold, black rock.

As Grizelda finished packing away her trinkets, she saw out of the corner of her eye a movement on the path ahead. Looking up, she peered into the distance. Coming from the direction of the village was a character she recognised. It was Rufina, the golden feather hammered into her tunic. The crone scuffed her foot angrily, sending dust into the air, and cursed.

Rufina was on her way to the banquet. As she approached the fork in the path, she stopped. There was trouble in the air. Ahead, she could see an old woman. It was Grizelda Folly. Rufina knew her, and her tricks, very well.

Grizelda was surrounded by a circle of rocks. In the centre, two academy apprentices were frozen. They were a dull shade of grey.

Petrification! Rufina's eyes flashed.

Quickly, she pulled her sword from its sheath. At the Academy, Rufina had been part of the Department for Overcoming Monsters. This was text book. Raising the sword above her head, she turned its point to the sky.

'By the pen of the Storyteller,' her voice rang, 'I call upon the western wind.'

From beyond the mountain pass there was a rumble and then a strong gust of wind blew down the valley, tossing scrub from its path and making the river leap white with spray. The clouds between the mountain peaks parted and the last rays of evening sun shot through the ravine. The shard struck Rufina's sword, reflecting a bolt of light back towards the hills.

Like a scythe, the light sliced Grizelda's eyes. Shocked, she cried out, falling backwards, her cloak slipping from her skinny body to reveal a wrinkled, emaciated face.

Her crows fled in different directions, some dispersing over a ridge towards the foothills of the mountains, others scattering towards the Puddles of Plot.

As they left, Grizelda became weaker.

The image of the golden feather, hammered into Rufina's armour, glinted in the sunset. Grizelda staggered back to her stool and sat down. Seizing the initiative, Rufina ran towards the circle of rocks.

Fletcher was conscious.

What's going on?

His body was heavy, as if he'd been bulldozed to the ground.

The pendant was in his hand. It made his arm ache with dreadful pain. His whole being was numb. He tried to open his fingers, but they were stuck. He pushed with all his might. With a cracking sound, a little feeling returned. He wiggled his fingers and slowly the chain of the amulet slid through his palm, hitting the floor. Fletcher felt immediate release. Painfully, he turned his head. The old woman was on her stool, her face now visible. She was ancient, wrinkled and bony, her black eyes glaring from sunken pits.

Fletcher started. He recognised her.

A memory!

But where from? He couldn't think. It felt as if his head was being squeezed by a vice. He strained to connect eye and brain, but the impression died away.

I'm clutching at straws, he fumed. *She could be anyone.*

Grizelda snarled. It looked as if her cover had been blown.

The boy must recognise me!

It had been a long time since Grizelda had looked into those piercing eyes.

Not long enough, she cursed, inclining her head in grudging acknowledgment. She expected the same in return, but Fletcher looked blank.

She leaned forwards.

Wait a moment. He doesn't recognise me. But how...?

Something flickered through the old crone's memory. She'd heard about it before: characters who'd been cast aside, their stories de-activated, only to return with blank minds – the trauma of the transition back to life too great.

The boy looked sickeningly well; healthy even. Not as she remembered him – the little runt. This was the Storyteller's doing, she had no doubt.

Fletcher caught sight of someone running towards him.

'Get up!' Rufina cried.

He strained, pushing his body from the ground.

Next to the old woman, Scoop stood frozen.

'The tiara!' Rufina pointed, 'Knock it off!'

Sensing the urgency, Fletcher pushed with all his strength, moving towards his partner. The old woman was beginning to recover. One by one, crows flew back, wheeling around her head. Reaching Scoop, he lunged at the tiara.

'Ouch!' he shouted, his fist connecting with stone.

'Again!' Rufina cried.

Fletcher struck the tiara once more. With another crack, it fell from Scoop's head. Rufina grabbed the two apprentices and dragged them towards the right-hand fork. Scoop moved slowly, her body stiff.

The old woman stood up. With a toothless grin she reached out and grabbed Scoop's hand.

'This way, Scoop my dear!'

How does she know my name?

Scoop was being pulled in both directions. The old woman let go. Released, the apprentices followed their rescuer, beginning to climb the steep path. At this, Grizelda cackled again.

'Oh, my dears, you're not intending to take that forgotten path? It's full of briars and thorns. Carry on to my left, the path is much more travelled.'

Scoop was waking up. She was being dragged uphill, brambles tearing at her legs. She felt awful. Hearing the old crone's voice, she looked to her left – a path rose gently into the mountains.

'It looks easier that way.'

'It may be easier, but it leads in the wrong direction,' Rufina called.

Although every part of Fletcher wanted to disagree, he knew Rufina was right.

'Cover your ears to this nonsense. Don't be misled by foolish words.'

Ignoring the old woman's cries and laughs, Fletcher and Scoop began to climb. Thorns poked between the boulders, grabbing their legs and catching their clothes. With a ripping sound, Fletcher freed himself from one, tearing a hole in his tunic. Nettles stung Scoop's legs. Nevertheless, they pushed along the narrow gully into the hill, careful not to slip from the footholds and crevices the rocks provided. Finally, out of breath, they heaved themselves onto a flat boulder, which jutted out from the hillside.

Before them Rufina stood, looking down to the valley with a grim expression. Wind lashed upwards. Beyond her, a horde of crows circled menacingly, and below, Grizelda could still be heard.

'Each to his own. I've heard that path's a dead end!'

Her voice rose unnaturally, carried by the wind.

'*A dead end*, I tell you!'

'Keep climbing,' Rufina said, without turning.

'What about you?' Fletcher asked.

'Don't worry about me. I know how to look after myself. I'll stay here and keep her crows at bay. You make some headway. I'll see you at the banquet. Now, go!'

Silently, Fletcher and Scoop turned, scrambling over another boulder and continuing.

After a while, the track levelled off, curving inwards. Ahead the Mysterious Mountains rose, their snow-capped peaks disappearing into the clouds.

The two apprentices moved quickly, Grizelda's cries fading. The only noises that remained were the brushing of the long grass and their own deep, worn-out breaths.

They rounded a bend and stopped. In front of them was an awesome sight. The steep slope of a mountain stretched upwards, battle-armoured scree guarding its ravines, its snow-capped summit distant and ethereal. Jutting out from the mountain's rain shadow, above Fletcher and Scoop, a craggy rock formed a solid grey plateau. On the plateau, overshadowed by its foreboding neighbour, was a stately house. It seemed to be suspended in mid-air, an illusion created by the fact that the house was built upon seven stone pillars. Its long, stained-glass windows pointed skywards. The whole edifice looked immovable, rooted and strong. Yet a low mist hung around its base and in the fading light, it looked as though the whole building was floating on the clouds.

'The house of Wisdom,' Fletcher whispered.

'Yes,' Scoop answered.

'We're here.'

In front of them, a long, spindly staircase started its winding ascent to the house. Stepping forwards, Fletcher began to climb.

Scoop hesitated. She could feel something in her hand. Opening her fingers, she looked. It was a small, black pebble. The old woman had pushed it into her palm when she'd grabbed her. Scoop knew she shouldn't have it, but for some reason she didn't want to let it go. Touching the smooth rock made her feel far away, as if she was floating over her own body. Somehow that comforted her. She gripped it tightly. As she did, a flock of crows flew silently over the ridge and descended on the mountainside. Scoop paused, unsure of what to do.

I'll think about it later, she told herself, although deep inside she didn't really want to think about it at all; she just wanted to keep it. Pushing the reservations from her mind, she slipped the black pebble into her pocket and followed Fletcher up the steps to the house of Wisdom.

Back in the valley, Melusine had returned to the fork in the path.

'So they've slipped through your fingers,' she hissed, a faint smile visible. 'And so it falls to my snake charms to finish this – just as I anticipated.'

'Oh I don't think so, my dear. You keep yer little snake brain occupied, be my guest. But I've got a backup plan, and it's not gonna be *stopping* the apprentices now, neither. No!' The old crone grinned. 'I'm goin' to the feast myself. And when I get to the banquet – if the princess really is there – I'm gonna claim her for our master – the lord of the Abyss. Then we'll see who his favourite is!'

Melusine threw her head back, revealing razor sharp teeth. She let out a noise that was half laugh, half hiss. 'You're sanity is more unsssteady than I sussspected. You are aware we cannot cross the threshold into the cassstle of the Storyteller?'

'Oh, I'm not intending to waste my energy even walking to the castle, let alone trying to cross its threshold by myself. I'm going to arrive by carriage! And just like a princess,' Grizelda began to dance and turn, her cloak spinning outwards and her voice rising to a shriek, 'Grizelda will go to the ball!'

Chapter 14

The Treasure of Miyanda

Fletcher and Scoop edged nervously up the stone staircase towards the thick wooden door of Wisdom's house. They appeared small against the backdrop of the stately building, the dusky, patchwork landscape stretching out in the valley below. In the distance, they could see the fires of Bardbridge, and beyond, the rain-shrouded sea.

Drained from the steep ascent, they neared the doorway in silence. It looked cold in the fading light. Above it, Scoop noticed a motto emblazoned in elegant letters. It read, "Let all who are simple come here."

'You should be welcome here,' she said, nodding at the words, trying to lighten the gloomy mood.

'What's that?' Fletcher asked, staring at the writing.

'Look, it says, "Let all who are *simple* come here".'

'You'd be welcome, more like!'

Scoop punched him playfully on the shoulder. Just as she did, the door swung open. Fletcher, already slightly off balance, nearly fell off the staircase in surprise. There, looking even tinier than usual in the enormous doorway was a familiar face.

'Yarnbard!' Scoop cried in astonishment.

The old man raised an eyebrow. 'I thought I could hear some noise.'

'What are you doing here?'

'Well, I said that I had a friend to visit. That friend just happened to be Wisdom.'

'But...'

'And the sign above the door is proof that Fullstop Island is a topsy-turvy place. Remember, the foolish things of this world are often chosen to shame the wise.'

Behind the Yarnbard, there was a flash of green and Scoop caught sight of a child dashing away. 'You're it,' a girl called from inside.

The Yarnbard span around. 'Oh bother! They were distracting me. That's not fair!'

'Na-na-na-na-na-na,' the girl called. 'Catch me if you can!'

Quickly, the Yarnbard vanished inside, leaving the door open. Through it, Fletcher could see the most bizarre sight. The house was a single hall, but its decor wasn't ordinary. Instead it was filled with trees that appeared to be growing out of the floor. The apprentices tentatively peered through the archway. In the centre rose a pine, its crown ducking below the high rafters; hawthorn and whitethorn crouched like chicks with scruffy hair; and an old blind oak stretched its crooked fingers out, exploring its surroundings.

Between the trees, rope ladders hung and precariously-balanced planks created air-bound pathways. Climbing nets dangled from branches and a treehouse hugged the trunk of the great pine. The room was a giant adventure playground. It was the outside, indoors.

There was a buzzing sound and the girl suddenly whizzed through the air on a zip wire, somersaulting onto a platform halfway up the pine.

'Come in; you'll make it cold.'

Leaping with the suppleness of a leaf blown by the wind, she caught a dangling rope and whooshed onto an adjacent branch. There she balanced, camouflaged, her green tunic blending into the tree.

The Yarnbard stood at the bottom, hopping from one foot to the other and jumping pointlessly.

'That's not fair. You know I can't climb.'

'Come on, old man, I keep winning this game! It's about time you won one.' She glanced at Fletcher and Scoop. 'You can join in too.'

'I think she's talking to us,' Fletcher mumbled.

'Of course I'm talking to you – who else?' She sprang to another branch, slipped through a tunnel between two of the trees, slid down a pole and flipped forwards, landing just in front of Fletcher and Scoop.

'Hello,' she grinned. 'I'm Wisdom.'

'You're Wisdom?'

'Oh, I'm sorry,' the Yarnbard squawked, joining the group. 'I should have introduced you. This is Lady Wisdom – the Guardian of the island's hidden treasure.'

'But she's just a girl.'

'And *you're* just a boy!'

'Actually, she's as old as I am. All the Guardians of the island possess youth and age in equal measure.'

'Well, I wish she'd act it.'

Wisdom giggled.

The old man grinned. 'But time has treated her so much more kindly than it has treated me, don't you think?'

'Stop sucking up to me, Yarny. I'm still not letting you into the treehouse.'

'Aww,' the old man pouted.

'My house, my rules.' Leaning forward, she tagged Fletcher's arm and back-flipped away.

'Now you're it. Catch me if you can!'

'I'm not here to play games!' Fletcher bristled.

'Spoilsport.'

Fletcher was getting annoyed.

'We've been sent here by the Storyteller,' Scoop butted in. 'We need some help.'

'Come on then. Let me show you some of my treasure. I've got food too – you must be hungry. We can talk about whatever up there.' Wisdom pointed to the treehouse.

Skipping to the pine's trunk, she nimbly swung up a rope ladder and ducked into the little hut. A second later, she emerged with a harp. It was as big as her and ornamented with gold and jewels.

'This is Dagda's,' she called, resting it on a branch. 'Play harp!'

Instantly, the most delicious music began to issue from the instrument.

'One of my favourite treasures – it plays music of healing, music of tears, music of mirth *and* music of sleep – awesome!'

Scoop felt her feet begin to tap, shuffling gently to the rhythm.

Fletcher resisted. He was in no mood for frivolity. They had just escaped being turned into stone. Tomorrow evening they needed to be at Alethea and time was running out. He had to get whatever information this girl had, and he had to get it fast.

'Come up. It's great up here.'

Feeling weariness washing away, Scoop smiled and began to jig to the rope ladder.

'Come on, Fletcher,' she said over her shoulder. 'can't hurt to have a look.'

As she turned, a sudden rush of air surprised her. There was the sound of flapping and a little yellow bird flew past, landing on a nearby branch. Looking up, Scoop noticed other birds bobbing in the trees. Some of them were ordinary brown sparrows, others were large, colourful and exotic creatures. The yellow bird peered at her, puffing itself up and ruffling its feathers with curiosity.

'I want to come up too,' the Yarnbard whined.

'Ok, if you promise to play blind man's bluff, later.'

'Ok, I promise!'

Wisdom dropped a rope with a wooden seat tied to the end. The Yarnbard sat on it, his staff on his lap, and Wisdom began to winch the tiny man up to the platform. Scoop climbed after him.

Fletcher glared. Things weren't going his way.

'You not coming then?' Wisdom called down.

He stuck his hands in his pockets and stared at the floor,

stubbornly.

'Please yourself.' She disappeared into the treehouse.

Fletcher felt something in his pocket.

What's that? he wondered. Pulling it out, a mischievous grin spread across his face.

You want to mess about, do you? Well, two can play this game.

Inside the treehouse, a fire blazed, crackling from a wrought-iron fireplace built into a hollow in the trunk. Above it, a large hole in the roof acted as a chimney, the smoke winding up passed the branches of the tall pine. Outside, the harp was now playing a merry folk-dance.

In the flickering light, some very curious objects were visible. There were piles of precious stones: rubies and sapphires, gold nuggets and silver ore. There were sea chests, alabaster jars and padlocked trunks. From the wooden walls antiques of different ages and sizes hung – lamps, keys, strings of pearls, goblets, horns and shields. And there were maps – many maps – fragile and yellowed, blotted and torn.

'Wow,' Scoop whispered.

'Yes, it's an impressive stash, isn't it?' the Yarnbard agreed, sitting on one of the trunks.

'That's part of Alaric's horde in there,' Wisdom winked. 'It's full of Spanish doubloons and gold ingots.'

'Oh?' The Yarnbard wiggled his bottom. 'It's a very comfortable hoard, if I do say so.'

Wisdom giggled.

'But, why have you got all this?' Scoop asked, sitting on a basket by the fire.

The Yarnbard leaned over. 'I told you, she's the Guardian of the island's hidden treasure.'

'And Keeper of the mines.'

'Ah yes, Keeper of the mines.'

'Mines? What mines?'

Wisdom leaned towards Scoop, her voice low. 'The island is

riddled with underground tunnels and secret caverns. The silver mines to the west; the gold mines of Rainbow's End; the Cliffs of Uncertainty, where iron is taken from the earth and copper is smelted for ore. Places forgotten by the feet of men. That's where my treasures are to be found.'

As she spoke, Scoop caught a flash of Wisdom's age in her youthful eyes.

Suddenly, the girl picked up a dagger from a pile of swords and swung round, causing the Yarnbard to almost topple from the trunk.

'This is the knife of Llawfrodedd the Horseman – found by the famous treasure-hunter, Matthew Saith-Wyth. Watch.'

She lowered the blade to the surface of a sea-chest and, using it as a table, began to chop.

Scoop gasped.

Appearing from nowhere, as the blade touched the wood, there were slices of meat.

'Where did they come from?'

Wisdom's eyes glistened. 'see – I told you I had food!'

Below, Fletcher was stomping through the trees. He had a plan to make the annoying girl talk, but to make it work, he needed water.

There must be some in this ridiculous indoor forest.

A bird flew past his face and he waved it away, irritably. Rounding the trunk of the old oak, he ducked under a low branch and stopped. Somewhere towards the back of the room there was the sound of trickling water.

Got yer, he thought, triumphantly. *I'll soon have you telling me everything you know.*

By now, Scoop, the Yarnbard and Wisdom were tucking in to a sumptuous feast. The harp had settled into a charming love ballad and the knife of Llawfrodedd the Horseman had conjured a meal for twenty-four soldiers. There was more than enough to go round! Musepig pie, fresh fish, tomatoes, roast potatoes – the knife didn't seem to tire. To accompany the food, Wisdom reached up and unhooked another treasure – the horn of Bran Galed.

'Hold this and make a wish,' she said, thrusting it into Scoop's hand. 'Go on – ask for any drink you want.'

Grasping the horn, Scoop closed her eyes.

Instantly, she felt something spill onto her lap. Looking down, she saw froth on her tunic. The horn was full to overflowing with Noveltwist Cordial.

Scoop looked dazed.

'Drink,' Wisdom laughed. 'It's real.'

Fletcher reached a little stream that tumbled from some rocks at the far side of the hall. Among them was a flurry of flicking feathers and spraying water – a flock of tiny shrewd-a-birds hopping about, bathing themselves. Fletcher clapped his hands and the shrewd-a-birds shot away as quickly as a volley of darts.

Kneeling down, he placed his new found discovery into the flowing water and set about his task.

As they ate, Wisdom told Scoop and the Yarnbard treasure stories. One by one she picked up precious artefacts and opened caskets, luxuriating in the secrets they hid. She told of the treasure of Aruba, the four jewels of the Tuatha De Danann, the white hilt of Rydderch Hael and the Jinni lamp.

Scoop watched, transfixed, all thought of why she had come to the house of Wisdom vanishing. She was captivated.

Outside, Fletcher was focused on one thing alone, finding out what Wisdom had to tell them. They needed to know how to turn the silver thread of the Storyteller to gold. The annoying girl had answers and Fletcher didn't intend to let her keep them to herself.

Finishing at the little stream, he stood up. It was time to climb. He had already mapped out his route. He would start on the low branches of the oak, ascending steadily. A ladder would then take him up to a platform level with the treehouse.

Fletcher glanced up. There was a window in the side of the hut. It overlooked the platform.

I'll have to be careful not to be seen.

From there, he would scale a climbing net to a log suspended at the top of the tall pine. From it, he would be able access a mid-air plank that provided a pathway across the branches to a position directly over the treehouse chimney. That was exactly where Fletcher needed to be.

But it's not going to be easy with just one hand, he thought, looking at the package now carefully stowed under his arm, making that hand redundant for climbing.

There aren't any safety nets, either.

He looked up at the spindly planks high above. Fletcher wasn't one for heights. He gritted his teeth.

I'll just have to make it work.

Carefully, he pulled himself onto the first branch of the oak and began to climb.

'This is the Halter of Clydno Eiddyn.'

Wisdom reached up to a rope that hung from a nail, high on the treehouse wall. She unhooked it.

'What's a halter?' Scoop asked.

The Yarnbard's hand shot up. 'I know, I know,' he strained. 'It's for leading horses – a bit like reigns.'

Wisdom laughed. 'Yes, but this isn't an ordinary halter. If you hang it at the end of your bed, any horse you wish for will appear in it.'

Scoop clapped her hands.

'You want to try it?' Wisdom asked.

Scoop nodded.

Fletcher was now climbing the ladder to the platform opposite the treehouse. This was harder than he had anticipated. It jutted out over his head. To get onto the terrace, he was going to have to lurch from the ladder and grab the edge of the platform, before pulling himself up. He wasn't cut out for this sort of thing. He looked down and instantly regretted it. Below, sharp branches spiked up. If he missed the ledge making such a move...

It's not worth thinking about, he told himself, *there's no going back now.*

Taking a deep breath, he released his fingers and lunged towards the platform. Catching it, he gripped with all his might.

Suddenly, there was an enormous commotion in the treehouse. Great thumps echoed from the hut and Scoop yelped. The little house shook and the pine tree rocked. Scoop's face suddenly appeared in the window. Fletcher ducked down, not wanting to be seen. His partner seemed to be riding a horse.

A horse?

It was sliding about on the floor of the little hut, making it sway. In shock, Fletcher's feet slipped from the ladder, leaving him dangling from the platform by one hand, the package still gripped under his arm. He could feel his fingers slipping.

I'm not going to make it.

All of a sudden, Fletcher's finger's dropped from the ledge. There was a buzzing noise behind him and something whizzed through the air. Instinctively, he reached out and grabbed whatever was flying past. His fingers closed around a handle. It was the zip wire. It yanked him to one side and he plunged across the indoor forest, passing under the treehouse and through a cluster of leaves to safety.

That was close, Fletcher thought, jumping to a platform that nestled below the zip wire's destination. *The handle must have got dislodged in the commotion. Why on earth was Scoop riding a horse? And how did it get up there!*

He wondered for a moment and then decided not to let it distract him. The undamaged package was still tucked under his arm, so his task hadn't been scuppered.

Next to him, balanced on a branch, was a chair. Fletcher studied it and smiled. The chair was attached to a rope, the cord stretching upwards to a bough at the top of the tree, where it passed through a pulley and fell back down to the platform. It was a self-operated lift – with it he would be able to pull himself up the trunk. This was a *much* easier way to access the high branches.

Inside the treehouse, the horse had disappeared. The room was a mess, trunks and treasures having been kicked across the floor. Next to the fire was a steaming pile of horse dung. The Yarnbard lay sprawled in an open sea-chest, his hat knocked to an awkward angle and one of his pointed slippers swinging from a hook above his head. Scoop's haywire hair covered her face, shooting out in random directions. Only Wisdom was unscathed. She stood in the centre of the treehouse grinning widely.

'That was fun!'

The Yarnbard groaned.

'Luckily, I have a treasure that will tidy this up.'

She clapped and a broom shot out from the wreckage. It began to frantically sweep the floor, ushering the horse dung into a dustpan.

'We'll soon have this cleared up and then I can show you the treasure of Kaida – it's used to summon the Leviathan Dragon.'

'No!' Scoop and the Yarnbard moaned in one voice.

'Aww.' Wisdom looked disappointed. 'But I love to play with the Leviathan Dragon.'

Fletcher had now pulled himself up the trunk of the tree. Tying off the chair-lift, he studied a thin plank just below. It led to the crown of the pine. Tentatively, he stretched his foot out and slowly lowered his weight onto the fragile wood. Balancing himself, he began to inch along it.

Below, the enormous trunk stretched dizzyingly downwards, the birds on the lower branches no bigger than specks. The air at this height was lonely. He could see the treehouse beneath, the hole in its roof almost directly below. There were no rails or handholds. Fletcher had to trust his feet.

The plank wobbled and he froze. Surely, there had to be an easier way to discover Wisdom's secret. Momentarily, he wavered.

Don't panic. Whatever you do, don't panic.

He took a deep breath, his feet shifting. Adjusting his weight, he balanced himself with minute sensitivity. He had to hold his nerve. He knew if he looked down before feeling secure, or thought too much about the situation, he would end up swaying.

And then I'll topple off this matchstick and plummet to my...

Stop it, he silenced his fears. *Don't even think words like 'topple' or 'plummet'. Think safe, think confident, think almost there.*

He *was* almost there. Near enough anyway. Slowly, he crouched down. He needed to sit on the plank so that he could take a proper aim. Carefully, he balanced the package next to him. It squelched, bulging onto the hard wood of the plank.

I hope there are no splinters. I haven't climbed all this way for things to go pop.

With both hands free, he lowered his body, sitting on the plank. His legs dangled in the chiffon air. He picked up the package again and it wobbled in his hands. Through the hole in the roof he could see Wisdom and Scoop pulling the Yarnbard's frail arms. He seemed to be stuck in an old sea-chest.

What are they doing?

Fletcher held the package directly over the hole.

My aim needs to be perfect.

He waited. The old man was groaning as the girls pulled him to his feet. When he was finally upright, Scoop and the Yarnbard sat on a trunk and Wisdom moved back to the fireplace.

Ok, now's the moment, Fletcher thought. *She's directly below.*

He leaned forwards, taking aim. In his hands, a purple Gush Bomb quivered. Silently, Fletcher thanked his neighbour from Scribbler's house and released the package. It fell, plunging through the branches of the tree, wobbling with liquid, its target directly below.

'What I'm going to show you now is one of my favourite treasures,' Wisdom said, warming herself by the fire. 'It was discovered in...'

Suddenly, something flew through the chimney. Before she could move, it hit her squarely on the head and broke with an enormous splosh.

'What..?' she cried, taken aback.

Looking up, she saw Fletcher sat on a plank above the treehouse. He waved at her.

'Rascal!' she called, shocked. 'Why did I say that?—what sort of word is "rascal"?—I sound ancient—why am I talking?—I only meant to think.' She looked up. 'Hooligan—scoundrel—reprobate—how come I'm saying what I think and not thinking before I speak? Think before you speak—that's wise, isn't it? And I'm Wisdom, aren't I? Why can't I stop myself from speaking my mind? It's disturbing.'

She looked down.

'Water—on the floor—I'm dripping—my hair's wet—and my clothes—urgh, I can feel it running down my back—braggart—delinquent—chump—it's a Gush Bomb—oh, I see—clever—you want information—good focus, arrow-boy—good shot—I'm speaking a stream-of-consciousness—risky strategy—maybe I'm too annoyed to think anything of worth—but I'm not—Gush Bombs are fun.' She grinned. 'I like you, arrow-boy—you obviously want to hear my wisdom more than play with my treasure, don't you? Good choice—well, you shall hear it—but I warn you, you may not find its message comforting.'

She waved her hand and instantly the harp stopped playing. Without warning, Wisdom's playful countenance slipped away. The Guardian of hidden treasure grew in height, her face darkening, becoming serious. The fire sparked and spat behind her.

'What question do you ask of me, apprentice?'

Fletcher was listening from the top of the tree.

'The Storyteller's asked us to bring his story back to him — to bring him the silver thread. But we have to make it glow. How do we do that? He said you would help.'

'I will—The task he has asked of you is not an easy one—It will require courage and strength—The final part of the silver thread's story has seeped into the very core of the island, carried by the river—It is buried beneath its soil, in the depths of the land—There in the darkness, it hides—To see it burn, you must face that darkness—You must travel underground—into the very heart of the shadow—to the place where only dust remains, and bring it back.'

Underground? Scoop shivered. She hated the dark. For the first time that day, she'd been feeling relaxed. She'd even been having fun! Why did Fletcher have to spoil it?

'What are you doing?' she mouthed at him, scowling.

He shrugged back, moodily.

'Ríoghbhardán,' Wisdom spoke with command. The Yarnbard looked up, the scatty manner with which he had been conducting himself dissipating, a serious expression on his face.

'Stand,' Wisdom said, firmly. At once the Yarnbard rose to his feet.

The light of the indoor forest dimmed, Wisdom's words triggering a change in the hall's ambience. A cloud began to form, brooding and overcast. The birds squawked and screeched, thrashing through the branches.

Scoop was nervous. The atmosphere had changed so quickly.

Why couldn't she have some fun, just for a little while? She was so tired. Feeling sorry for herself, a dull thought crept into her mind. It tugged at her, fuzzy but irresistible. Slipping her hand into her pocket, she found the little, black stone that nestled there. She clutched it and felt instantly better – somehow less present, less sensitive.

Outside, the crows that clung to the grey mountainside began to leap and hop, ragged scavengers throwing themselves towards the house of Wisdom.

The Guardian of hidden treasure fixed the Yarnbard in her sights. She looked much older now, stern and foreboding.

'Ríoghbhardán,' she repeated, 'in your possession you have one of my treasures. Is that so?'

'Yes,' the Yarnbard replied.

'Give it to me.'

The old man lifted his staff and held it out. Wisdom and the Yarnbard looked at one another, their eyes filled with knowledge. In that look, the long years of their friendship could be seen, a friendship that traced its way back to the very birth of the island.

Taking the stick, Wisdom held it in the air.

'This is the treasure of Miyanda. It was plucked from the forests of Nitara and is able to penetrate the depths – to expose the roots of the mountains. With it, a pathway can be made into the heart of the island.'

She finished speaking and suddenly brought the stick crashing onto the treehouse floor, making Scoop jump.

Releasing the staff, it stood rigid, as if driven into the ground. The little hut shuddered and there was an almighty crack.

Without thinking, Scoop let go of the stone and grabbed the Yarnbard's kaftan. He glanced at her, unembarrassed as she tightened her grip, the feel of the cloth between her fingers, comforting.

For a moment, nothing happened.

Scoop looked to Wisdom for reassurance, but the Guardian of hidden treasure didn't flinch.

Looking down, Scoop stared at the floor around the staff. She noticed a fine black line, no thicker than a hair's breadth, beginning to creep from its base.

The Yarnbard edged away.

'What's happening?' Scoop asked, letting go of his kaftan.

He didn't reply.

The black line grew, spreading across the floor, forging a path through the grain of the wood.

'What's happening?' Scoop asked again, her voice more urgent.

Nobody spoke.

Above, Fletcher could see what was happening. The treehouse floor was beginning to crack.

What on earth...?

He hadn't expected this. As he watched from the heights, the black line thickened. Something dangerous was happening. Fletcher felt vulnerable in the tall pine.

The fracture spread, the riven wood beginning to whine and grate, creak and crack.

'I asked, what's happening?!' Scoop snapped.

A convulsion suddenly shook the treehouse and it lurched. Scoop stumbled forwards. The floor of the hut buckled and a chasm appeared in the centre of the room. The little treehouse was cracking open; it was being ripped apart.

Scared, Scoop pushed herself back against the wall, clinging to a hook for support. Her feet slipped towards the chasm, treasure sliding to the centre of the floor and tumbling through the crack.

From above, Fletcher could see through the rupture. From the end of the Yarnbard's staff, roots were emerging – living roots. They grew downwards, wiggling like snakes, advancing at an amazing rate. They burrowed through the floor of the treehouse with incredible force, breaking it apart. Then, free from restraint, they twisted downwards, surging towards to the earth.

As they wound towards the ground, Fletcher could see them twisting together, creating a long tube. They smashed past thick branches, snapping them like twigs, causing the birds to dive into the air.

Reaching the stone floor, the roots punched into it. It buckled and cracked as if it was no stronger than the wooden treehouse. The hall shook with the force. Fletcher's plank swayed and teetered. He clung to it, praying it wouldn't slip from its fixings. A great slab of masonry fell away from the floor, hurtling down past the pillars that supported Wisdom's house and shattering on the plateau below. Mountain wind whistled through the breach in the house, whipping up leaves and sending them swirling in frantic eddies. The birds screeched, flapping in the chaos.

Beneath the house of Wisdom, the roots curled past the seven pillars, heading towards the side of the mountain. Growing in size, they weaved around each other. Within their twisted mass, there was a space – a gap just big enough for a person to climb through. The roots were creating a pathway into the earth.

With a colossal thump, they hit the side of the mountain. Thunder rolled down the valley. Stone spewed from the mountainside, great shards of rock shooting from the hole as the roots drilled, forcing a way into the depths of the hill.

After an ear-splitting tumult of crunching and grinding, the noise abated. Loose scree showered the hillside, the hail-spray echoing, until the valley fell still once again.

Scoop was speechless. Shivering, she gripped the side of the treehouse, the wind whistling through the floor.

Wisdom reached up, unhooked a coil of rope and threw it up to Fletcher. Catching it, he knew what to do. Tying the rope around the plank, he scaled down, joining the others.

As he reached the buckled floor, Wisdom began to speak. 'You have sought my advice, apprentices. You have desired it more than gold or silver. In this, you have done well. The pathway these roots have opened will lead you to the heart of the island. You have already uncovered part of the Storyteller's tale and the silver thread has started to weave through your robes. But the last part of the tale is still hidden. To discover it you must travel into the darkness, where it is buried. When you have heard all there is to hear, the silver thread will be yours – the thread of his story. You will carry it wherever you go. It will be woven through you, a rich seam in the fabric of your lives. But that is not the end of your task. To enter Alethea, the thread must burn again. To make it glow, you must face the Shadow itself.'

Wisdom fell silent, allowing her words to sink in. Scoop and Fletcher looked at one another.

Wisdom continued. 'From the darkest place, you must take dust. Throw that dust into the silver lake. Only as it mingles with the thread of the Storyteller at its source, will the thread burn gold once again.'

Wisdom reached forwards and grabbed the Yarnbard's staff. Pulling, it broke away from the roots and she handed it back to the old man.

'This is your path. It is time to take it.'

'Now?' Scoop asked in disbelief.

'Yes. It is less than a day until the banquet starts. There is no time to lose.'

'But I'm tired!'

Scoop felt her cheeks flush.

Wisdom didn't reply.

'I want to go home,' Scoop's voice wavered.

'And where exactly is your home, apprentice?'

Scoop felt a lump in her throat. She couldn't reply.

I don't have a home, she thought, agitated. *I don't have anything.*

She fought back angry tears.

The Yarnbard stepped forwards. 'Wisdom, my dear...'

Wisdom's eyes flashed. 'Sometimes I am playful and sometimes fearful. That is the way it is. I speak the truth. The journey into the earth is not pleasant, but it is necessary.'

Fletcher walked over and put his arm around Scoop, hugging her gently.

'Come on, partner. I know it's late. I'm tired too. This time tomorrow, we have to be at the banquet. We have to finish this now. I know how you feel, I feel it too, but we can't go anywhere but onwards. At Alethea, we'll find out how we got into this mess. We'll find the Golden Feather. We have to. And then we'll know who we really are and where our home is.'

Scoop looked at him, tears visible behind her eyes.

'Enye!' Wisdom called.

The little yellow bird Scoop had seen earlier flew through the treehouse window and flitted to Scoop, perching on her shoulder. It cocked its head and stared at her. Scoop looked back. The bird was comical, trusting. She felt her heart lift a little and smiled, weakly.

'Enye is a gift to aid you on your journey. She will be your guide. Follow her.'

The little bird hopped from Scoop's shoulder and flitted to the entrance to the tube of roots, where she sat for a moment and ruffled her feathers. Then she hopped into the tube and disappeared.

Without speaking, Fletcher walked to the roots. Reaching them, he turned and nodded at Wisdom, silently acknowledging her help. He stepped into the tube and began to climb down, leaving the treehouse.

The Yarnbard looked kindly at Scoop and held out his hand for her to follow.

Scoop rubbed her eyes. Fletcher was right; what choice did they have? They had to see the silver thread turn gold. They had to reach the banquet.

Steeling herself, she stepped towards the path into the earth. It was time to begin the slow descent into the bowels of the island, to seek the last part of the Storyteller's tale. It was time to face the shadow.

Climbing into the tube of roots, she disappeared from sight.

Chapter 15

Into the Story Caves

High on the mountainside, an owl hooted.

Bleary eyed, Scoop climbed through roots, ducking and weaving across the tubers, lowering her hands first, then her feet. Like a spider she edged along the tangled drainpipe, careful not to slip from the footholds it provided. Moonlight criss-crossed its aperture, seeping through the chinks in the tube's wooden skeleton.

Ahead, Fletcher slowly picked his way along the roots, every so often crossed by a flash of yellow as Enye flitted in the moonlight. Behind, the Yarnbard wheezed.

Through the gaps, Scoop could see where the roots hit the mountain – a rocky mouth, its wrinkled lips wide open. She swallowed. In the dark, it appeared to have flinty teeth. Scoop didn't want to be eaten by the mountain. She didn't want to brave this rock giant. She wanted her cosy bed at Scribbler's House.

In silence the three pressed on towards the hillside. The roots creaked, swaying in the wind. Below, glimpses of the steep slope they had ascended earlier were visible, the valley dropping away in the distance. The tube hung suspended over a deep ravine that plunged between the plateau of Wisdom's house and the rock face of the mountain. It felt fragile.

Don't look down, Scoop told herself, moving quickly towards the dark opening.

After clambering hard through the tube, she reached the mountainside and stepped into the darkness of the hill. Under her feet, fallen rocks shifted.

The tube opened into a cave, the roots unwinding and disappearing into the mountainside.

Scoop shivered. The cave was dark and damp. Darkness

scared her; it made her feel anxious and alone. Reaching into her pocket, she touched the black pebble and a dull feeling crept over her, covering her nervousness.

Beyond the rock face, black shapes descended, perching on the twisted bridge. They burrowed through the gaps in the roots and began to hop along the inside of the tube towards the mountain.

Fletcher walked forward and stood in the middle of the cave, Enye flitting ahead of him. He looked small – the fissure in the rock was at least four times his height, but it narrowed quickly and disappeared in the gloom.

'Ah yes,' the Yarnbard said, entering the cavern, 'it's just as I thought. The roots have led us straight to the nearest under-ground cave. They are charged to find the fastest way into the earth.'

His voice echoed and some scree fell from the top of the chamber, hitting the floor and making Scoop jump.

Fletcher looked up. The cavern was supported by thick wooden struts that formed beams across the top of the cave. They were decaying and sagged dangerously. One had snapped, buckling under the vast pressure of the mountain. Looking closely, Fletcher noticed the broken beam was spotted with dark patches of black.

Shadows, he thought, edging away.

The Yarnbard studied the chamber. 'It appears there is some disrepair in this part of the caves. When we return to the village I will report it to Vim and the Cartographers – they look after the map room.' The old man sighed and shook his head.

'What do you mean, "...this part of the caves"?' Scoop asked, nervously.

The Yarnbard hesitated. 'Well...it's not usually something apprentices are taught at the start of their training.' He paused. 'But it appears that you and Fletcher are an exception to the rule.' Looking around furtively, he lowered his voice. 'You must promise not to share this information too freely.'

Fletcher and Scoop glanced at each other.

'Promise,' the old man repeated.

'Promise,' the apprentices whispered.

'Well, under the island, a labyrinth of caves and tunnels exist. The mines Wisdom spoke of are part of these. They are all connected by one Central Chasm that runs along the entire length of the island. There are two openings to the Central Chasm – one of them you have already been close to.'

'Where?' Fletcher asked.

His voice bounced from the walls and more scree showered the floor. The three ducked, covering their heads with their hands.

The Yarnbard spoke quietly.

'At the Academy – surrounded by the three towers. The southern entrance to the Central Chasm is at the heart of the ancient site on which Blotting's was built. Some say it's the mouth of the island itself. It constantly emits a subterranean rumble so low that it is silent to the ear. In ancient legends this is called the Well Whisper – the voice that guides stories quietly towards the place in which all things are reconciled.'

'And the second opening?'

The Yarnbard gave a grave look. 'The northern doorway is a counterfeit well – a deep pit that seeks to drag everything into its own emptiness. It is known as the Abyss.'

Fletcher started, an image from his dream flashing through his mind – the beast plunging into a dark hole, carrying its prey.

'Between these two ancient openings,' the Yarnbard whispered, 'lie the myriad of tunnels and passages like this one. These are the Story Caves.'

'The what?'

'The Story Caves – so named, as in them you can find any story you want, if you know where to look – any story, including your own. One of the great wonders of Fullstop Island grows from the rocks of the Story Caves – it is known as the Glowing Yarn. It is a network of fine threads that carry the island's tales, and imprints them in the different chambers.'

Fletcher wondered if he'd heard his mentor correctly. *Did he say any story, including my own?*

The Yarnbard continued. 'And so in the Story Caves you will find characters running through passageways and sitting on rocks. You may stumble across a carriage with footmen and white horses that suddenly transforms into a pumpkin and mice, or you may meet a talking rabbit, or a walking puppet.'

'Are there monsters?' Scoop interrupted, an irrational fear erupting without warning. She surprised herself with the ferocity of the question.

'Well, yes,' the Yarnbard was taken aback, 'but there is nothing to be afraid of.' He smiled at Scoop, reassuringly. 'The caves are merely the place to *observe* stories – to follow their twists and turns. The characters that dwell in them cannot see or hear you – for they are not in your story and you are not in theirs. Because of this they will pass through you, as if you are merely a ghost. So you see, they cannot hurt you.' The old man paused. 'But you are right to be cautious. The caves are dangerous and shouldn't be ventured into without a trained explorer. Below ground, the boundaries between the mines, the Abyss and the Story Caves are unmarked, and you may stumble from one to the other without warning. In the subterranean realm, treasure and danger abide together. So, it's lucky I'm here with you.'

The Yarnbard began to tiptoe towards the wall of the cave, the rocks crunching under his feet.

'Come. This way.'

Fletcher followed. Enye flitted past him and disappeared into the tunnel ahead.

Scoop's heart was beating fast. She didn't want the others to know how scared she was. As Fletcher and the Yarnbard neared the rock at the back of the cave, she reluctantly crept after them.

'Now, place one hand on the side of the cave,' the Yarnbard said. 'Let it be your guide into the depths of the mountain. Your eyes will soon adjust. As we move deeper into the caves, the Glowing Yarn will light the way. Fletcher, you first, then Scoop, and I will bring up the rear.'

Fletcher laid his hand on the rock and began to move into the darkness.

Nervously, Scoop let go of the pebble in her pocket, placed both hands on the cave wall and followed. The rock was cold and slimy. It felt so different to the black pebble. As she edged forwards, the cave began to narrow. In the gloom she could hardly see the others. The darkness closed in, making her feel claustrophobic.

She stopped.

'Keep going,' the Yarnbard whispered from behind. 'The opening is narrow, but once we're through, I'm sure it will open into a bigger chamber.'

Scoop turned sideways to push herself through the tight gap. Something dripped and icy liquid slid down the back of her neck. She reached forward, hoping to feel Fletcher's hand on the wall just in front, but there was nothing – just cold, hard rock. Closing her eyes, she reached into her pocket again and touched the black pebble. For a moment the world felt far away.

Suddenly, a cacophony of flapping and cawing disturbed her trance. In the confined space the noise was deafening.

Scoop stumbled, shocked.

'What's that?' Fletcher called from in front.

High-pitched shrieks echoed along the tunnel walls. Disorientated, Scoop raised her hands to cover her ears.

The noise was coming from the entrance to the cave. She could hear the muffled sound of the Yarnbard, his voice raised amid the scream of crows.

Crows? But how...?

Through the confusion, she could make out the old man

waving his staff. Bird after bird was diving angrily at his head.

Stumbling, she moved back towards him, but before she could reach the mouth of the cave, one of the wooden beams snapped. The wall quaked and rubble thumped down, exploding in a cloud of dust. Thick air swirled. Scoop coughed and gagged. She couldn't breathe. She reached out, but the cave dissolved. A searing pain split her head, and then darkness filled her vision.

Scoop felt warm breath on her face. She opened her eyes. It was pitch black. The sound of the crows and of the Yarnbard's cries had disappeared.

'Scoop, are you ok?'

Fletcher was kneeling, his face close to hers. She was lying on the floor. The cave was quiet now; very quiet.

'I, err, I don't know. What happened?'

'It's the tunnel. It's collapsed,' Fletcher said, sounding anxious. 'Are you ok? You fell down.'

Scoop tried to get up. Her back was hurting and her knee felt painful. Reaching down, she touched her skin. It stung and she pulled back. With Fletcher's help, she stood up, aching. Her leg was grazed, but apart from some minor injuries, she was unharmed.

'I'm ok,' she said, shaken.

Scoop hadn't taken in what Fletcher had said about the cave. All of a sudden it hit her.

'The tunnel!' she spluttered, alarm in her voice. 'Collapsed?'

She turned and, reaching down, began to scrabble at the rock, pulling fallen stones away and throwing them behind her.

Fletcher put his hand on her shoulder.

'Hey,' he tried to calm her.

Scoop carried on, frantically shifting the stones.

'Hey stop, there's too much. Too much has fallen.'

Scoop span round, another thought striking her: 'The Yarnbard...'

'He's...'

'Where is he?' She was panicked.

'He's on the other side of the fallen rocks.' Fletcher was trying to stay calm.

'But...'

'We're going to have to try and find our own way.'

'But the Yarnbard...'

'He'll be ok. He knows what he's doing.'

'But maybe he's...The rocks...'

'He'll be ok,' Fletcher repeated, his voice reassuring, although underneath he also felt worried. So much rock had fallen. The Yarnbard was frail. Fletcher couldn't bring himself to think of the old man hurt.

'What are we going to do?' Scoop's voice quivered.

'We need to keep going.'

'But how? We don't know the way. Don't you remember what the Yarnbard just said? The caves are dangerous – it's easy to get lost. I think we should just wait here until someone comes to get us.'

The two apprentices stood in silence, neither knowing what to do.

Scoop tried to control her breathing.

As they waited, Fletcher glimpsed a movement ahead of them. They weren't alone.

'Did you see that?'

'What?' Scoop flinched.

'Something just up there – I saw it move.'

It was almost impossible to see in the dark. Scoop edged away, her back against the fallen rocks.

'I think...' Fletcher paused, and then a smile spread across his face. 'Yes, of course.'

'What?'

'It's Enye. She was ahead of me.'

Scoop exhaled.

'We can follow her – she will guide us.'

'Oh, I don't know. I still think we should wait here.'

'You want to get out of the caves, don't you? Come on, Wisdom said we should follow her.'

Scoop really *did* want to get out of the caves and although she wasn't sure they should move, warily she agreed.

Slowly, the two apprentices began to edge along the tunnel, following the little yellow bird.

After a while, a hazy, twinkling light began to glow. As their eyes adjusted, they could see where it came from. Hanging from the walls and ceiling of the tunnel, growing out of its rock, were thousands and thousands of tiny hairs that swayed and whispered. Every hair was fine, and each shone with a dim half-light.

'They must be the Glowing Yarn,' Fletcher whispered. 'Do you remember? The Yarnbard said they would give us light. I wonder what they are.'

In the light, the apprentices could see a large cavern ahead. It glimmered, invitingly.

On reaching it, they stopped. The floor to their tunnel dropped away abruptly and they found themselves standing on a high ledge, halfway up the wall of the cavern. It was cathedral-like. Pebbles fell from the ledge, bouncing down the rocks. Quickly, Fletcher and Scoop stepped back.

Around the walls of the grand cavern, hundreds of dark recesses opened to other tunnels. It was like a rabbit warren. There were passages next to them, above them, opposite and below. Narrow, worn, staircases and ledges hugged the walls of the cavern, providing pathways to each of the tunnels. Some of the gateways yawned, unencumbered; others were guarded by thick wooden doors.

To their side, Enye bobbed along the ledge and hopped onto a rock next to a dangerously eroded staircase. Fletcher and Scoop glanced at one another and then, pressing their backs against the wall, started to sidestep after her.

'Look,' Fletcher nodded as they edged along the narrow shelf.

Scoop looked to where he signalled. On the far side of the cavern, large spots and patches of black were slowly spreading, withering the Glowing Yarn. It looked like a disease.

'Shadows,' Fletcher said. 'We'll have to be careful.'

They continued through the chamber, helping one another down the slippery stairs, following the little bird. After they had passed a number of other tunnels, Enye reached a door. It stood slightly ajar. She flitted through the gap and disappeared. Fletcher, who was ahead, reached the entrance while Scoop was still picking her way down some steep steps. He examined the wood. Thick iron bars fortified a small, square window in the door. It reminded him of the entrance to a dungeon.

A faint cry drifted through the barred window and Fletcher thought he heard a voice.

'Leave me alone.'

It was a child, crying.

Instinctively, he froze.

'What are you doing?' Scoop whispered, catching up to him.' We don't want to lose Enye. Hurry up.'

Glancing at Scoop, Fletcher decided not to mention the noise. Her nerves looked frayed enough as it was. Anyway, he could have been mistaken – the caves were having a strange effect on his imagination.

Tentatively, he prodded the door. Its hinges were rusted and it didn't budge. Scoop joined him and together they shoved the wood. The door gave way with a grinding noise and swung open.

Behind, a long passage stretched gloomily away. Enye darted forwards, the sound of her wings startling Fletcher.

Taking a deep breath, Scoop stepped forwards. 'Come on,' she said, following the little bird along the narrow corridor.

In the quiet, the apprentice's footsteps echoed.

Something was irritating Scoop – she couldn't quite put her finger on what. It was in the background, constant, vexing.

'Hissing,' she said under her breath.

'What?'

'I can hear hissing.'

'Oh it's me, I think. I'm just a bit out of breath, that's all.'

They carried on in silence. There didn't seem to be any doorways or exits in the corridor, just the impenetrable rock of the mountain either side of them.

But as they reached the middle of the tunnel, Scoop noticed that there *was* one door, hidden in a recess to the left of the passage.

Suddenly, she stopped.

'Did you hear that?'

'I said it was me.'

'No, not that. Listen.'

Fletcher strained to listen, his breathing loud.

Along the passage, a ghostly wailing rose and fell. It drifted through the tunnel, distant and lonely. Wide-eyed, Fletcher and Scoop looked at one another. It seemed to be coming from the other side of the door in the recess – it was the unmistakable sound of a young woman crying.

Chapter 16

The Girl in the White Dress

'Who's that?' Fletcher asked, straining to listen.

The sobs echoed through the passage, thin and heart-rending.

'I don't know, but we should keep going.' Scoop stepped past the recess and continued along the corridor.

'Wait,' Fletcher stopped her. 'Someone's in trouble. We can't just leave them.'

'We can,' Scoop snapped. 'I need to get out of here. What can we do, anyway?'

'I don't know – but we should help if we can.'

'But we're following Enye. I don't want to get lost!'

'Me neither. But look – where's Enye gone?'

Scoop looked around. The corridor appeared to be empty.

'Are you sure she went straight ahead?'

The little yellow bird was nowhere to be seen.

Where is she? Scoop's eyes darted.

She *couldn't* be sure.

Behind the door, the sound of weeping rose again, clearer than before.

Fletcher stepped towards it. 'Listen,' he said, turning to Scoop. 'Whoever it is, they're in trouble. We should look. We can come back after.'

Scoop glared at Fletcher, the apprentices holding each other's gaze for a moment. Then, breaking eye-contact, she stepped back towards the hidden door.

'Thanks,' Fletcher nodded.

Stepping into the recess, he carefully pushed the door. It swung open easily and he ducked through. Scoop followed, moodily. On the other side, a small, square chamber was hidden, a rusty iron door with barred window built into the opposite wall.

In the centre of the chamber, a flat boulder jutted from the ground. On it, her back turned, a young woman sat. She was weeping, her shoulders shaking as she cried. Golden light emanated from something on the other side of the boulder, just in front of the girl, making the chamber glow.

Fletcher moved towards her, eager to tell her about the fallen tunnel and ask for help, but before he'd taken a step, Scoop grabbed his arm.

'Stop,' she hissed. 'We don't know who she is or what she's doing here. She could be dangerous.'

'Dangerous?' Fletcher said, unconvinced.

He studied the cave's inhabitant. She wore a long, white dress that flowed over the boulder, onto the cavern floor. It had obviously been rich once. In the glow, Fletcher could make out gold patterning.

No, he stepped nearer. *It can't be.*

The dress was dirty, smeared with grime and ragged at the edges, but the pattern was unmistakable – it was golden feathers.

The girl from the forest clearing.

Fletcher's heart leapt, the deep connection he felt to the young woman suddenly rekindling.

But I can't be sure it's her, he told himself, restraining his emotion.

The girl's head was bowed, her matted, golden hair falling in dank curls, covering her face.

Fletcher edged across the chamber to get a better look, hoping not to be seen.

The girl's hand came into view. In it, a long quill moved quickly. She was writing. The golden light that illuminated the chamber appeared to be flowing from the quill. It shimmered with an iridescent glow. Fletcher blinked.

Long and slender. Jewel-like swirls.

As if in slow-motion, he made the connections. Then, hitting full speed, Fletcher reeled.

The Golden Feather! He recoiled. He recognised it from his dream. It was unmistakable.

At once, a barrage of emotions assailed him. The feather was here – in the cave – the answer to his questions, right in front of him. He wanted to possess it, to own it – he wanted to *steal* it. He pulled back.

But it's hers.

The young woman seemed totally unaware of Fletcher's presence. As she cried, tears fell onto the page of a writing book that rested on her lap, and as she wrote, her sobs rose with increasing distress.

In the distance, there was a commotion. A heavy door slammed, echoing through the tunnels. The sound ran through Fletcher's veins, making him shudder.

The girl looked up. Fletcher could see the side of her face. Her skin was soft, her cheeks red from crying. She was beautiful. His heart leapt. It was definitely her.

Scoop tugged his sleeve.

'We should go. Did you hear that?'

'Yes,' Fletcher replied, captivated.

Scoop followed his gaze. The girl *was* strangely beautiful. She looked fragile and broken. Scoop watched for a moment. She hadn't really looked at her – not properly – she'd been too angry with Fletcher and frightened of losing her way. But now as she did, her desire to leave ebbed away. There was something in the girl's face, in her eyes, that drew Scoop to her. She was beautiful, radiant even, and yet she wasn't simple. In her, Scoop could see conflict: questions and regrets, innocence, sorrow, even hardness – and yet such beauty. The girl in the white dress seemed to be full of contradictions. Scoop thought of the pebble in her pocket. She understood contradictions.

Again, the girl looked down and began to weep. Fletcher couldn't bear to see her in this state. Without thinking, he moved towards her, reaching out to her shoulder. Scoop darted forwards to stop him, but it was too late. Fletcher lowered his hand. But instead of connecting, it passed straight through the young woman, as though she were a ghost. Momentarily, he looked thrown.

'Of course,' Scoop whispered, 'it's a story. She's not really here, or we're not really there, or whatever it was the Yarnbard said.'

Another slamming door echoed through the chamber and the thudding of slow footsteps began to reverberate, pounding ominously.

At the noise, the girl leapt from the boulder. Putting the book and quill down, she lifted her dress, and opening the iron door, ran out of the chamber. As she did, the book tumbled to the floor, one of its pages falling open. Fletcher caught a glimpse of its cover – it was decorated with a crest – a golden feather.

'The journal,' he blurted. 'It's the journal!'

Scoop had seen it too.

Without hesitating, Fletcher ran to the boulder and leant over to read.

'Let's see what it says.'

'Do you think we should?' Scoop asked, still apprehensive.

'Of course! We might not get another opportunity.'

She hovered for a moment and then curiosity got the better of her. Glancing nervously at the iron door, she dashed to join Fletcher.

The words were packed tightly and written in silver ink.

I am sorry my love. Sorry that I allowed myself to be captured. Sorry that I did not trust. Can you love me for who I truly am? Can I still be yours? Now that I see myself clearly, I wonder.

And yet, I remember the long summer evenings we shared beneath the high boughs of the eaves. I remember the sunlight, dappled on the grass. I remember the fragrance of the fruit and you by my side. My doubts flee, and I know that you do love me, and I, you, although many times I have not shown it.

I hear him speak. My captor. I do not see him, but I hear him, whispering on the walls of the dungeon. He dwells in the depths of the Abyss. He accuses me; reminds me of my betrayal — my ripped and tattered robes. He says that you have forgotten me.

Perhaps I could cope with my own misery, but my fate is worse. I don't know if you will ever read this, if you will ever know, but there is something I must tell you. Here in the caves, two children have been born to me — a boy and a girl. They know nothing other than this darkness. I long for them to see the light, to breathe the air above. He has taken them — locked them away! I cannot bear it. My heart is broken. I hear them calling, but he will not allow me to see them. I cannot bear this wicked imprisonment.

But there are other whispers — even here. I know that you will come for us — save us. I hang on to the promise that you made — that we would never be parted, not even by death.

I am writing this journal as a record of our love, lest I forget. I keep it hidden. It is not an unblemished story; you know that full well. It is no longer filled with the innocence we first shared. It is written on scarlet paper. But these are words of love. In this place of broken dreams, I see what I have lost.

I cling to the gift you gave me — the feather of the Firebird. With it, I have written this journal. It *is my emblem and my standard. A golden feather – it gives me light.*

I hear his servants coming through the tunnels once again. Come quickly...

Reaching down, Fletcher tried to turn the page, but his hand passed through the book.

'It's a story, remember,' Scoop whispered.

At that moment, a gust of wind blew through the chamber. The Glowing Yarn swayed, its light shimmering. The cave dimmed. In front of them, the journal and the Golden Feather vanished, leaving Fletcher and Scoop crouched in the stillness.

Neither of them spoke.

Suddenly, from beyond the iron door, a child's cry cut through the silence.

'Put me down!'

It was a boy. He was in distress, his shrill howl chilling the lonely caves.

Fletcher and Scoop sprang up.

There was the sound of approaching footsteps. Two sets this time, one heavy, one hobbling.

The boy cried out again, rage in his lungs, his voice cracking.

Fletcher felt a stabbing pain in his chest.

A girl joined the commotion, crying, terrified.

'Shut up, the pair of yer, or I'll have yer thrown to the monster.'

The apprentices recognised the cruel voice instantly. It was the crone who'd tried to turn them to stone.

Scoop felt her stomach lurch.

The girl's cries quietened to a timid whimper. Everything in Scoop wanted to find her, to reach out to her, to comfort her.

'I don't believe in monsters!' the boy yelled.

'Oh don't you now, well we'll soon see about that!'

Without warning, the old woman appeared beyond the bars of

the iron door. Fletcher and Scoop sprang back, fearful. Grizelda was younger than when they had seen her on the path. In her arms, the boy kicked and struggled.

Passing the window, she disappeared. A moment later Knot followed, the girl child clinging to him, her cheeks dirty with tears.

At the sight of them, instinct kicked in.

'Come on,' Fletcher said, scrambling to the door.

Scoop joined him, both apprentices filled with the powerful impulse to follow the children, to protect them.

Their thoughts frantic, they flung the door open. Grizelda and Knot were disappearing along the corridor, their backs lit by fiery torchlight. The boy's legs thrashed at the old crone. Stopping, she hitched him up, squeezing him close to her bony body to stop him flailing.

Fletcher felt sick.

The girl's heart-rending sobs rang along the rock walls.

Quickly, the apprentices followed.

Grizelda and Knot reached a crossroads in the tunnel and stopped.

'Right, say goodbye to your brother, my dear – you're not gonna see him again,' the old woman smirked. 'Don't cry, lovely – he's not worth it, the little runt.'

She turned to Knot.

'Take her that way. There's a cell three doors down. Lock her in there. I'll go down here.'

Knot grunted.

Fletcher and Scoop watched as the children reached out, straining towards one another, their fingers grabbing, trying to clasp one another's tiny hands.

'Aww, ain't that sweet,' Grizelda chuckled, leaning so that the children's fingers touched. They closed their hands around each other, gripping tightly.

'Well, that's enough of that,' she barked, pulling away from

Knot.

The children held tight.

'Let go of her, you little runt!' Grizelda yelled, yanking harder.

As they scuffled, Scoop looked at her own hand. She could feel the little girl's pain – somehow she knew her fear. Coldness flowed from her chest, flooding through her. As she watched the children being torn apart she could feel her heart breaking.

Fury rose from Fletcher's gut. He ran towards the old crone, his fists clenched. But as he reached them, the children's fingers slipped from each other and the two kidnappers disappeared in different directions, the children's outstretched hands the last to vanish.

Their fading cries echoed along the desolate corridors.

Fletcher froze. He looked one way and then the other. He was stuck. Caught in an impossible trap. As Scoop reached him, he pointed to where the boy had disappeared.

'I have to...' his voice withered away.

Scoop stared in the other direction. She had to follow the girl, she just had to – she had no choice. She turned to Fletcher, lost for words. They were being separated – again. She had been so thankful that he'd come back to her at the Academy.

Fletcher stepped into Grizelda's tunnel. For a moment, he stared at Scoop. Then turning, he disappeared into the gloom.

Alone, Scoop wavered. She could still hear the sobs of the young girl through the caves. Her legs unsteady, she turned to face the cries. Vanishing into the dismal dusk, she left the cross-roads in the opposite direction to Fletcher.

Chapter 17

Darkness

Scoop followed the sound of the young girl's crying along the corridor. As she passed the locked doors that lined the passage, she had a strange sense of recognition. She'd been here before.

Reaching the third door, she peered through a prison hatch that rested open. Inside, the ragged girl was huddled in a corner, the gigantic man kneeling in front of her.

Scoop froze. She did recognise this. It was the image that had flashed into her mind as she'd waited to enter the Hall of Heroes at the Academy – the image she'd seen again as they met Grizelda at the fork in the path – the ragged girl, huddled in the corner of a dark cave.

How have I seen this before?

Silently, she opened the door and slipped inside.

The man-mountain was crouching, the girl cowering away from him. As if she were a frightened mouse, he held out his hand to her. In it, a tattered piece of knotted string hung limply.

It's a doll, a string doll.

All at once, Scoop remembered. She remembered holding the doll. She remembered the sensation of it in her hands. She remembered talking to it – feeling that it was her only friend.

Silently, a tear fell from her eye and rolled down her cheek.

The ragged girl reached out and snatched the doll from Knot, retracting her hand quickly.

Knot rose to his feet and grunted. Walking to the door, he looked over his shoulder and gazed at the girl in the corner. Scoop thought she could see sadness in his eyes. Turning, he left the cell, the door slamming behind him. The sound of a key rattled in the lock and heavy footsteps faded along the passageway.

Scoop looked back. The girl was playing with the doll, untangling its coarse hair. Walking over to her, Scoop crouched down and reached out, her hand hovering just before the little girl's head. She imagined actually being able to touch the fragile child, being able to hold her, to feel her warmth.

Scoop's fingers moved forward. Without resistance they passed through the mirage and her heart sank.

Turning round, she lowered her body into the same position as the child, the two sitting as one, the ragged girl's image inside her own. The child's arms reached from her body like alien appendages, holding the string doll in front of Scoop's face. Scoop held her own arms out, trying to replicate the moment, mirroring the girl's position perfectly. She wanted to feel close to her. She wanted to reach beyond the boundary of time and be there with her.

She is me, after all, Scoop thought, allowing the truth that had been plain for a while to fill her consciousness. *This is my life. This is it.*

Under the doorway, darkness was beginning to seep. It inched forwards, spreading like spilled ink.

'Snicker snick,' the sound rustled quietly.

'Snicker snick. Snicker snick.'

The dense black edged across the room, rising up the walls, great blotches of nothingness eating away the cell. The doorway vanished into blackness, sections of the wall and roof nearest to it, disappearing. The shadow crept closer to Scoop and her younger self, crawling across the floor.

'Snicker snick.'

The young Scoop continued to play with the string doll, oblivious.

The darkness reached her toes. She was being eaten, consumed by the nothingness. Slowly, it spread to her feet, silently creeping up her legs and over her body.

It was painless. Scoop didn't feel a thing. She leaned back

against the cold rock of the cell and closed her eyes.

Now I know. I remember everything. This is how my story ends.

A few corridors away, Fletcher was watching his younger self. Grizelda had brought the boy some gruel on a battered plate. In a rage he had flung it against the wall. Now, the congealed contents slowly ran down the rock, slopping onto the floor.

'I'll teach you some manners, you little runt,' Grizelda yelled in fury, raising her hand to strike the boy.

As she approached him, the little lad threw himself across the floor, grabbing her bony leg. Drawing his face close, he sunk his teeth into the old crone's flesh, biting hard.

Grizelda screamed in agony, grabbing her ankle. She hopped around the cell, a tirade of expletives pouring from her wrinkled lips.

'You ain't getting any more food – not for a week – not a month. Not ever!' she limped manically out of the cell, crashing the door shut. Locking it in three different places, she hobbled off, her curses resounding through the caves.

Young Fletcher ran to the bolted door and strained up to the bars. Furiously, he rattled them, shouting and screaming for the old woman to come back and let him out.

Fletcher looked on in despair. He had wondered why such deep anger bubbled beneath the surface of his heart. Now he knew. But he wasn't angry anymore; his fury had ebbed away. All he felt now was numb.

His memory had returned. With it, the answers he'd longed for had vanished into the ether. This was his life. This was it. There was nothing else. He knew that at any moment, shadows would spill through the tiny window and engulf this cavern – his tomb – in darkness. He remembered everything. That was all there was.

Sitting on the floor, he buried his head in his hands. What had it all been for? The silver thread? The banquet? The feather? He felt cheated. As his younger self vainly fought the iron door, Fletcher covered his ears and waited for the inevitable blackness to descend.

Chapter 18

The Storyteller's Gift

Scoop opened her eyes. She was unsure how much time had passed, but she was still there, stranded in the darkness. Her body was visible. Everything else was black.

How is it I'm I still here?

It felt as if she was sitting on cold rock. Her back was still supported too, but she couldn't see by what. Cautiously, she lowered a hand to where the floor should have been. Sure enough, her fingers met the resistance of unyielding stone.

What is this place? Is this what it's like to be dead?

Scoop was surprised by her own calmness. All her striving had drained away.

As if I've passed the point of fear, she thought, pensively.

Looking down, she examined her body, her arms and legs. They were definitely real; physical.

But she's gone, Scoop suddenly realised, noticing the image of her younger self was no longer there.

Her heart sank. She was truly alone.

The beating of swift wings disturbed her thoughts. Without warning, Enye flitted out of the darkness. The little yellow bird landed on Scoop's shoulder and ruffled her feathers. Tilting her head, she looked at Scoop, just as she'd done at Wisdom's house.

'Enye!' Scoop blurted, surprised. 'What are you doing here? Where did you go?'

The little bird looked at her, almost reproachfully. Hopping onto Scoop's lap, she began to peck.

'What're you doing? Get off!' Scoop waved the little bird away.

Enye circled up, hovering for a moment, before flying back to peck at Scoop's leg again.

'Tink – tink. Tink – tink.'

'What is it? What are you doing?'

The little yellow bird looked up, her black eyes entreating, and then turned back to her task.

'Tink – tink. Tink – tink.'

What's that noise?

Enye pecked harder.

'Tink – tink. Tink – tink'

Reaching down, Scoop laid her hand where Enye was pecking. Under her tunic she could feel something cold and flat.

The mirror, she suddenly remembered.

Enye darted away, hovering to one side. Scoop reached into her tunic pocket and pulled out the looking glass.

In the blackness, reedy light shone from the mirror; it was dim, but it created a hazy beam. Something was reflecting from the glass. Tilting the surface towards her, Scoop jumped. From the mirror, the cave reflected, its image clear. The Glowing Yarn swayed gently above her and ahead, the thick wooden door stood ajar. Scoop adjusted the angle, looking around. It was all there, exactly as it had been before the shadow engulfed her.

What am I seeing?

Scoop was confused. She'd watched the room being eaten, hadn't she? The blackness that surrounded her felt as real as her own flesh.

She studied the mirror.

What was it the Storyteller said again – when we saw him through the glass?

She thought back, trying to recall his words.

"Take this mirror with you. In the darkest place it will reflect the truth."

Truth? Is this truth then? She looked into the glass, unsure whether to hope in its vision, despite the evidence of her own senses.

If the mirror did show the truth, it would mean the blackness surrounding her was a lie – the cave was still there.

'Not a lie,' Scoop thought out loud. 'It's a story! Of course, we're still in the Story Caves.'

How could I forget? What I'm seeing is a story – my own story. But it's my past. Right now, Scoop hesitated, hardly daring to breathe for fear of losing the thought. *Right now, I'm still in the caves – still alive.*

She struggled to work out how.

I know my story did end here – I was swallowed by the shadows – I remember it now. But somehow I've been given a second chance.

Scoop cast her mind back, remembering waking up at Scribbler's House, feeling as if the whole world had been created in that instant. Somehow she'd been taken from this cell, this place of darkness where she knew her story *had* once ended, and she'd been given a new beginning, a different story, another chance.

She didn't know how.

But I don't care! she thought with sudden excitement. *I'm still alive!*

She leapt to her feet. The blackness that surrounded her was still overwhelming, but summoning all her courage, she stepped into it. Her foot touched solid rock and she transferred her weight. Using the mirror, Scoop began to pick her way out of the chamber. She had to find Fletcher. She had to tell him the good news. She had to let him know they still had a chance.

With the mirror as her guide, Scoop made her way back to the crossroads where she and Fletcher had been separated. Working out which of the tunnels Grizelda had vanished along, she began to navigate the passageways looking for her partner. Her thoughts were disjointed as she navigated the darkness, struggling to make sense of the last few hours. Her mind turned to what they had read in the journal. She stopped, a strange thought occurring to her.

Not just my partner – my brother.

She giggled in shock.

No.

If she was the ragged girl that meant her and Fletcher were the children – the two children born to the woman in the white dress – a boy and a girl. Like a tsunami, the full force of the revelation hit Scoop, a wave of emotion rolling over her.

Born to her...But that means the girl in the white dress is my...

She froze, not knowing how to react. She couldn't even bring herself to even think the word.

How on earth will Fletcher cope with this?

'Fletcher!' she called into the darkness, her voice echoing along the passage.

'Fletcher, are you there?'

Not fully aware of what she was doing, she edged along the tunnel, her legs shaking. All she knew was that she had to find Fletcher. In a haze, she stopped at each door, using the mirror to examine the cells.

'Fletcher!' she called again. 'Fletcher!'

From somewhere ahead, there was shuffling.

Scoop froze.

'Scoop?' a voice murmured, unsure. It was him.

Quickly, she stumbled along the corridor towards her partner's voice. Reaching an iron door with a barred window, she looked through. Sitting in the darkness, his knees drawn to his chest, was Fletcher.

'Fletcher!' Scoop cried, flinging the door open.

'What's going on? How..?'

'It's not real – this darkness.'

Without trying to explain, Scoop handed him the mirror. Fletcher peered into it and then looked up, confused.

'Do you remember what the Storyteller said when he spoke to us through the mirror?'

Fletcher was blank.

'He said it would show us truth in the darkest place. Well,

that's the truth.' She tapped the glass. 'This darkness isn't real – it's our past. Right now, we're still in the Story Caves – it's just that we can't see them because we're in a story – our own story.'

At that moment, a gust of wind blew through the cave. Around them, the apprentices heard the rustle of the Glowing Yarn ripple along the walls and gradually light began to return to the caves, the shadow fading away.

Fletcher blinked.

Scoop was right; they *were* still in the Story Caves. He was on solid ground.

Without a moment to gather their thoughts, a wretched cry filled the caves.

'Noooo!' a man's voice echoed with devastation.

Fletcher and Scoop looked at each other, fatigue on their faces.

'What now?' Scoop whispered.

'How should I know?'

'Maybe we should go and see?'

Fletcher was still numb from the darkness. 'I'm not sure I can.'

'Noooo!' the cry came, again.

'Come on,' Scoop whispered, 'if there's more to see...well I'm not sure I can ignore it.'

Weakly, Fletcher nodded, his face pale.

Leaving the cell, the two apprentices headed in the direction of the cry. They quickened to a jog. The tunnel curved away. As they rounded the bend, Fletcher jumped to one side. In the middle of the passageway was a pool of dark, red liquid.

'Blood,' Scoop gasped, covering her mouth and stepping backwards.

'Look,' Fletcher pointed. Coming from the pool of blood was a trail. It led into a narrow chasm. 'Someone's been hurt. It looks like they're on the move.'

They followed the trail of blood into the chasm – a deep scar in the rock that rose vertically either side of them, its apex high above. Squeezing through a cleft at the end of the chasm, they found themselves in a large stone chamber. In the middle of the chamber, the trail ended. Kneeling on the ground was someone Fletcher and Scoop recognised instantly. It was the Storyteller.

Around the stone chamber signs of a vicious battle were visible. Blood spotted the rocks at the other end of the chamber, next to a tunnel that led away. Marks on the floor signalled the presence of another body, a body which had been dragged into the darkness, pieces of torn cloth clinging to sharp stones as witnesses of its path.

The Storyteller was wounded. Dark liquid oozed from a deep gash in his side, a pool of blood spreading slowly across the stone floor where he knelt.

In his hands he clutched a piece of cloth – it was white with gold patterning. It was ripped to shreds. Beneath it, the crested journal nestled. The Storyteller pressed the cloth to his face and cried. Slowly, he rocked back and forth on his knees.

'Gone,' he sobbed. 'Gone. She is dead.'

Then with a great sigh he collapsed and sank into the spreading pool of blood.

Chapter 19

Worms and Whispers

Another gust of wind blew through the chamber and the Glowing Yarn swayed. The Storyteller's fallen body faded and disappeared. The two apprentices were left in the dismal gloom, cold and empty.

'Dead?' Scoop repeated. 'She's dead?' Her voice was hollow.

'Perhaps we misunderstood – perhaps the Storyteller got it wrong and...How do we know...?'

'I know,' Scoop said, definitely. 'I can feel it. She's dead.'

'Yes,' Fletcher agreed, his voice dropping, 'I feel it too.'

The two apprentices stood in the stone chamber, staring at the place where the Storyteller had knelt.

'Why does it feel like this?' Fletcher asked, barely audible.

Scoop looked at him. Had he still not realised?

'Because...'

She hesitated. Should she say? The girl in the white dress was gone, after all.

'Because...' her voice cracked. 'Because she was our...she was your mother.'

Fletcher stared at her, fixed to the spot. The truth oozed through him, too deep to form as a conscious thought, but saturating him completely. He stood in the centre of the chamber, unable to move.

'Think about what we've seen, Fletch – what we read in the journal. They were her children. We were – *are* hers.'

'But she's dead,' Fletcher repeated.

Scoop nodded gently, her head hardly moving.

She gazed at the place where the Storyteller had collapsed. After a moment, she walked to where he had vanished and kneeling down, began to brush the stone.

'What are you doing?'

'I'm collecting dust,' she replied, closing her fingers around a little pile of soil.

'Dust...? Oh, I'd forgotten all about...' He trailed off.

The journey to the banquet was far from Fletcher's thoughts. It seemed like a past life. Treasure and weddings were futile. He knew his history now – his past was empty, hopeless.

Fletcher wanted to stay in the darkness of the caves. 'You're carrying on?'

Picking up the dust, Scoop tipped it into her pocket. 'There's nothing else for us to do.'

As she spoke, a flutter broke the stillness. Enye flew out of the chasm into the chamber. Circling, she disappeared again through the narrow entrance.

Without speaking, Scoop followed.

Fletcher was too tired to argue. His head hung low, he left the chamber after her.

They walked in silence, following Enye through the labyrinth of caves. As they trudged on, Scoop became aware of the hissing she'd heard earlier. She rubbed her ears.

'I wish you wouldn't breathe so loudly,' she said tetchily, her tiredness overwhelming.

'What?'

'You're hissing again. I wish you'd stop it.'

'I'm not, leave me alone,' Fletcher snapped. The fact that Scoop could think something so inane angered him. He wasn't hissing.

Hanging back, he allowed Scoop to move ahead. His thoughts were fragmented. If the girl in the white dress was his mother, it meant Scoop was...He stopped. It was too embarrassing. He didn't know how to deal with this. He didn't *want* to deal with it. He was tired now, too tired. And hungry too. He hadn't eaten since Quills' Quenching Tea Rooms, whenever that was – he'd lost all track of time.

She got to eat at Wisdom's house, he thought, irritated.

Beginning again, he dodged passed the waxy fingers of stalagmites and stalactites that punctuated the long, narrow cavern they were in.

Scoop had disappeared through a door in the end of the cavern.

When Fletcher reached it, he threw it open. It swung back quickly, blasted by a strong gust of wind. Caught off-guard, he swore.

Evening light streamed through the opening and the wind whistled. Fletcher blinked, raising his hand to his eyes. On the other side of the door was the valley once again. They were back above ground, but much higher than before. The sides of the hill were steep, forming a ravine. In front, a path clung to the side of the mountain. Beyond it was a sheer drop. Fletcher stepped out just in time to see Scoop vanish around a bend. Not caring if he fell, Fletcher stomped after her.

He followed the narrow track along the mountainside. Just before the bend, something caught his eye. It stood out against the monochrome grey rock. It was sitting on a stumpy boulder that poked up from the ground. As Fletcher drew near, he could see what it was.

An apple.

He looked around. There was nobody in sight and no apple trees nearby.

How did that get here?

The fruit was inviting, blood-red and fresh. Fletcher picked it up. It was firm in his hand.

He smelt the skin. The fruit was ripe.

Going to take a bite, he stopped.

he'd seen an apple like this before. The girl in the forest clearing...

He had to stop calling her that.

She was...

He froze. It wouldn't sink in.

In the forest clearing, he'd watched her eat fruit just like this, given to her by the beast. His skin crawled as he remembered the scene.

Beside him, unnoticed, a snake slipped to his side. It had been shadowing the apprentices ever since they'd entered the Story Caves, waiting for an opportunity to strike. Scoop had heard its hiss, but Melusine was crafty and it was easy to stay hidden while they'd been in the dreary caves. The boy, however, wasn't able to sense her. Certain people were oblivious to her presence and so she could speak to them without being seen – her voice disguised as a thought in her victim's mind. The boy was susceptible to her charm. Melusine transformed, standing up just behind Fletcher's shoulder, close enough to touch him. He didn't notice her. He stared at the apple, conflicted. He was so hungry, but it made him uneasy.

'Your father would desssire you eat it,' Melusine breathed, her lips almost touching his ear.

My father..?

Fletcher looked up, an awful thought striking him.

If the girl in the forest clearing was my mother, then my father must be... he stopped.

He could see the beast, its hand outstretched, the apple in its palm. In his dream Fletcher had felt as if *he* were holding out the fruit – as if he were *one* with the beast.

That can't be...I'm nothing like that monster.

'It is no use resssissssting,' Melusine whispered, her voice indistinguishable from Fletcher's own thoughts.

Deep unease accused Fletcher. All his defects assaulted him.

In disgust, he threw the apple down. It rolled to the edge of the precipice. He wasn't like that monster. He wasn't.

'It is simply an apple.' Melusine hissed.

Fletcher looked at the fruit.

What am I doing? It's just an apple.

He picked it up again, his hand hovering.

Below, the River Word rushed, leaping over the rocks, its white water swirling and surging, the roar filling Fletcher's ears. He looked up. Above, a bare tree clung precariously to the side of the mountain, its roots exposed. He felt so torn.

Just decide! He snapped, his frustration turning to anger.

'Surrender to your rage. Let it blossssom,' Melusine coaxed. 'Your father is a massster of rage. He is anger itssself.'

'No!' Fletcher hissed.

He fought the dark thoughts. But it was no good, they were too strong. Melusine's poison flowed through his veins.

Fletcher's chest tightened. He hated everything he'd discovered about himself – his dead-end history, a murdered mother. He hated the rage that lingered in him. Most of all, he hated the thought that darkness itself flowed through his veins, that it was inescapable – it was in his blood.

Melusine drew closer. 'Life is no more than decay – the end of the story is darkness and death.'

The end of the story is darkness and death, Fletcher repeated, the image of the Storyteller holding his mother's torn and bloodied dress pressing in on him. It was inevitable.

What does it matter? I might as well just accept it.

'Eat.'

Lifting the fruit, Fletcher took a bite.

The apple was crisp and fresh. Hardening his thoughts, he lifted his head and marched on.

There's nothing wrong with it. See, what were you worried about?

Melusine smiled, revealing razor sharp teeth. Once Fletcher tasted the apple, she knew she would be able to whisper his thoughts whenever she wished. Transforming, she slipped away.

Fletcher rounded the bend and stopped. Below, the valley opened out, the path descending to a lake. Its water shimmered silver. Fletcher recognised it. It was the place they'd watched the Storyteller drag his boat to; the lake formed by the thread from the journal. But the desert was gone now. Lush green circled the water. The valley had been transformed, fed over many years by the river's flow.

At the far side of the lake, a white cliff rose. Its rocks sparkled, as if they were sharpened diamonds. Over it, a swirling mass of water tumbled into the lake. The sound roared through the valley.

Just visible beyond the brow of the cliff, a magnificent golden dome shone. It looked as if a Phoenix had laid a giant egg above the waterfall. In the dome, a single window looked out across the valley, and at its top, a golden bell glistened in the sun.

Alethea, Fletcher thought, numbly. *We're here then. Fat lot of use it'll do.*

Setting off again, he began to tramp down the path towards the silver lake. He took a second bite of the apple, then another.

At first he didn't notice the change in the fruit's texture, but slowly its crunch was lessening, making it soft and mushy. Its pulp became sticky and stuck to Fletcher's teeth like fudge.

That must have been a bad bit.

He forced it down and took another bite, hoping to rid himself of the taste of the last mouthful. But instead of the badness passing, it grew worse. A horribly bitter flavour spread across Fletcher's tongue. He spat, sending a spray of mushy chunks into the air.

That's horrible!

He wanted to gag. Breathing deeply through his nose, he tried not to give in to the reaction.

Disgusting!

Lifting the apple, he looked at where he'd bitten it.

'Ugh!' he cried aloud, throwing it at the ground. It exploded onto the shale of the lake's bank where Fletcher had arrived, its rotten contents splattering everywhere.

Scoop, who was at the water's edge, heard the commotion and turned back.

At Fletcher's feet, a writhing mass of grubs squirmed, burrowing their way under the stones that lay strewn on the bank.

Maggots! Fletcher thought, with horror. *It was full of maggots!*

He stopped, bending to gag again, breathing heavily.

'Are you alright?' Scoop called.

What's it to you? Fletcher thought, spitting on the floor.

Rushing back, Scoop laid a hand on his arm, trying to comfort him.

'I'm fine, go away!' Fletcher snapped, pushing Scoop away and straightening up.

'Oh, it's just that…'

'Shut up and leave me alone!'

Scoop lashed out. 'But I was only…'

Fletcher cut her down with a chilling look. She stepped back. His eyes were filled with malice.

'Fletcher,' she whispered.

With a snarl, her brother stormed off, heading to the water's edge.

Scoop was devastated by the outburst. She had hoped that the discovery that she and Fletcher were brother and sister would have drawn them closer together. But he was more distant than ever. She had lost everything – her mother was dead and she had watched her own story being eaten by darkness. The outburst was the last straw in a day of unbearable sadness. Scoop sank to the ground, tears streaming down her face. On the grey, scaly bank of the silver lake, she hugged herself for comfort and emptiness overwhelmed her.

Fletcher stared into the silver water as it lapped. It couldn't be true. The beast couldn't be his father.

The thought wormed under his skin, burrowing into his chest.

He looked at the tower, high above the cliff. It was so close.

But what's the point, a voice in his head whispered, as if his thoughts were detached from him. He stared at the cliff. It cut the valley off completely.

How are we supposed to get up there? We'd be smashed to pieces if we tried to climb. It's a dead end, just like the old woman said.

He felt leaden.

Staring at his reflection in the water, his mind turned to the story the lake contained – the silver thread of the Storyteller.

What's it brought me? Nothing but misery. That's all that's in this lake – misery and death.

He hated everything the Storyteller's thread had revealed.

An empty history, a dead mother and a father who...

He couldn't bring himself to think the words again. Looking into the lake, he saw the face of the beast forming and dissolving in its waters. Wherever he looked, all he could see was the monster.

That's all it's taught me, he spat, angry with the Storyteller.

He had to get away from the oppressive tale of the silver lake. Turning, he began to march back to the path. On the bank, Scoop was still huddled like a bundle thrown against the cracked rocks. Without looking at her, Fletcher walked straight passed.

'Where are you going?'

He turned. Scoop was staring up at him, her face streaked where she'd been crying.

'Back,' Fletcher replied, monotone.

'What do you mean?'

'I'm not staying here.'

Without explanation he turned again.

Scrambling to her feet, Scoop grabbed his arm.

'What do you mean, you're going?' she spoke through gritted teeth.

Fletcher shrugged, moodily. 'We've come all this way for nothing. It's a dead end. The old woman was right.' He pointed at the cliff. 'If you think I'm climbing that, you've got another thing coming. We'd be smashed to pieces. Let's face it – we've failed.'

Scoop didn't let him go.

'And I've been thinking,' Fletcher said, emphasising his words, almost relishing the argument. 'We're supposed to be going to a wedding, aren't we?'

Scoop didn't respond.

'But what have we just seen?' Fletcher raised his voice, pointing angrily in the direction of the Story Caves. 'She's dead, isn't she? Dead! It's all a lie! There is no wedding. What have you got to say about that?'

Scoop tightened her grip. 'I've made a decision.' She reached into her pocket and grabbed a handful of dust. Her fist clenched, she held it in front of Fletcher's face. Wisps of soil blew into the breeze.

'I'm going to throw this into that lake, if it's the last thing I do. I'm going to do it for my mother and I'm going to do it for the Storyteller. You might want to leave me here for dead, but I've made my choice.'

Fletcher glared.

'Because you know what – *I've* been thinking too.'

Fletcher sneered. 'Oh yeah, what about?'

'The Auracle. When he made the announcement about the wedding, everything went quiet, as if a ghost was in the room – you remember?' Scoop drew her face close to Fletcher's, speaking her words slowly, her eyes fixed on his. Fletcher didn't move. 'They knew at the Wild Guffaw. They knew she was dead – they knew how ludicrous the Auracle's words sounded. And yet many of them still believed the proclamation – many decided to make the journey to Alethea. And so despite all we've seen, despite that cliff and despite *you*, I've decided I'm going to be one of *them*.'

'Well, you're a fool,' Fletcher shouted, lashing out, breaking free from her grip. As he did, he knocked her hand. Scoops fingers flew open and the dust whipped up into the air.

'No!' she cried.

The two apprentices watched, open mouthed, as the wind caught the cloud of dust, blowing it upwards. It flew into an eddy, swirling above their heads, swept into a battle, just as they were. Then a strong gust blew from the ravine and the dust whirled out over the water. The wind abated and it fell noiselessly downwards, sprinkling into the silver lake.

'Well, it looks like despite all your efforts we've done what the Storyteller asked of us,' Scoop snapped. 'We've thrown dust from the darkest place into the silver lake. So now we'll find out who's right, won't we?'

Fletcher didn't reply.

The apprentices stared at the lake. At first, nothing happened. The waterfall tumbled hypnotically. But then, beneath the surface, there was a movement. It was fleeting, a surge of white water deep below. A shimmer swept across the lake and disappeared. Something was in there. Whatever it was had been dormant, but as the dust mingled with the silver water, it was waking from its sleep.

Chapter 20

The Silver Lake

The water swirled again, the lake sighing. It sounded almost like a whisper, as if the pool were alive, as if it were welcoming the apprentices. Scoop stepped forwards, a powerful feeling suddenly sweeping through her, drawing her on. The depths of the lake were calling; calling to the deepest part of her.

Fletcher felt it too, but the lake's magnetism sent terrors through him. He feared the water and hated the story it contained. As the force of the lake pulled him towards its edge, another equally powerful force repelled him. He felt trapped, torn between two unseen titans. His body ached and his mind felt dislocated. He didn't know what to do. The strain made him want to crumble.

Beware the siren of the silver lake, his thoughts hissed. *Resist its pull.* Stumbling, Fletcher stepped backwards, shivering.

Scoop, on the other hand, was edging further forwards. Stepping right up to the water's edge, she looked into the silvery liquid. Her face reflected back.

Again in the deep, the water swirled, a ribbon of bubbles fizzing to the surface. The sense that the lake was calling them was palpable. As Scoop stared at her reflection she heard the lake whisper again; it murmured, life...life...life.

Fletcher's thoughts were loud and angry. *What's this? Lies! The silver thread is a story of death. This place holds nothing but misssery.*

Above the cliff, the evening sun had touched the top of the Alethean tower. Its descent to the underworld had begun.

The intensity of the lake's attraction grew. It enticed the apprentices, pleading with them to abandon themselves, to enter the water – to swim.

Scoop stepped into the silver liquid, her feet becoming wet.

The water lapped around her ankles.

There is death in the water, Fletcher's thoughts goaded. *The lake is dangerous. It's full of destruction.* He shook himself, breaking free from the lake's hold.

'There is no way I'm swimming in there!' he shouted over the roar of the waterfall.

Scoop looked at him. 'You heard it too? I thought only I could hear what it was saying.'

'No, I can hear it,' Fletcher shuddered. 'We have to go!'

'I'm not going anywhere!' Scoop said, resolutely. 'I'm going to swim.' Turning, she took a deep breath.

Fletcher rushed forwards. 'Stop!' he yelled, grabbing her arm.

She span round, furious. 'What now? Let me go.'

'No! It's not safe!'

'What are you talking about? I'm sick of you, let me go!'

'The lake, don't go in it – it's full of death!' He dragged her out of the water.

Scoop tripped, stumbling to her knees. 'I hate you!' she screamed. 'Leave me alone. Just go away!'

As the apprentices argued on the banks of the lake, behind them, a transformation was beginning to occur. The setting sun was passing through the Alethean window, its rays making their way from the west through an oculus in the roof of the circular hall. As it passed through the glass, it focused a bright beam of light onto the lake. Where it fell, the lake became clear, a tunnel of light slicing through the water.

All at once, the sound of a single bell thundered through the valley.

Fletcher and Scoop froze.

The peal echoed down the ravine, ricocheting from the rocks. For a moment, the whole island fell still, everything resonating with the note, as if all things were connected.

'Alethea! The wedding!' Scoop said, looking panicked. 'It's starting.'

And then she noticed the beam of light hitting the lake. Fletcher had already seen it. Where the light punctured the water, they could see right to the bottom. Half submerged in the sand was their mother's journal. It was open, threads still pouring from its pages. Next to it, shining, was the Golden Feather, its jewel-like swirls shimmering in the lake's motion.

'The treasure,' Fletcher gasped, 'it's right here.'

With a flash of clarity, he knew what he had to do. The Golden Feather would settle the question that accused him once and for all – he would be able to see into his heart – to know who he truly was.

It's not real, his thoughts hissed.

But Fletcher had reached the limit of his resources. *I don't care!* This was his last chance. If the Golden Feather was in the lake he would find it. If it wasn't, well, he would let the lake take him into its depths.

Without pausing, he launched into the water. The lake resisted his leaps, but he pressed on, wading towards the centre.

All of a sudden, Fletcher lost his footing. The lake's bed fell away and the water wrapped itself around him. His hair washed upwards. The sounds of the world faded as the liquid slid about his ears. Fletcher felt himself being pulled into the lake's under-current. Rolling over, he dived, trying to reach the bottom. The water was dark. He kicked his feet, pushing down. His hands reached the bed and sunk into the sand, the grains flowing through his fingers. There was no journal, no feather. He grabbed out in different directions, sinking his hand into the mud again and again, grabbing frantically, clutching, fumbling in the dark, but his fingers found nothing but grit and mud.

I need to know, Fletcher pleaded. *Tell me! I need to know.*

Victorious, Melusine's words mocked him. *You fool. You've been tricked. There is no feather. You've been deceived.*

Fletcher stopped thrashing. He wasn't going to find the treasure. The last of his energy ebbed away and he let go, abandoning himself to the current, allowing his body to sink into the water's embrace.

He drifted into the liquid cushion. Melusine's poison drained from his body, the coldness that had coiled around his heart loosening and slipping away. His mind became unusually still. His body swayed, one with the gentle ebbing and flowing of the water.

Then the lake brushed his body, circling gently.

It was whispering again.

Were there words? Even here?

A voice?

Fletcher.

His name sounded strange.

There was a flash of silver. A face.

It swirled transparent and fluid, and then vanished again. Delirium was making him hallucinate.

The whisper came again.

Life...

The lake flowed and bubbled in shifting patterns.

Life is more than just your own story.

There was the face again. He recognised it. It came close to him.

I am who I am because of the gift given to me by my love – the gift of the Golden Feather.

I am who I am, the lake repeated.

That voice. *Her* voice.

She came close, whispering in his ear.

You believe all is lost, that the Golden Feather is not here. But you are wrong. Believe, Fletcher.

The words felt warm, as if water was seeping into his soul, as if he were becoming one with the lake.

She was there; the princess, his mother. Fletcher's thoughts were clear. How could she not be, the lake was created with the thread from her journal. He was floating in her story.

He heard her breathe. The lake sighed, the water rippling with her voice.

There is something you must understand about the Golden Feather. It comes from the tail of a special bird, Fletcher – a bird that is known by many names – the Ember-Bird, the Immortal-Bird, Adarna or Bennu. It is the feather of the Firebird.

As she spoke, Fletcher saw the bird, blazing red and gold at the top of a great oak.

Listen...

He opened himself, his senses more alert than ever.

He could hear the Firebird singing. Its song was so sweet, so precious. It was unbearable. The lake caught his tears. As the Firebird's song grew, its feathers glowed brighter and brighter.

Gentle whirlpools formed and skipped around Fletcher's body.

This is the firebird's last song. She sings only seven. After her last, she shines with such brilliance that the creature knows, with its next song, it will burst into flames and die.

Like a firework, Fletcher saw the Phoenix explode. The warmth brushed his skin. Flames blazed upwards, one with the sun. Then, as suddenly as it had exploded, it fell still, darkness descending.

The lake swished and the whirlpools subsided.

The water was silent.

Fletcher listened. He strained, his heart aching for more.

He could feel his confidence ebbing away, flowing into the lake. It was dark, cold. Just as he was beginning to panic, the water stirred again. The voice was still there.

All that is left is ash, it whispered. *But although this is an ending, it is not the finish, for from the ash a new Firebird will arise, young and strong – the same, and yet different from that which went before.*

Fletcher felt a little kick of excitement. He could see movement at the top of the great oak. There in the branches, something was stirring. Life – a new Firebird?

The gift the Storyteller gave me was not only a feather – it was the essence of the creature from which the feather came. He has given this gift to you also – although you do not know it, you already posses it.

Fletcher imagined the Golden Feather glowing in his hand, but it shimmered, vanishing into the water.

You doubt me?

The lake whispered and lapped, rocking Fletcher in its flow.

Then, so that you might be sure, hear this...

Water swirled towards him, spinning, the image of the princess forming, her hair white in the surging waves. She drew close. The lake breathed. And then she whispered.

Fletcher felt that her words were fire. He was glowing on the inside. In that moment he knew. He knew the answer to the question that had gnawed at his heart, accusing him, making him doubt himself. In the depths of the silver lake, as his mother whispered those secret words, Fletcher knew, once and for all, that the feather was indeed something he could find, something he could treasure, something he could hold without shame.

At that moment, a hand reached through the water and grabbed Fletcher's shoulder. It pulled him upwards. Fighting the water, it dragged him through the liquid, straining against the current. It hauled him from the lake's depths, towards the light.

Fletcher's head split the surface of the lake. As he exploded into the air once again, the sounds of the valley flooded back. He took a gulp of air and kicked his legs, pushing upwards to keep his head above water.

Fletcher wasn't sure how long he'd spent under the lake. It felt like an age. But as he trod water, he knew something amazing had happened. It was as though he was a different person – or perhaps he was fully himself for the first time.

'Are you ok?' Scoop asked. She was gripping his shoulder, also treading water. She shouted over the roar of the waterfall. 'I was worried. I thought you were hurt, that you were...'

Fletcher could see the distress on her face.

'I'm ok.' He touched her hand.

More than ok, actually, he thought, recalling the secret words his mother had spoken.

Scoop breathed deeply, a tear of relief falling into the water.

'I'm sorry,' Fletcher said. 'I'm sorry I shouted at you.'

'It's ok, we're both tired.'

'Yes.'

Fletcher paused. He still felt awkward at the revelation that Scoop was his sister.

'And it's a bit weird, don't you think – finding out that we're...' He trailed off, blushing. 'You know.'

'It's ok,' Scoop said, smiling. 'Yes, it is weird. But I'm glad.'

'Me too.'

Scoop changed the subject. 'Have you noticed?'

'What?'

'Look at the water.'

Fletcher looked down. Below the surface of the pool, Scoop's clothes were twinkling. Golden threads wove through the fabric of her tunic, swirling with the lake, connecting her to all that surrounded.

'We've done it!' she beamed. 'We made the thread glow gold again.'

Fletcher looked across the lake. It shone as liquid gold, the last rays of the sun brushing its waters.

'And,' Scoop sounded excited, 'I've worked it out.'

'Worked what out?'

'How to get to Alethea. We don't have to climb the cliff after all. Remember when we saw the Storyteller in the desert? There was a cave in the cliff, right where the waterfall is now.'

Fletcher stared at the rock face. Sure enough, through the great glassy sheet of liquid there was a dark shape.

Scoop continued. 'We must be able to get to Alethea *through* the cliff. We just need to swim past the waterfall. But we'd better hurry up, the sun has almost set.'

Fletcher nodded and they began to swim.

As they approached the waterfall, they could feel its power. The same liquid that moulded itself so easily around their bodies was fashioned as a hammer. It pounded against the surface of the lake. It was hard to not to be dragged down again in the current, but in turn, each of them took a deep breath and swam through the falling water. It crashed about their ears for a moment, and then the hammering stopped.

On the other side of the waterfall, it was darker. Through the tumbling liquid they could see the blurred image of the valley. Under their feet was a shelf of rock. They stood up, their robes dripping.

Along the walls of the tunnel that led away from the waterfall, torches flickered. In the distance, there was the sound of festive music. The passageway was nothing like the Story Caves. The rocks glimmered and glistened, sparkling with a thousand points of light. They were made of crystal, carnelian, onyx and jasper. The apprentices began to make their way along the tunnel. It headed gently upwards. The sound of the waterfall faded, and the music grew louder. Water gave way to dryness and the comforting crackle of the flames. Their tired, aching muscles, began to warm, finding renewed energy. Their clothing and hair dried unnaturally quickly and they felt comfortable once more.

The last part of the tunnel was steep. It led upwards and emerged into a rocky antechamber.

In awed silence, Fletcher and Scoop stepped into the sparkling grotto. In front of them an ancient door stood open. They'd made it in time. Finally, they had reached Alethea.

Chapter 21

The Storyteller

The instant they stepped across the Alethean threshold, Fletcher and Scoop were swept into a sea of music and dancing.

Someone hooked Scoop's arm.

'Ah ha!' they shouted, whisking her into the great circular banquet hall of the Storyteller. Scoop whirled round to see Nib grinning at her, his face scrubbed clean.

'You made it then?'

He grabbed her hands and swung her out, spinning her in time to the music. 'You're just in time – the party's getting started!' His grin widened. Scoop blushed. She didn't know why, but she felt instantly safe in his company.

As Nib swung Scoop across the floor, his knees bobbing high, she soaked in the atmosphere.

The banquet hall was full to overflowing. A banjo player, a fiddler and two drummers strutted on a long wooden table close to Scoop. Around them, throngs of islanders stomped and clapped to their tune.

Across the hall, a vast cheer shook the air. Scoop twisted round to see Wisdom hanging from a chandelier. The Guardian of hidden treasure somersaulted to another of the suspended candelabras, to rapturous applause.

All around, couples cavorted and hopped, bounced and kicked, twirling each other across the dance floor.

Through the revellers Scoop caught sight of Fletcher. He was being spun across the ballroom by the taller of the two Quill sisters, his face a mixture of bemusement and fear.

I wonder if he's worked out if that's Molly or Mable yet? she smiled.

'Jump!' Nib shouted. Obeying, Scoop found herself bounding

over a stream of water that bubbled through the hall.

'What?'

'That's the River Word.'

'What, indoors?'

'Yes. You have to be careful not to fall in when you're dancing – plenty of people have – look out for the wet trousers!' He laughed. 'That's its source over there.' As he do-si-doed around her, he nodded towards a pool of crystal water. From the pool, the river wound through the crowd to a huge arched window, underneath which it disappeared.

'From there it flows over the great white cliff, becoming a waterfall. Then it begins its descent across the island to the Oceans of Rhyme.'

That must have been the waterfall me and Fletcher just swam through, Scoop thought in amazement. She remembered what Mythina had said about the Hall of Heroes being built to look like Alethea. She glanced round, wondering if the Head Girl was there.

Despite the jollity, in the back of Scoop's mind something niggled her. She couldn't work out what it was.

'Pass on, pass on!' a cry rippled around the hall.

Nib stepped back and bowed.

'What's going on?'

'We're passing on – moving to the next partner. It was lovely dancing with you.'

Scoop blushed again.

A fat hand with stubby fingers reached out.

'Hello, Scoop.'

Scoop looked up to see Mr Grammatax in front of her.

'I hope you're enjoying the dance.'

'Oh, of course, sir,' Scoop replied, gingerly taking the Headmaster's hand. 'You know my name?'

Mr Grammatax smiled. 'Indeed I do. I know all my students' names.'

Bowing, he began to step and hop in time to the music. Scoop followed his lead.

At the other side of the hall, Fletcher was now dancing with the second Quill sister.

'Hello there, duckie – nice to see you made it,' she said, her brown hair bobbing. 'It's very raucous isn't it?'

'Yes,' Fletcher replied. He hadn't had time to catch his breath since being swept into the castle.

'You know why, don't you?'

Fletcher shook his head.

As Mabel sidestepped and kicked, she held up her sleeve. It sparkled with gold.

'The threads – they turned gold just as the sun sank behind that window.' She leaned forward, whispering. 'Rumour has it, somebody travelled right into the heart of the shadow to make it happen. But nobody knows who. It's wonderful isn't it?'

Fletcher looked around. Everybody's robes were shimmering.

Right into the heart of the shadow? Did we do that? Surely not.

Mabel grabbed Fletcher's hands. The dancers were splitting into two big circles, one inside the other. Hooking her arm over his shoulder, she began to promenade around the outer circle.

Scoop passed on the inner circle, walking in the opposite direction.

'Look!' she nodded across the hall. Dancing a frenetic jig on one of the tables, his arms above his head and his legs flying out dangerously, was the Yarnbard.

The circles changed directions.

'He escaped the fallen rocks,' Scoop shouted, passing Fletcher again. 'He's alive!

'Pass on!' one of the musicians called. There was confusion as the islanders tried to work out who they should be dancing with next.

Fletcher grabbed Scoop's hand. 'Let's go and see him,' he whispered, pulling her away from the dance. Weaving around the merrymakers, they made their way towards the old man, narrowly avoiding being ushered into a tunnel of raised hands.

As Scoop crossed the floor, the niggling feeling returned. *What's wrong?* she asked herself. She still wasn't sure.

The Yarnbard seemed to be dancing the hornpipe in front of a group of pirates from the School of Seafarers (a subset of the Department of Quests). They were playing accordions and singing sea shanties. They roared loudly. As Fletcher and Scoop drew near, they could see their mentor trying to heave a stocky man onto the table next to him. The man's evening jacket was bulging and his monocle threatened to pop from his eye. He was resisting the Yarnbard, but Fletcher and Scoop's mentor was not taking any excuses.

'Who has better reason to dance than you!' he cried.

'Arrr!' the pirates agreed in one voice.

The stocky man huffed, but there was no getting out of it. He was cajoled onto the table where he teetered awkwardly, his walrus moustache twitching and his cheeks flushed from a mixture of whiskey, embarrassment and exertion.

The apprentices dodged past the last couple of dancers and reached the table. The Yarnbard spotted them instantly.

'Ah, Fletcher, Scoop – salutations and a capital hello to you!' He held his hands up to greet them. 'These are my apprentices,' he announced, proudly.

'Arrr!' the pirates roared again.

'You made it. I knew you would.' Leaning down to them he whispered, 'In fact, I knew you were very close when our threads turned to gold.' He winked.

'You're alive!' Scoop smiled.

'Indeed I am. I still appear to be very much alive. Yes, definitely alive. A good reason to dance, don't you think?'

'Arrr!' The pirates raised their tankards.

'But how rude of me. Let me introduce you to the man of the moment – Mr Bumbler.' He wheeled round, holding his hands out towards the stocky man.

Mr Bumbler coughed. 'Oh no, Yarnbard, you go too far. I am in no way the man of the moment.'

'In no way?' the Yarnbard chuckled. He turned to Fletcher and Scoop. 'We all feared Mr Bumbler was dead. Well, in fact he *was* dead, but he has been revived!'

Fletcher stared at the Yarnbard's portly partner. 'How?'

'From his book – the famous Bumbler's Guide to Bardbridge,' the Yarnbard announced with a flourish. 'You see, our words carry a trace of who we are – as Mortales, they are our lifeblood. We managed to distil Mr Bumbler's words into a rather fine whiskey. Mr Bumbler is very fond of his whiskey.'

'I am,' Bumbler agreed.

'And then we fed it to him. Revived him in an instant, clearing the poison out of his system completely. Which means, Mr Bumbler has a better reason than most to enjoy the party, don't you think?'

Turning, the Yarnbard began to cajole Bumbler again, prodding his legs to make him jump.

As they watched Mr Bumbler reluctantly begin to hop and dance, Scoop started to feel uncomfortable again. Her body was heavy. Something wasn't right.

Come on, she thought trying to shake the feeling. But no matter how hard she tried to enjoy the entertainment, she couldn't. She felt at odds with her surroundings – the dancing and laughing, the roars of the pirates. Scoop noticed that her cheeks were burning. Glancing round, she wondered if anyone had noticed. But the wedding guests were completely absorbed in the celebration. *What's wrong with me?*

Her leg was stinging. She lowered her hand to touch it and realised there was something in her pocket. It was making her leg burn.

Her stomach lurched.

The black pebble!

She'd forgotten about it. Instantly, she knew she had to get rid of it.

Feeling ashamed, she scanned the hall. Why hadn't she thrown it away earlier? Slipping her hand into her pocket, she touched the stone. It was red hot. She bit her lip. Her hand was stinging now.

Trying not to make a noise, she pulled the pebble out. It was unnaturally heavy. Hoping that nobody would notice, she lowered the pebble and released it.

As it hit the floor, there was a crack. It shot through the ballroom as if a gun had been fired, the sound ricocheting from the walls.

The fiddle player span round and the music petered out. Everyone looked to where the noise had come from.

Oh no, Scoop thought in horror. She could smell burning behind her.

Suddenly, the wedding guests gasped. Benches scraped as islanders rose to their feet. A few people squealed in shock.

Scoop turned. She felt sick. Stood where the pebble had hit the floor, a crooked smile on her face, was Grizelda.

The old woman bowed. 'Grizelda will go to the ball. Thank you, my dear,' she whispered to Scoop. 'And look who I've brought with me.' Pulling a piece of knotted string from her pocket, she placed it on a bench. Knot suddenly appeared. He looked round, startled.

'Get up,' the old woman commanded. Those in the vicinity edged quickly away.

The man-mountain lumbered to his feet, knocking the bench over. It fell to the floor with a clatter.

'We've come to claim our prize!' the old crone shouted, her voice echoing. The wedding guests stared at the intruders, open-mouthed. 'Where is she?' Grizelda yelled. 'Come out, come out, wherever you are.'

Something shifted in the centre of the room. It was a figure.

He had been hunched beside the crystal pool. Now, all eyes turned towards him. His auburn hair flashed with fiery light.

'The Storyteller,' Scoop whispered.

Slowly, the wedding's groom turned to Grizelda, the silver cane hanging by his side, his shoulders low and relaxed, his eyes sad.

'Where is she?' Grizelda repeated with menace.

Knot stepped nervously forward.

The Storyteller dropped his head. He stared into the crystal pool and stirred the water.

What's he doing? Scoop wondered. The wedding guests held their breath, waiting for their host to speak.

As the Storyteller stirred the crystal water, he tried to sense the presence that usually flowed from beyond the Un-crossable Boundary. It felt distant. *Where are you?* he wondered. *I need you now more than ever.*

He stopped stirring and looked up.

'That is a question many are asking.' His voice echoed around the circular walls. 'Although you, Grizelda, are the one to speak it aloud.'

The old woman bowed. 'Well, I'm not here to mess about, am I?' she spat. 'You know full well why I'm here. I've come to reclaim *her* – your *princess.*' A sneer crossed her black eyes. 'As you know, she is the property of my master, the Lord of the Abyss. I don't know if you've forgotten, but many years ago she chose *him*. She chose *his* gift over yours. So now *we* have come to take her back.'

The Storyteller spoke quietly. 'She did choose him, that is true, but she regretted her decision.'

'Makes no difference to me. She made her bed, now she has to lie in it.'

'No longer,' the Storyteller raised his voice, anger flashing across his face. The wedding guests looked uncomfortable. 'She has been freed from your master – freed by that great leveller, death – for as you know, death breaks such bonds that are made in life. Your master now has no rightful claim over my love. She is free to make her own choices.'

After a moment of silence, Grizelda cackled. She looked at the faces of the assembled crowd and roared with laughter.

'Did you hear what he said? Can you hear what he's saying? She's dead! You fools – what are you doing, dancing and carrying on like this? You're at the wedding of a dead bride.' Laughing again, she turned back to the Storyteller. 'Whatever next?'

'She is indeed dead,' the Storyteller responded quietly. 'Killed by the beast that gave me this wound.' He lifted his shirt to reveal the scarred gash that marked his side.

As he touched the wound, he could feel the presence from beyond the Un-crossable Boundary flowing again, growing stronger.

Inside me, he realised. *You're inside me. I trust you.*

The Storyteller looked up. 'But I made a promise, a promise that is deeper than death, a promise that we would never be parted – that I would bring her back.'

Shuffling, the audience looked about, expectant of a miracle, hoping to catch a glimpse of the Storyteller's bride; but she was nowhere to be seen.

Snorting, Grizelda shook her head.

The Storyteller scanned the hall. 'Words are powerful things,' he said, addressing his guests. 'You have all made the journey to my home. Each of you has taken a different path to get to Alethea. Some have come together, others alone. And yet each of you has one thing in common. You have all embraced my story, a story of love and of death. The robes you wear are witness to that.'

The Storyteller waved his hand and a ripple of gold spilled across the room as the robes of each guest shimmered.

'As Mortales, stories are our blood, for life is held in our tales. In bringing the thread of my story back to me, you have brought a great gift – the greatest wedding gift you could offer. You have brought her lifeblood to Alethea. The threads you carry hold the seed of her return. Tonight, through you, she will be brought back to life.'

A buzz of excitement spilled around the hall.

'Only one thing is needed to fulfil that promise. The ancient rhyme speaks of it:

When Alethean bells chime,

And the Golden Feather shines,

All shadows will hide and flee,

And her face again we'll see.'

As he finishing speaking, the Storyteller looked at Fletcher and Scoop.

They peered over their shoulders.

'Is he looking at us?' Scoop whispered.

'I think he might be,' Fletcher replied, nervously.

The Storyteller held them in his sight. 'Apprentice Adventurers, you bring a treasure with you, I believe – the gift that many years ago I entrusted to your mother – the feather of the Firebird! This treasure will unite the golden threads, drawing them to it. As they meet, your mother will be reborn.'

Delighted applause rippled through the crowd.

'The time has come for you to bring the treasure to me.'

All eyes turned to Fletcher and Scoop. The crowd parted, creating a pathway to the Storyteller.

The apprentices' eyes moved across the waiting assembly.

'What does he mean, we have the Golden Feather?' Scoop said out of the side of her mouth.'

'I don't know,' Fletcher whispered back.

'Come.' The Storyteller held out his hands. He looked at the apprentices, his expression reassuring, encouraging.

Not knowing what else to do, Fletcher and Scoop began to walk through the crowd. They felt exposed. But ahead, the Storyteller smiled at them, kindly.

'I hope he knows what he's doing,' Scoop muttered under her breath, 'because we certainly don't.'

Now is the time. The Storyteller directed his thoughts to the one who was with him, filling him, from beyond the Un-crossable Boundary. *The appointment is now.*

As Fletcher and Scoop reached the Storyteller, he leaned towards them.

'Take my hands,' he whispered. 'There's someone I want you to meet. We don't have long.'

Reaching forwards, Fletcher and Scoop grasped the Storyteller's hands.

As they did, Alethea vanished.

Chapter 22

Stolen from the Shadows

Soft music was playing.

'Hello,' a voice said.

Fletcher and Scoop opened their eyes. The Storyteller no longer held their hands. Instead they were being gripped by a small, slight, girl. She was about seventeen years of age. In shock, they pulled away.

'Where are we?' Scoop spluttered.

They were in a tiny, simply decorated room. It was gloomy, dingy even, but it was unlike any place they'd seen – the colours were different.

In the middle of the room was a dining table. On it, a writing book and piles of paper were scattered. Next to them, a screen glowed. Heavy raindrops splattered a small garden outside the window.

Scoop's eyes darted. 'Where's the Storyteller?'

The girl walked to a shiny white box and pressed it. The music stopped.

'You are beyond the Un-crossable Boundary,' she replied, matter-of-factly.

The apprentices looked confused.

'I know what you're thinking – it's not possible.' She paused. 'Well, that's what everyone thought – but for a while I've suspected that perhaps the boundary isn't as impenetrable as people believe. In fact, I've been banking on it.'

'Who are you?' Scoop asked, bewildered.

'My name's Libby. And in answer to your second question, I'm still here.'

'My second question? What was that?'

'You asked where the Storyteller had gone.' Libby paused.

'Well, I'm still here.'

'What? What do you mean?'

'I *am* the Storyteller,' Libby said slowly, allowing her words to sink in. 'He is me. I am in him. On Fullstop Island, that's how I look – he's like my avatar.'

Scoop frowned. 'Avatar?'

'Doesn't matter,' Libby replied, shaking off the question. She fixed the apprentices in her sights. 'You're in my world now, so you see me as I am. This is what I look like in my world.'

Fletcher and Scoop stared.

Suddenly, Scoop recognised Libby.

'I saw in the silver tunnel,' she blurted. 'Inside the Storyteller, or somehow through him – it was you I could see.'

'But she's just a girl,' Fletcher interrupted.

'And *you're* just a boy!' Libby replied with a smile.

'Wisdom said that.'

'I know.'

Fletcher studied Libby. He could see Wisdom in her face. In fact, he had the strange sense that he could see a lot of the island's inhabitants in her.

'Sit down,' Libby said, holding out her hand. 'We don't have much time and there're lots I want to tell you.' She signalled to a long, wide seat.

Without speaking, Fletcher and Scoop shuffled to the sofa and sat down. It was soft. They sank into the cushions, awkwardly.

'Where are we again?' Scoop asked.

'You're in a place called Yorkshire – in England. That's where I live.'

'Beyond the Un-Crossable Boundary?'

'Yes.'

'But how? Why are we here?'

Libby paused. 'To answer that, I need to tell you a story.' She sat at the table, looked down and took a deep breath.

'A year ago my mum disappeared. One morning in December

I came down for school and she'd gone. She'd left the breakfast on the table – that was strange. Nobody knows where she is. She's classified, missing.'

At her words, the bright red letters of a 'MISSING' poster flashed through Fletcher's thoughts.

Libby glanced at him and then looked down again. 'It happens to a lot of people; I never realised. I was devastated, obviously. It turned my whole world upside down – left a hole in me that try as I might, I couldn't fill – still can't. I just couldn't work out why she'd gone. Was it me? Was it Dad? He says some things just happen.' A look of disappointment crossed her face.

A cat brushed past Scoop's feet.

'That's Alphabet,' Libby said. 'Mum named her.'

She looked out of the window, staring at the hypnotic rain.

'Anyway, one day about a month later, we were clearing out the spare room and I found these down the back of a chest of drawers.'

Libby picked up the writing book and a pile of papers from the table. Moving to the sofa, she sat on the arm and placed the papers on Fletcher's lap.

Fletcher stared at them.

On the pages were scribbled notes and diagrams, pictures and maps. There was a line drawing of the Wild Guffaw, the barman sketched next to it, his apron blue and white. "Noveltwist" was written above in scruffy letters and underlined a number of times. There was a box, in which the old island rhyme had been written. It had been crossed out and altered. A title read, "Design for Quills' Quenching Tea Rooms." Below was a sketch of the large pink cupcake that Fletcher and Scoop had peered around as they'd sat in the bay window of Molly and Mable's shop.

Libby shuffled through the papers.

'These were my mother's,' she said. 'She never told anyone that she was writing. None of us knew. She spent all this time scribbling, creating this whole world in her head – but she never said. Why wouldn't you say?'

She looked at Fletcher and Scoop. They didn't reply.

'Dad said that maybe she was scared – that she didn't want anyone to know, like it was a secret she had to keep. I'd always thought of mum as a bit straight-laced – just work and looking after us. But when I found this, well, it was like I was getting to know her for the first time. As I read, it felt as if I was travelling into her world, into her mind – as a stranger. The more I read, the more connected I felt to her, you know? But the story was only half-finished. She'd obviously abandoned it halfway through – hidden it away behind the drawers – given up.'

Libby pulled out a few crumpled sheets of paper.

'This is your story. Mum started it, but never finished – two children born in an underground dungeon, guarded by a crone and a giant. When I found the papers, these sheets were screwed up, stuffed in an old envelope. I felt as if I was stealing them from the shadows.'

Fletcher and Scoop glanced at one another.

'So,' Libby said, looking up. 'That's when I decided to carry on with the story – to finish it. Well, I sort of started it again actually, using all the ideas mum had left. I know it sounds strange, but I thought that maybe writing it would help me feel close to her – somehow the story would reunite us.' She paused. 'I feel in some way that it has.'

Scoop looked at her hopefully.

'Oh, I don't mean she's back – we're still looking for her,' Libby said, sadness in her voice. 'But I do feel closer to her – as if I've got to know her properly for the first time. I know it's odd, but you've both given me a lot of hope. We will be reunited again – I know it. We will find her.'

Fletcher and Scoop didn't know what to say. As they thought about it, the pieces fell into place: the missing characters, the shadow eating their half-finished stories, the deep chasm beneath the island, and the new story they'd been given – the second chance.

'I'm on the last chapter now. I've almost finished it,' Libby said, smiling. 'There's only one piece of the jigsaw left.' She reached across the table and picked up a pen. 'This is something that's been with me the whole time I've been writing. It was my mother's – the pen she used to write the start of your story. It reminds me of her – keeps me hoping. This is what you need to finish your quest. Take it back with you.' She handed it to Fletcher.

Fletcher looked at the pen. It was ordinary; a plastic biro. But printed on the side he noticed a small logo. It was a tiny, golden feather.

'Come, take my hands again,' Libby said. 'It's time for you to return. We have a story to finish.'

'But...' Scoop started. The revelation that a whole other world existed beyond the Un-crossable Boundary didn't feel like an end – there were so many new questions.

'I know,' Libby said. 'We will meet again, I am sure of it. But that will be another tale. Now, you have a task to complete. The islanders are counting on you – your mother is counting on you. I'm counting on you.'

She held out her hands, kindness in her eyes.

Tentatively, Fletcher and Scoop reached towards her. In his fingers, Fletcher clutched the pen – a pen that had given birth to his whole world, to his sister – to himself. A pen that now had to finish the story it had started.

As their fingers connected, they felt the warmth of their creator's hand for just an instant, and then the room vanished.

As one, the wedding guests gasped.

In Fletcher's hand, shimmering with fire, was the Golden Feather. It had appeared out of nowhere.

The audience broke out in joyful applause, cheers echoing around the banquet hall as islanders threw their hats in the air.

Fletcher looked at the feather; it was just as he had seen in his dream – long and slender, shining with a thousand shades of glittering gold. Jewel-like swirls rippled along its spine. It was beautiful.

Around the ballroom, a murmur arose. Something strange was happening.

Scoop's tunic was being tugged. She looked down. The gold thread that wove through her robes was being pulled out. It floated into the air, drawn to the Golden Feather. Other guests were experiencing the same thing. Across the hall, gold floated from its bearers. The threads wiggled outwards, causing laughter and joyful yelps to break out. From above, the hall looked like a giant spider's web, shining with morning dew.

Suddenly, the threads broke free from their bearers. To delighted gasps, they floated towards the feather. As Scoop's thread left her, she felt light, as if she were floating with it.

The gold threads neared the feather and began to circle, spiralling around Fletcher, Scoop and the Storyteller. They gathered speed, spinning faster, growing in number as new threads joined the glowing mass.

Soon the air in the centre of the hall was thick. The threads whirled about the apprentices, forming a pillar of gold.

Fletcher and Scoop were inside the spinning pillar. Gradually, the wedding guests disappeared from view, the apprentices hidden at the centre of the cyclone.

Then suddenly, bursting upwards from the golden pillar was a flame. It shot into the air and spread across the ceiling, splitting into two great pinions.

At once, Fletcher recognised it.

'A Firebird,' he whispered in awe.

Its wings spread, covering the banqueting hall, its feathers like flames.

The wedding guests gasped.

In a flash, the threads stopped spinning. Spellbound, the

crowd watched as gold began to fall like rain. The hall was filled with 'oohs' and 'ahs' as the Firebird hovered peacefully above.

Out of the shimmering stillness, a cold hard voice arose.

'She is *his*.'

Grizelda was standing, unflinching. She was staring at the centre of the hall. Fletcher and Scoop looked round. Beside the Storyteller was a sight they would remember for the rest of their lives. Held captive by the Storyteller's gaze, her dress shining as new, was the wedding's bride – their mother.

'She's back!' Scoop whispered.

As the words left her mouth, warmth flooded through her, all the emptiness she'd felt in the Story Caves transforming into joy. She wanted to jump, to leap into the air and dance.

Beneath the Firebird's wings, golden threads still fluttered through the air. As they reached the ground, they fizzed and disappeared – all except the ones that landed on Grizelda and Knot. Slowly the pair were being drenched in flecks of light. As the threads touched them, they began to wriggle again, joining together in cords of gold.

Knot tried to step away, but the cords stuck to him. He flicked his hands erratically over his clothes, as if trying to brush away a swarm of flies.

The threads circled the two gatecrashers, crawling across them, tightening and binding them as ropes.

Grizelda stood defiant.

Slowly, the threads twisted around the pair.

As they did, Grizelda could feel the Storyteller's story trying to connect to her garment. She resisted, but an image flashed into her mind – the Storyteller and his princess, before they had been separated, lying beneath a high tree. Momentarily, she felt a pang of love. Her heart cracked. The pain was excruciating.

She heard herself cry out.

Battling, she fought the story. Another image assaulted her – the Storyteller on his knees, clutching a piece of white cloth. His pain was inside her. Her body wrenched and she lurched.

The guests watched as Grizelda writhed and jolted, the thread of the Storyteller wrapping around her, reaching her heart.

Above, the Firebird's eyes blazed.

Through the cords that bound her, Grizelda could see the Storyteller and his princess consumed by one another. The old crone had travelled too deeply into the Abyss for too many years to be able to cope with such a vision. Overwhelmed by seeing two people so abandoned, so completely given away to one another, she threw her arms into the air.

'No!' she cried.

The golden threads broke, falling from her.

For a moment, Grizelda felt relief. But this wasn't the end of the old crone's troubles. Where the threads had fallen away, black liquid started to ooze from her skin. She looked at her hands, panic written across her face. The liquid was steaming, causing smog to rise from her body. She waved her arms, as if trying to put out a fire, but the more she waved, the thicker the cloud became. It seeped from her pores, rising through the hall, swelling to a nebulous tumour suspended in the centre of the great ballroom. Below, wedding guests choked and coughed.

Above the old woman, the poison cloud seethed. It was morphing, slowly transforming, taking on shape. A black eye appeared, stormy and swirling. Hunched shoulders became visible. The crowd screamed, as deadly claws swiped the air. Grizelda ducked. From nowhere, a powerful tail lashed out, sending tables flying. The guests scattered.

As Fletcher and Scoop ran to the side of the hall, Fletcher recognised the animal. *The beast!* Panicking, he and Scoop dived for cover, shielding their eyes.

Then, with a rumble that made the hall shudder, the cloud began to speak. 'She is mine,' it snarled, ash spewing from its squally mouth, showering the terrified crowd.

Grizelda cowered as debris showered, crackling as it fell.

The beast looked directly at the Storyteller.

'She is mine,' it repeated.

All at once, there was a piercing screech. Fletcher peeked through his fingers. Above, the Firebird was diving, its great wings spread, its talons bared. Screaming, it flew at the beast. Enraged, the creature turned, its claws scything the air, its jaws opening to reveal razor sharp teeth. It leapt at the bird and fire and cloud swirled into a deadly ball.

Above the crowd the creatures fought, a smoking blaze of ash and fire. The wedding guests pushed backwards, pressing against the circular walls. Through the turmoil it was impossible to tell which of the creatures was winning. Claws and talons, teeth and beak plunged and swiped. Smoke belched and fire shot out in all directions. Only Grizelda knew – only she could sense the beast was losing its power. She felt the release. As she did, she knew the time had come to make her escape. Turning frantically, she looked for a way out. There was none. The door through which Fletcher and Scoop had entered was blocked. There was only one other break in the solid stone wall – the great east window.

Without thinking, Grizelda began to run.

Wildly, she darted towards the window of Alethea, pushing her frail body with all her might.

In the air, the Firebird screamed. It had inflicted a deadly wound. The beast let out a howl of horror and rage.

Grizelda reached the window and leapt. She hit the glass and it shattered, shards raining down, chiming as they hit the floor. She dived through the window, tumbling down. Past the cliff she fell, through the waterfall. With a deep splash, she hit the lake below and disappeared into its depths.

Wind whistled through the shattered window.

With a sickening cry the beast transformed again. Taking the body of a raptor, it fled from the banquet hall, sweeping over the mountains. It soared across the island, spewing ash onto the village as its great wings beat its course, driving it away from the island, out to the Oceans of Rhyme. The Firebird followed as far as the shoreline, but as the beast disappeared into the horizon, the great phoenix reared up, its flaming wings spreading magnificently. It pulsed for a moment, its neck craning triumphantly and then it exploded, crackling into sparkles of light that showered the sea.

In the banquet hall of Alethea, a great cheer split the air.

The beast had left the island.

Across the land a metamorphosis was taking place. The shadows were transforming. Shadow Beetles leapt into the sky, becoming visible, taking to the air as fireflies, their little lights blazing. Where they had grazed, leaving piles of nothingness, life appeared once again.

Archie Squiggle picked up his ball and ran to find his mother.

The caretaker at Scribbler's House shouted at an apprentice for running along the corridor.

Out of the Abyss a myriad of butterflies fluttered: Red Admirals and Painted Ladies, Purple Emperors and Swallowtails filled the air, dispersing across the island to grace its meadows.

At the fork in the path, on the way to Wisdom's house, a group of academy students awoke – the fossilised dull worms that had turned them to stone having lost their effect. They stretched.

'What are we doing here?' Mythina asked, dazed.

An apprentice next to her shook her head, bemused.

In Alethea, the celebration exploded to life once again. The fiddle player whooped and launched into a scorching reel. The whole hall leapt as one, dancing.

On a bench among the revellers sat Knot. He looked different, his face changed. He appeared relaxed, at ease. A golden thread shimmered through his clothes. Looking at the dancers, he smiled. Grizelda had always kept him from knowing the tale of the Storyteller, but as the golden threads had surrounded him, he'd experienced it – he'd allowed it to flow into him. For the first time he felt truly free. This was his home now.

'Wahoo!' he cried, jumping to his feet. Linking arms with Mr Snooze, they began to thread around the hall, islanders joining the chain in their droves.

In the centre of the hall, the Storyteller was crying. His bride reached out to wipe his tears away. Taking her hand, he held it to his face and whispered, 'Now, at last, we are together.'

Fletcher and Scoop remained fixed as the dance whirled around them. They didn't take their eyes from the Storyteller and his bride.

But even as Scoop watched the two lovers, she couldn't shake a question from her mind. It had surfaced a few times, but she hadn't had the opportunity to pay it any attention. Now she couldn't ignore it.

Turning, she tugged Fletcher's sleeve.

'Hmm,' Fletcher murmured, still captivated by the image of the couple in the centre of the hall.

Scoop tugged his sleeve again.

He turned to her, dazed. 'What?'

'There's something I need to ask you,' Scoop said, a slight frown on her face. 'What made you change your mind?'

'What? When do you mean?'

'In the silver lake – when you resurfaced, you'd changed. Before you went under, you were so angry with me, you wanted to turn back and give up the journey. Something happened down there, didn't it?'

'Oh.' Fletcher pulled his attention away from the scene in the centre of the banqueting hall. 'Err, well – it was just that before, I didn't know.'

'didn't know what?'

Fletcher paused, nervous to admit his struggle. 'I didn't know,' he looked down. 'I didn't know who our father was.'

'Oh.' For some reason the question had never occurred to Scoop. She could see how much it affected Fletcher, though – it was written across his face. 'But now you do know?' she asked, gently.

'No, not exactly,' Fletcher stopped again. 'Down there I was told something, you see – something I hadn't seen before – something that changed me.'

Scoop was intrigued. 'What?'

'I was reminded that the Storyteller made the journey to the caves to rescue our mother – to rescue us. He battled for us to the point of spilling his own blood. He was wounded for us.'

Scoop glanced up at the man her mother had chosen to marry, the scar he carried hidden beneath his shirt.

Fletcher continued. 'When I saw that clearly, something changed in me. His actions speak more to me than a thousand words. And so I made a decision. I think it's the most important decision I've ever made. At the bottom of the lake, I decided to let go of my fear – of everything that condemned me – everything that said I wasn't good enough. It doesn't matter if there's darkness in us. It doesn't matter what led us to being born, does it? We don't have to be held back by that. That's not what's important. Down in the lake I worked out what really matters.' He looked at his mother and the Storyteller. 'Their story – that's what's important. The story of their love. That's what I'm going to build my life around. And I know that's where I'll find my real father, I'm sure of it.'

Scoop looked at the couple standing beside the crystal pool. Fletcher was right. They were connected to the Storyteller now, their lives woven together with his. He and their mother were their home, their future. Things would never be the same again.

In a tower high above, the Alethean bells began to chime.

As the wedding guests looked on, the Storyteller turned and kissed his bride.

It felt to Fletcher that in that kiss, the scars of the whole world were being knitted together – as if every story on the island would somehow find its rest right there.

'I suppose this is the end of our quest,' he said quietly. Despite the joyful pealing of the bells and the sense of achievement that burned in him, he was sad that the journey had finished.

'Yes,' Scoop agreed. She looked at him. 'But it's not over, is it? we're Apprentice Adventurers, remember?'

Fletcher smiled. He knew exactly what Scoop meant. This was the end of their first quest, yes, but every adventurer knew that an ending carried within it the seed of a new story.

He held out his hand to his partner. 'Shall we?'

Scoop was just about to take it when a voice squawked behind them, making them both jump.

'Aha, there you are. Congratulations to you both.' The Yarnbard was standing behind them balancing three foaming tankards, filled to overflowing. 'Noveltwist Cordial?' he grinned, reaching out his hands.

Fletcher and Scoop took a tankard each.

'Cheers,' the Yarnbard said, raising his tankard with a broad grin.

Just as Fletcher and Scoop were about to take a sip, the Yarnbard interrupted. 'Oh, those tankards are not for you – whatever gave you that idea?

His apprentices raised their eyebrows. Even now the old man had the ability to surprise them.

'No, no,' the Yarnbard continued. 'Those tankards are for the bride and groom. I thought you might want to give them to the happy couple yourselves. I imagine you have an awful lot of catching up to do.

Fletcher and Scoop looked to where their mother and the Storyteller stood. They were beaming back at them, their eyes glistening.

'I'm nervous,' Fletcher whispered.

'Well I'm sure they wouldn't mind if you had just a little sip of Noveltwist – to give you courage.

Fletcher raised the tankard to his lips and took a swig. The liquid warmed him instantly, flooding him with confidence.

'Come on, partner.' He reached out his hand.

'Sister,' the old man interrupted.

'Yes,' Fletcher agreed with a shy smile.

Scoop took his hand.

Although they had travelled for many miles to reach this place, along rivers, across mountains and through caves, both of them knew deep in their hearts that the next few steps were the most important they would ever make.

As they stepped towards their destiny, the Yarnbard looked at the third tankard of Noveltwist with relish.

'This one's mine,' he grinned. 'And you deserve it old man, if I do say so myself.' He raised the tankard towards the four figures who were now greeting each other at the centre of the Alethean Banquet Hall. 'Cheers,' he whispered, 'long life, good health and a rip-roaring, full-hearted story to you all.'

**OUR STREET
BOOKS**

Our Street Books for children of all ages, deliver a potent mix of fantastic, rip-roaring adventure and fantasy stories to excite the imagination; spiritual fiction to help the mind and the heart grow; humorous stories to make the funny bone grow; historical tales to evolve interest; and all manner of subjects that stretch imagination, grab attention, inform, inspire and keep the pages turning. Our subjects include Non-fiction and Fiction, Fantasy and Science Fiction, Religious, Spiritual, Historical, Adventure, Social Issues, Humour, Folk Tales and more.